Waking Up in Vegas

Brittany Arreguin

Contents

To Por Por and Gung Gung: who took me on my first trip to
Las Vegas many moons ago.
And for everyone who's given this girl with big aspirations a
chance. Let's go on an adventure.

Content Warnings

This book has the following content warnings that may not be suitable for all readers:

Harassment, kidnapping, physical violence, gun violence, hospitalization, anxiety and on page panic attacks, racism, mentions of food and eating, drinking and alcohol, and gambling.

Chapter One

Marissa

I should have expected that during tonight's shift I would have to call in reinforcement on the floor. I just didn't think that it would be because of me.

Here's the thing about waitressing in Vegas: you do so with the predisposed notion that some dramatic event will ensue. It's Vegas. What happens in Vegas...well, a lot of regrettable stuff, so it's best if it stays in Vegas. There have been plenty of movies made with some action-packed, Vegas-set plot to prove that point. There's never a dull moment here. And, being a cocktail waitress, whether it's in a nightclub or on the casino floor, means that you're wearing a dress that hugs every curve in your body, and you're gonna shine bright like a diamond from the sequins sewn in, specifically a bright pink color for the dresses we wear. I'm happy I've finally reached a point where I feel confident in it, but in my short stint working as a waitress, I've never had to call security. Karma really bit that bullet right in its ass today.

I walk up to a man I've kept my eye on for a bit. He's been at the same machine for two hours now, loading a hundred dollar bill each time, and furrowing his brow when that number gets smaller and smaller without a sound marking a big win. Each time I round the floor asking if he'd like something to drink, he tells me the same thing: "whiskey neat." I didn't stop serving him because he tipped well, but maybe I should have paid more attention to the signs that there was a breaking point.

It's probably the third or fourth drink in when I make my round again and ask if he wants a refill. He has a lost expression on his face and is slumped in the casino chair that's purposefully so plush to the point you could fall asleep in it. After a time spent pondering about who knows what, he finally nods and leans forward toward me.

"You got some good curves," he slurs. "It's so hard to not want to touch that ass."

Oh. So that's what he's thinking about. I swallow and cower back from him, making a small step backward from the machine while he continues staring at me with hungry eyes, like I'm delectable enough to eat.

"Uh, thank you," I say, even though I'm far from thankful for the compliment he's giving me.

"I could win a lot of money, this next one feels like a big one." he says, grinning. "And when I do, I'm going to treat you right." He leans forward to try and touch me, but I step back, almost stumbling on that ass that's apparently so touchable to him.

I grit my teeth and look around frantically for a security guard to catch the uncomfortable expression across my face and put two and two together that I am in need of help. Once I see someone in a brown suit jacket walking toward me, I flag them down.

"Hey now," the guy says once he sees what I'm trying to do. "I'm just joshing here. There's no need to make a scene."

I don't say anything because one of the guards, Victor, steps in between me and the guy and tells him that it's time for him to vacate the premises.

"Hey man, I didn't even touch 'er!" His yell is almost as loud as the machine. "I'm a paying customer here, you can't tell me to leave!"

"You come to our casino, you obey the rules. That includes not touching the waitresses. Come on." Victor grabs him by the arm and pulls him off the chair while I watch, clutching my serving tray. The guy shoots me a menacing look and I cower for a moment, but I just tell myself that I will probably never see this guy again, and he'll probably forget everything that happened while in a drunken state anyway.

"Are you okay, Marissa?" Julie, one of the bartenders asks me after Victor takes the man out of the hotel.

"Yeah," I sigh. Unfortunately, I can't say it's anything that surprises me. There's always an instance where a player is escorted because they've lost a lot of money, and even if there's less of an instance where flirting with the waitresses goes too far, it still happens. I mean, we wear the dresses to attract people to spend more money. Sometimes things will take a turn for the worst. My time had finally come. "Shit happens."

I technically signed up for this when I decided to take a second job waitressing. Anyone that knows me should know that I'm on the more introverted spectrum for a Vegas inhabitant. I would rather spend the night cooped up inside my apartment eating a bowl of instant noodles and watching K-dramas than bumping elbows in a nightclub with hundreds of strangers. I know that being a cocktail waitress seems like the complete wrong job for me, but I couldn't say no to good tips from people who either drink more because they're irritated or excited. Plus, I don't have a boyfriend, my parents live in California, and my fellow hotel coworkers-slash-friends work odd hours so making some extra money beats being alone at home.

"Yeah, but still." Julie rolls her eyes to the ceiling. "These men don't know how to keep it to themselves."

Julie is one of our seasoned waitresses. She's only been at the Blossom for a little over a year, but she came to us with over five years of Vegas waitressing experience from day and nightclubs to a brief stint at a gentlemen's club she has no desire returning to. She's kind of the big sis of the Blossom casino waitress crew, and somehow still sticks around when shit like this happens. I know she's dealt with worse than what happened to me—stupid things that stupid people do—but she's somehow grinned and bared all of it. I know she gets super good tips that easily bought her everything she's ever wanted and then some, so she's been able to grow thick skin. Whereas I am wondering if I should have just applied to be a table attendant. But then I'd have to unearth my secret, that I'm actually more of a Vegas implant than what everyone thinks, and we can't have that happen.

"Marissa," Julie begins. "I'm going to tell you one thing, and I want you to carry it with you, whether you stay being a cocktail waitress or don't. No matter how your body reacts to what just happened, you just need to tell yourself to stick your head up high and fuck anyone who tries to mess with you."

"But it sucks," I mope. "I know we're supposed to be selling a good time here, but sometimes it feels like the cons outweigh the pros."

"Hey. I know that you're doing this as a second job to make some extra pocket money. Your life isn't going to be waiting machines or nightclubs. But not many people can say they've persisted through typical Vegas visitors. You can!"

I shrugged, even though she made a good point. Persistence through tough times is important in a job, and I've definitely persisted. I'm certain that eventually, when I work my way up in the hotel world, this one blip on the timeline of my life will be a good talking point and hopefully give me the edge if I'm up against someone else who may not know the "explosive" life of a Vegas hotel employee.

"You're right," I tell her. "My customer service skills are on another level."

"Exactly!" She pats me on the shoulder and pulls me into a side hug. "It'll get better, Marissa. And when you've made it in the Vegas hotel sales world, promise you won't forget about us down here."

I laugh. "I could never. There might be hard days but this job really helped me start to break out of my shell."

"Yeah! I mean, come on, you didn't move to Vegas for nothing. Embrace everything Vegas has to offer. Have you even been to a nightclub?"

I lower my face and quietly bite my lip before shaking my head at her. "No," I whisper.

Her eyes widen and when her mouth opens, her jaw sticks. "You've..."

"I know," I butt in before she finishes that sentence.

You can ask me all you want why I decided to move to Vegas, why I was so excited to be in the hotel capital of the United States, and I will give you a genuine answer. I wanted to live and work somewhere where I knew I was going to move up in the hotel world, and I could have lived anywhere: New York, Los Angeles, San Francisco. They all have bustling hotel scenes, but in the end, I chose Las Vegas because I was mesmerized by the grandeur of the Strip. Thousands of rooms towering over one street, the beauty of lobbies that are designed with such elegance it's like you're in a rich person's garden, all of it. Even if I didn't like going to nightclubs or couldn't afford a meal at a high-end restaurant, I couldn't help but feel mesmerized by their grand interiors. I just hate large crowds. How I walk down Las Vegas Boulevard every day when there are show girls asking for photos or people lugging coolers in the summer, I don't know. I just know that a confined space with no lighting except for a strobe here and there with blaring music makes me want to immediately flee and jump under my bed sheets.

"Not your thing?"

"I don't do great with crowds," I tell her. "Something about sweaty bodies touching mine and stepping on toes does not sound appealing at all."

"So what you're saying is, if you were in a state where you couldn't feel sweaty bodies or someone stepping on your toes, you might tolerate being in a club?"

I know what Julie is getting at. Sure, if I had a drink or multiple in a booth that only housed a few friends and acquaintances, then I could feel some kind of way that even a bump wouldn't phase me. I wouldn't be opposed to trying it, but drinks at a club cost a pretty penny and unless someone offers, I won't be handing anyone my credit card for a well vodka soda or bottle service.

"I mean maybe. That's a 'don't knock it until you try it' sort of thing."

She grins at me, perking her eyebrows up and down. "Well, I'll keep that in mind." She winks and soon leaves to make her rounds again to the new flock of people who are settling down at the machines, and once I do a round of deep breathing in place, I decide it's probably time for me to do the same.

Once it's time for me to clock out, I meet up with Kayley, aka my work wife, in the break room since she got off work around the same time as me. As I walk down to the room, Kayley scrolls through her phone, eating a plate of fried rice set aside from one of the restaurants for employees to grab.

Kayley waves at me as I sit down across from her. She's a front desk supervisor who started working at the hotel around the same time as me. We bonded over being young and newly moved to Vegas, but we couldn't be more different. It almost feels like Kayley took a majority of the social skills I had and doubled it on herself. She loves talking to anyone, which is good for her job and making friends. She's attempted to get me to go out with her many times, but I've always steered clear from it, even though I knew if I were to go out with anyone, she'd be the one I'd trust the most to make sure I was doing okay.

"So," she began, chewing. "A little birdie told me you had an incident on the floor today."

"A little birdie?"

She rolls her eyes and shakes her head at me. "Okay fine, it was Jeff. Victor told him after he had to escort the guy out of the hotel. He's not so much of a little birdie and rather a big eagle, spare me. But more importantly, how are you feeling? After everything's happened?"

I shrug, standing up to get myself a plate of food. "To be honest, I'm over it now. I mean, when it happened, sure it was kinda nerve-wracking. Especially because I saw how quickly it escalated. And I feel like I could've done something to stop it, maybe ignored him when he tried to flag me down, but I couldn't say no to the tips. I guess I'm grateful he didn't actually touch me. That I was able to get help before it got any worse." I sit down and shove a fork full of the fried rice in my mouth, groaning at how it suddenly made my body full just from one bite. I realize I hadn't eaten in eight hours and this comfort meal is really doing the trick at eleven o'clock at night.

"That's a plus. Still though, people just need to back off. Thank goodness there's a desk that separates me from anyone trying to get their hands on me."

"Yeah. I mean, I'm only waitressing three days a week. It's not like I'm stuck doing it forever. I'm doing it for now to put some money away in savings, and then we'll hang up the dress for good. Probably when I get promoted as Director of Group Sales."

"Or hang it up for a special occasion. Which brings me to my next point..."

"Wait," I drop my fork onto the plate and narrow my eyes at her. I don't like where this is going already. "What next point? There wasn't even a first point!"

She gives me a dumbfounded look. "Well sor-ry! I'm just trying to figure out a good transition to what I'm going to ask because I know you're not going to like it no matter what."

"Then why are you asking me?"

"Because I want you to say yes as a gift to me, your best friend-slash-work wife, for everything I've done since we moved here almost two years ago."

Oh no. I definitely know where this is going. "Kayley..."

She points a finger at me. "Don't 'Kayley' me! You don't even know what I'm going to ask."

"Of course I do! You said 'which brings me to my next point' in response to my cocktail dress. Where do you wear cocktail dresses? To nightclubs. What have I never been to, even though you have begged and pleaded with me every single time to accompany you to? A nightclub. You're going to ask if I can go with you to a nightclub, Kayley."

She slams the table, hard enough to jolt me upright. "You're damn right I was going to ask you to go with me to a nightclub! Come on, Mar. It's my 27th on Friday and for once I want to be able to celebrate with you at a nightclub in Vegas. And I already know you don't have to work Friday night so you can't use it as an excuse."

I groan and slump back into the hard plastic chair I'm sitting in. I don't even think I could use anything as an excuse because if I miss Kayley's birthday, it's just going to make me look like a shitty friend. Maybe if I visited my family last minute, but

Friday is in two days so that wouldn't give me much time to plan. So that means I have to tell Kayley that my schedule is wide open.

"Okay fine," I murmur. "I'll go. But only because it's your birthday. That's the only time where I'll sacrifice my dislike of nightclubs for you. That or your bachelorette party, whenever that will be."

"Hey!" Kayley shouts. "Rude. I just haven't had the best of luck in the dating pool. All the men I match with online are either fratty security guards or that club promoter who had the audacity to tell me that I was too much for him. Besides, you're not even looking for anyone to date and you don't hear me complaining."

"That's because I don't even have time to think about dating with how much I work." Plus, I don't want to try and search out "The One" through some online dating app. Kayley's right, the pool of dateable men around here hasn't struck her lucky yet and I know if I started to list all the qualities I want in a future partner, my findings are going to come up short.

"Yeah I know. You know I'm just messing around. No man in Las Vegas can even hold a candle to the Marissa Waters. And if there is someone out there, well I'll be damned."

"I'm sure that somewhere in this city, someone is probably at least worthy of a nice date out."

Kayley starts to laugh. "Yeah, and it better be at the fanciest steakhouse on the Strip. And he'd better be like, the next CEO of freaking MGM Group or something. Otherwise I can assure you, no one else is worth your time."

As long as he's smart, determined, and has a sense of humor, I think I'll fare okay. He definitely didn't need to be swimming in money, but if I was currently devoting most of my hours to make it up the Vegas hospitality ladder, I'd hope he would be too.

"Noted."

"So Friday," Kayley says as she props her elbows onto the table, leaning into me with her blinking green eyes. "You're coming?"

"I don't think I have a choice, do I?"

"Nope. Consider this my present. 10 PM, Omnia. Well, we'll meet here first. Dress to impress. Who knows, maybe you'll find what you're looking for where you'd least expect it."

"Doubt it." With my standards, I definitely don't think I'm going to find the love of my life at a nightclub that I'm being forced to go to. If he was anything like me, then he'd be spending his night being a completely boring soul at home, maybe reading a book or watching television. But being at a nightclub, probably wasted on expensive alcohol? That's a myth ready to be busted.

Chapter Two

Kellen

"And this is where you'll be staying until we talk about a more permanent location," the hotel's General Manager, Erick, explains to me and my dad as we step into one of the Blossom Hotel and Casino's luxurious villas. His voice is flat as he opens the door and gives us the grand tour of all the amenities the villa has to offer: motorized curtains that span from the floor to the room's high ceilings, marbling throughout the pillars and floors, a private backyard pool, and dedicated butler service. People pay thousands to stay in these villas for a night, and I get to stay here complimentary until we regroup to talk about what my future looks like, and if it'll even be in Vegas.

I can't seem to get a read on Erick and his thoughts on the whole situation, because this guy has yet to smile or spread any sort of cheer since introducing himself. Trust me, I'm still warming up to it too, buddy. I don't know why he's so cold, considering who he's talking to. My dad's kind of a big deal in Vegas, even though he's hardly even here. His name is Lawrence

Zhang, the CEO of Fortune Hotel Group. Who owns the Blossom? Fortune Hotel Group. The moment I graduated with my Master's in Hospitality Management from Cornell, my dad wasted no time putting me to work in one of Fortune's hotels spread across the globe. Lucky for him, an opening came to be the Blossom's Director of Hotel Operations.

So, he immediately phones Erick in Vegas and tells him, "My son is newly graduated and will be temporarily taking over the Director of Ops position. He'll be on a ninety day trial period, and after we will assess if he will be suited to continue." No ands, ifs, or buts about it. I didn't even need to show my resume or interview. That's how powerful my dad is. In his defense, it's not like I'm coming to the hotel with zero experience. I worked front desk summers throughout high school and college at our hotel in New York City and later moved into banquets. So, it's not like I'm going in with no idea what I'm doing. I'm just going in with less on my resume than what the job description says an ideal candidate should possess for this job. But despite what people might think of me—a spoiled know-it-all who's really getting whatever he wants right now—I do have some part of me that wants to try my very best for Fortune's top-ranked hotel in service, especially because that's my department that maintains it. That and I want to work somewhere where I don't need to be under the guise of my father dictating my every move.

"Looks good," my dad nods. He takes a walk around on his own, peering into the bedroom quickly by himself before rejoining us out here. "I think I am set. Erick, are you good to move on from here?"

"Yes sir." Erick nods.

"Good. Kellen, I will return to Vegas in ninety days. I expect a glowing performance review from Erick. If I hear you are not doing a good job, then I will have no choice but to have you stay home and work back at the New York property under my watch. I am giving you your chance to be independent, in Las Vegas of all places. Do not disappoint me."

"Yes, father." I nod solemnly.

"Excellent. I'm flying out to Hong Kong tonight. You will be reporting to Erick, but also will have a multitude of people working under you. Make them want to respect you."

And with that, he opens the front door and disappears as the door slams behind him, not even muttering a goodbye or thank you. I don't even remember the last time my father told me he loved me. Every major milestone of my life, I never heard a lick of affection from my father. It's just always work with him. When am I old enough to work for the hotel, when am I going to take over a hotel, take over the company? The moment he knew he was going to have a son, he crafted my life for me to be the perfect offspring to run his billion-dollar company.

"Thanks, dad," I murmur.

"Well then." Erick claps his hands together. "I need to get back to my office. Get settled, your first day is Monday where you're going to meet the team and get right into it. Make daddy proud, alright?" His condescending tone irks me to my core.

He follows the same pattern as my dad and heads out the door, without a mention of a "welcome" or "nice to meet you." Suddenly, the villa feels a lot more ominous as it's just me and the sound of the air conditioning whirring throughout the room. If there's one thing I wish I was right now, it would be not alone. I've spent the last few years in New York with my calendar booked every weekend, basking in the glory of bachelorhood at its finest, complete with exclusive clubs and weekend trips to the Hamptons with a different woman in my bed every night. I craved the desire to be like that again, especially when I'm somewhere where it can come so easily.

I stroll over to the couch in the living room area and turn on the tv to continue watching that show I started on the plane. Pulling out my phone from my pocket, I snap a photo of my feet propped up on the coffee table in front of me and type the caption, "Officially settled in the new place, HMU if you are in the Vegas area and want to go out," to post on my story. Last I checked, I have close to three thousand followers and I sure as hell do not know three thousand people personally, but out of that number are a select handful that I remembered moved to Vegas to continue their hospitality career. I just hope they remembered me. Hell, that they still liked me, to warrant a hangout in this new town I called home.

A few episodes in, and a call to the restaurant for dinner later, my phone buzzes with a DM from Taylor Cutler, a friend-slash-acquaintance of mine because his dad is also a hotelier.

> Taylor: Yo, you're in Vegas now??

> Me: Yup, new DOO at the Blossom.

> Taylor: Wow, congrats! I've been staying here for a bit now. We're about to announce a new acquisition. Wanna go to a club?

> Me: Let's do it

> Taylor: Cool. 10 PM Omnia. I can get us a table, no prob. VIP meet and greet with Zedd, the whole shebang.

> Me: Sounds good man, see you then.

I put down my cell and walk over to the landline located near the wet bar to place my dinner order. I dial the extension that transfers me to the butler service.

"Villa Guest Services, this is Frank. How may I assist you, Mr. Zhang?"

"Hello, Frank." I smirked. "I wanted to see if I could place an order for room service. And if it's possible for me to add a drink onto that dinner tab?"

When Frank and another banquets person open my door, they wheel in the many plates of food that I ordered for dinner. I figure because my tab is covered through the hotel, why not just order whatever I want?

Frank begins to lift up the cloche to my entrees: oysters on the half shell, filet mignon with mashed potatoes, seared scallops, and for dessert, creme brulee. I don't know if I will finish all the food, but damn, I will eat as much as I can inhale.

Frank finishes by putting a bottle of whiskey on the table and pours me a glass.

"As requested sir, a recommendation from our head bartender, Hakushu 12 Year. The best Japanese whiskey in our collection."

He waits for me to take a sip, and I melt once the smoky taste reaches my mouth.

"Excellent choice," I tell him.

"Wonderful," he nods in contempt. "Enjoy your meal, and please notify us should you need anything."

"Thank you, Frank."

When the door closes, I slice off a bit of filet mignon and shove it in my mouth. God. I know that different people have their feelings about red meat, but I can't help but moan at how tender the meat is in my mouth. I learned how to cook from my nanny, on nights when I felt alone because my parents were busy being hotel socialites almost every evening, and she'd teach me how to cook all the comfort Chinese food I wish my dad introduced me to, but as I grew up, the desire for cooking got lost somewhere along the way. I had the money to eat out at fancy restaurants, why would I spend time to cook? But now that I'm living somewhere, alone, for the first time ever, no parents, roommates, or a nanny, maybe it's time for me to reintroduce myself to cooking again. Try and understand what makes a piece of meat like this so melt in your mouth delicious.

Almost half the bottle of whiskey later, I grab my phone and check the time. Shit. Taylor told me to meet him at the club at 10 PM and it's already 9:30. I'm not even wearing anything remotely club appropriate right now. I stand up, and feel myself wobbling back and forth, definitely at a higher level of buzzed right now. I rush over to my closet and fan through all the shirts I own. I want to make some kind of impression. The clubs here in Vegas can be some of the most elite clubs in the country, and dressing to impress is definitely on the agenda.

I decide to pull out a navy blue suit jacket and matching colored pants to pair with a white button down shirt. I look at myself dressed in the mirror and brush my hands down my pants to get any excess lint off of them. I may not have worn a suit since my graduation day, but today may as well be the first day of many where a suit was going to be part of my daily wardrobe. So much for loose t-shirts and jeans, that wasn't the Blossom's brand.

I jog to the bathroom to put some product in my hair to keep any loose threads from sticking out and grab my wallet and phone before rushing down the long hallway that houses all the villas in the hotel and hoping there was a luxury car that was available to take me to the club. I could walk, but there are more people walking down the Strip right now than I want to deal with. Plus, I think if I tried to walk, I would be too buzzed to figure my way around.

Thankfully there's a car nearby that a bellman called for and within minutes, I reach Caesar's Palace. As I exit the car, I notice that there's a group of people who are also wearing similar attire to me - men wearing similar buttoned down shirts and women wearing body-hugging dresses. Some of the men wore prints that weren't really my style–a bunch of flowers that seemed too much for me, but I could appreciate that the women were wearing sequined dresses that accentuate the curves of their ass and the shapes of their breasts. I smirk, that sexy sort of grin I get when I drink enough that sends a tingle down to my hands. Oh, to touch those curves.

I walk up to the entrance of the club and meet eyes with Taylor who's propped up against the wall on his phone. It's been a few years since I last saw him; since then he's grown out a full beard and his voluminous hair is gelled back.

"Hey!" I walk up to him. He shakes my hand and we hug briefly. "Good to see you man."

"You too!" He grins back at me. "You look the same as you did when we saw each other last, like what? Six years ago now?"

"Yeah," I laugh. "Six years. We were at HX in New York. I was in my last year of undergrad. My dad forced me to go because he said it was going to be good for me to get myself out there before I take over a hotel."

"And look at you now! Director of Operations at the Blossom. People keep saying it's the hottest thing to come to Vegas since they opened the Wynn. Between you and me, my dad's pulling his hair out over whether or not opening a hotel here is going to bring us any business because Vegas is so saturated with good hotels already."

"Yeah, it's tough," I admit.

The Blossom has been open almost ten years now and when my dad decided to buy the land and break ground on the hotel, there was a lot of pushback from everyone whether or not it would be a smart idea to open a new hotel in Vegas when there are hotels that are well-established already, like Bellagio or MGM Grand. But he told investors that his property was going to succeed. Why? Because he was determined to bring a new face of luxury to the Strip with some Asian flair. The investors were beaming by the end of the presentation and decided they would fund the Blossom. Some of them I had to imagine were just excited to see cocktail waitresses wearing cheongsams because

I'm certain some of them have that fetish, but we ended up not even moving forward with the idea anyway because of cultural appropriation. Our architecture reminiscent of the inside of a palace speaks for itself.

"You kind of have to just hope you bring a sort of luxury that is going to attract people to spend money."

"Yeah. Have to admit, that blossom flower ceiling you guys do in the lobby is pretty dope."

I nod slowly. "Yeah, it is." I smirk at him while I picture myself standing in the lobby again. The cherry blossoms, which are actually just those fake plastic ones, are hanging from the ceiling and brighten the room with their light pink hue. It's my favorite part of the hotel, even though there are plenty of places that hold that "Instagram-worthy" charm.

We head inside the club without even having to wait that long because Taylor reserved a table diagonal from the stage that has a ten thousand dollar minimum spend. I don't know if anyone is planning to join us—maybe Taylor has a few friends in Vegas that will help us—because unless we buy a few bottles of the club's finest cognac, there is no way that we are going to meet that threshold.

As everyone starts flowing in, a few waitresses ask what we'd like to order. Before I can speak, Taylor immediately cuts in and lets them know we'll start with a bottle of Veuve.

"That works, right, Kell?"

I nod. I can't say my go-to drink is always champagne, but it's always the drink of choice at every social gathering I get dragged to by my parents. So, it's become one of those things that I tolerate. It's good, but a dark spirit like whiskey makes me feel warm inside and makes for a better thing to sip.

Once they return with a few chilled bottles, Taylor returns as well with two women, each one on each of his arms.

"Ladies," he yells as he sits back down across from me. "This is Kellen, he and I met because our dads are friends in the hotel world."

The ladies, who I soon learned are named Dani and Sophie, are two blonde women who tell us they're here on a girls' trip from Indiana. How did they get here at our table? Taylor spotted them while he was exiting the bathroom and something clicked in his mind that catapulted him into smooth talking his way to their party. I'm sure all he needed to say was "I have a table close to the stage," and they were literally running in their heels behind him.

Taylor calls dibs on Dani, which leaves me with Sophie, but I can't complain. She's beautiful, with her long, perfect curls and light blue eyes. When we talk, I don't feel like I'm in love with her, no love at first sight and butterflies in my stomach feeling either. But, as we're sipping on more champagne, my inhibitions flee from me and I scoot closer to Sophie until our lips are barely touching. I'll probably never see her again, but that doesn't mean we can't fool around and have fun right now.

"I bet you weren't expecting this when you woke up in Vegas this morning," I laughed.

"I've learned to not expect anything when it comes to waking up in Vegas," she chuckles back. Her hand slides up to my leg and I lace my fingers in hers. As we're leaning into each other, I feel the champagne bubbling up and warming my stomach. Our lips touch and for that brief moment, I feel like I'm the king of Las Vegas.

We blow through a few more bottles of Veuve, thanks to some more women Taylor's been able to round up, but I want to get up for a moment and decide to lead Sophie to the dance floor. Before we step on, she whisper yells at me that she has to use the bathroom first, so I nod and let her know I'm going to get a drink at the bar, because if I'm going to be at a club my first night at Vegas, I'm going to drink what I want, and I don't think I can get Taylor to budge from champagne. We've already met the table's minimum spend anyway.

"Whiskey, please," I yell at the bartender. He nods and asks me what kind of whiskey I had in mind. I tell him any top shelf is fine, so he rushes to make me a glass and I hand him my credit card. I quickly sign and grab the drink to hopefully find Sophie in the midst of people who are rushing to get to the bar.

I see her and as I'm stepping forward, I bump shoulders with someone and quickly let out a "Shit, sorry," when I feel that there's whiskey that's sloshed out of the glass and onto my hand and probably onto the person I bumped into.

I look at the person in front of me and see it's a dark-haired woman that had a frustrated look on her face morph into a soft look once our eyes meet. You know that thing earlier where I was saying I didn't feel that hint of "love at first sight" with Sophie the moment I saw her? Not with this woman. She's wearing a black, strapless dress that plunges into a deep V past her breasts and has her short bob styled like beach waves. The hairstyle meshes well with her round face. She's not wearing much makeup, just some eyeliner and mascara, and her skin is a nice olive hue that is slightly darker than mine. She looks like she can be half-Asian, like me, but I can't just lead in with "Are you mixed?" especially because I still look like a fool who spilled a drink on her.

"No, I'm sorry!" she says apologetically. "I tried to be sneaky to get my way to the bar and it backfired. Didn't mean to spill your drink."

"It's fine, it's just..." Top shelf whiskey that probably costs the price of a monthly car payment. "It's no big deal."

"Oookay," she says as a playful grin comes across her face. "Let me know if you want another one, on me."

I chuckle. I couldn't let her do that. "I don't think you should be telling me that without knowing how much I paid for this."

Her smile fades and she bites her lip. It's cute. I'm resisting the urge to kiss them. "Damn, just kidding then. I hate that these nightclubs charge damn near what I pay per month for my car."

"Hey, don't worry about it." I take my hand and grip it on her shoulder. "It's not the end of the world if I get another one. Here, how about I get you one? A drink."

She blushes and I see that grin again as she softens up. "That's nice of you, but I'm okay, thank you. These drinks are super overpriced anyway. Should've probably just drank more at home."

"Well can I get your name?" I ask.

"Marissa," she yells against the music.

"Kellen," I respond. "This might sound weird, but you're the most beautiful person I've laid eyes on all night."

I feel my hands clam up as I'm holding my drink. I don't know if it's the inhibitions or just the fact that I couldn't shake the feelings of fluttering in my stomach, but I couldn't stop looking at this girl and feeling like she was something special. Something more than a girl I met at a bar, and I wanted to do something that was gonna prove that point.

"Can I kiss you?"

She looks at me like she didn't just hear the question that I asked her, but she nods a bit to process it, and finally smiles.

"Yes, you may."

I bend down and lightly touch my lips against her. They're soft and I taste the hint of alcohol on them. Once we make that initial contact, she opens her mouth a little more and invites me in. I flick my tongue gently against hers and rope her in with my free arm snaking around her waist, while her arms wrap around my neck. She groans as we're breathing against one another and I'm starting to feel myself harden when she inches her hand up into my hair.

We break off from the kiss and I try to catch my breath for a moment. "Can I get your number? I can't go without seeing you again."

She breaks apart from my hold to take her phone out from her purse, and the moment she looks up, Sophie from earlier grabs a hold of me from my waist and plants a forceful kiss on my lips.

"Hey, there you are! So glad I found you."

Marissa looks at us, and back to Sophie being all affectionate with me, and scowls. I watch her sigh then roll her eyes. She puts her phone back into her purse and shoves a middle finger to my face before storming off.

"Fuck!" I mutter. My shit luck, well drunk decision making, just lost me the first woman that's made me feel butterflies for the first time in forever.

Chapter Three

Marissa

I t's a rare occasion that we're all pooled in a room for a hotel-wide meeting. Well, not the entire hotel, that would take up almost every seat in the Blossom's theater that currently houses Dua Lipa's first Vegas residency. Just the Hotel Operations team, aka guest services and housekeeping, plus Sales and Revenue.

Kayley leans in toward me and whispers close to my ear. "What do you think they want to talk to us about? Must be big if they want all of us in a room at once."

We're in one of the hotel's many ballrooms and there are coffee and breakfast items set out for us in the back of the room. Some people have braved the trip to the back, grabbing a plate full of breakfast because it's complimentary. Maybe the CEO of the Blossom is going to be here to tell us previously rehearsed praise like, "Good job everyone, we exceeded our goals for Q3!" or "You are all so special and make the Blossom what it is." Rich people who don't care about its people and only its revenue are not worth my false enthusiasm.

"I swear if they tell us we're all fired I'm going to riot," Kayley huffs and rips a piece of croissant with her mouth.

"I'm certain that is not the case. The hotel seems to be doing too well for a massive layoff."

"Well, that or we're all getting bonuses from the big man himself!" Kayley starts pointing to people I don't know super well, only that they work in housekeeping or the front desk. "You get a raise! You get a raise!"

Soon enough, we see Erick, the hotel GM, walk up to the stage in front of all of us. Erick only really associates with all the managers because he spends his day behind a desk, letting ownership know that yes, we're doing okay, and yes, we're making money. Of course, there are things we can be doing better, let's spend an exorbitant amount of time talking about it. Sales is doing rather well because we're booking a bunch of business, but as he likes to tell our Director of Sales and Marketing, Joelle, there's always more we can do to position ourselves well against the comp set.

"Good morning team," he says into the microphone. "Thank you all for being here this morning. It is not often that we need to gather in a room together, but I appreciate everyone for taking the time out of their busy schedules to be here. I will try to keep this meeting short as the week is just beginning but I wanted to do this in person rather than announce via email or travel from department to department. I am happy to announce that we have selected the Blossom's newest Director of Operations, Mr. Kellen Zhang."

Everyone claps as this new guy stands up from the front row and walks up to the stage. But I don't clap. I stare, using my cold dead eyes at the man making his way in front of me.

No fucking way.

In front of me and all the other hundreds of people in this room, is a familiar man dressed sophisticatedly in a dark navy blazer with a white button down that pops up a little at the collar. His slightly wavy hair is gelled to the side and he forces a dimpled smile out to his audience. The same dimpled smile that douchebag at Omnia flashed at me after kissing me and telling me that I'm beautiful, only to have a blonde woman kiss him like she belonged to him. Yes, the new Director of Operations, is the scumbag that I unfortunately fell head over heels at the club for before getting my heart broken minutes later. And now, after I told myself last night I don't have to worry because I'd never see him again, here he is. The new Director of Ops for my hotel. And now, I'm resisting every urge to rip my hair out and scream, "You bitch!" so loud the housekeeper on the 65th floor could hear me.

"Um, hi, everyone," he starts awkwardly while the ballroom is silent, sans the whir of the air conditioning. "I'm excited to be working with everyone here in Vegas. I know if I told you that my father owns the hotel, that you'd think I was given this job just for being my father's son. And you'd be right!"

Ugh, I'm actually feeling bad for how much he's floundering up there. He loosens his collar a little bit from nerves and as much as I want to roll my eyes, my mind keeps reminding me how absolutely delectable he is. How soft his whiskey-tainted lips tasted when we kissed. Shit, Mar, you're supposed to be hating him. I make a sour face to myself and see his awkward gaze stare for a moment right into me. I slowly watch as his eyes widen, like the puzzle pieces are coming together in his mind. He knows exactly who I am. And I don't know how exactly he feels, but he was definitely a little more friendly than any other male stranger I've met at a club.

"Well, if you have any concerns, please come and talk to me." He ends the talk abruptly and I can't help but think that I make him nervous. Good, serves you right for flirting with every eye candy you see at a club. That kind of thinking is not worth my energy.

Everyone soon gets up from their chairs to the exit. I take my time getting out of my seat because I genuinely wanted to see what everyone's thinking, if anyone has anything to say. The majority of people make a beeline for the exit, with no desire to come up to him and say "welcome to the team!"

"When your dad owns the place you just get whatever you want, eh?" one of the room attendants whispers near us.

"Dude looks like he's just graduated college. There's no way this guy has director-level experience."

"You know what," Kayley begins, "He is young looking. Wanna play a guessing game? I'll bet he's twenty-three. No, twenty-four. Took a gap year after graduating for a month and went on an escapade to Europe."

"You think so?" I wince. Well that's reassuring–or both his capability to run a hotel and for my potential newfound taste in younger men. In reality, I don't care that much. I could play devil's advocate and say if he's the son of a hotel owner, he probably has years of experience assisting his family with whatever startup hotel they had. Also, despite me being closer to thirty than twenty now, as long as someone's mature enough, age is just a number.

"What daddy's boy wants, daddy's boy gets. Just seems like he's going to get a lot more than smiling faces who delight in coming to work every morning."

"Yup," I nod. I finally get up from my chair and make my way out of the ballroom, quickly turning to see his face, which remains expressionless as he was nodding to whatever Erick was telling him. We meet eyes for a minute until I speed walk out, wishing I could erase him from my mind at the same time. Of course, the first time I fall head over heels in years and it has to be with someone I can't even have.

As I'm sitting in the back office where I'm housed with the rest of the Sales team, I watch as the door to our office opens up and it's Erick and Kellen walking in. Must be making the rounds, I assume. Erick nods at us in our cubicles and introduces Kellen again.

"Hi team, I'm just bringing Kellen around to meet each department. This is our Sales team..." he begins listing us off one by one, and everyone waves as he calls our name.

"Marissa, one of our group sales managers," he motions to me and I plaster a wide grin, no teeth. He's not deserving of my somewhat pearly whites.

"Um, hi," Kellen waves awkwardly. He tenses up as he looks at me. "Nice to meet you." He gulps and promptly turns his gaze away from me and to the wall of the cubicle in the complete opposite direction.

Once introductions are over, Erick leads Kellen into our boss Erica's office.

"Wow, Marissa." I jump and turn to see one of the sales coordinators, Leo, standing at the edge of my cubicle with his arms crossed. "The new DOO has got it bad for you."

"What?" Shit, was it that obvious? "I don't even know the guy." I'm not lying. I don't know anything about him other than his name, a slight history about his family, and that he has the most electrifying touch on my skin. That's not that much in hindsight.

"He obviously knows you. Or knows that he wants to get in your pants."

"Aw, love at first sight," someone else chirps up. "How romantic."

"It's not love," I roll my eyes. "It's probably first-day jitters."

"Well, he didn't even bat an eye when I was introduced," Leo chimed in. "Or anyone else for that matter. Are you sure you've never met the guy?"

I make a mental note to myself to buy Kayley a drink later, because she's going to be fuming if word gets out and I'm not the one telling it to her first, but I should come clean.

"Okay, fine, I've met the guy. But, it was brief! And at Omnia! I could barely hear what the guy was saying anyway. And turns out shit doesn't matter because he's a total player that can't keep his hands on one woman. So there! He can't be nervous meeting me because he just wants a good time."

"Well if he knew better, he'd quit his ways ASAP because it looks to me like he's hopelessly devoted to you."

"Whatever." This isn't some Danny Zuko, Sandra Dee story-line. I roll my eyes and quickly resume the report I have to finish by our strategy meeting. It's not that I don't think my coworkers are lying about what they noticed regarding our first encounter, it's that I wish it wasn't true, because I've already had my heart broken once, I don't think I want it breaking again.

I pack up and bid the office farewell for the day. Thankfully I'm not scheduled for waitressing until Thursday because I feel like I need to step away from the hotel for a bit. As I walk down the corridor to the employee entrance, I see a figure walking in the direction opposite of me. I roll my eyes quickly. Of course.

Life just has a funny way of pressing your buttons and pointing you in the wrong place at the wrong time.

I try to avoid eye contact with Kellen as much as possible until I hear my name.

"Hey, Marissa," he says, lightly touching my arm. "Um, do you mind...if we can talk for a moment?"

"Why? I have nothing to say to you," I say gritting my teeth.

"Please," he begs. "It won't take up much of your time. I can walk you to your car if that helps."

"I can't say that it will, actually. If you haven't noticed, not many people seem particularly enthused that you're the new ringleader."

His shoulders slump and he gives me an exasperated look. "I'm aware, alright? I didn't exactly get to pick and choose my career."

While I have the urging desire to scream at Kellen for bombarding me to talk to him, I know that his life right now is nothing but easy. While I love my job, I recognize that not everyone feels the same way about it. I mean, there are so many other jobs in the world. And maybe he has a dream job, but got stuck pleasing his father and carrying on the family legacy.

"Sorry," I whisper, the guilt seeping in. "I'm sure it's not fun having your dad bossing you around."

He softens up. "It's okay. So can we talk for a sec?"

I don't want to, but since I've given him a hard time since the moment I saw he was walking opposite me, I owe him my ears for a minute.

"Sure," I murmur.

"Look." He scratches the back of his head nervously. "I just wanted to talk about the night at the club. And apologize."

"It's fine," I quickly reply, starting to get nervous. "You were drunk. We make dumb decisions when we're drunk, right? Besides, I was foolish to think I could find someone I like at a club. That's my drunk mind playing games with me too!"

"Wait...can I..."

"But it doesn't matter anyway, because you're technically the boss. Not my direct report, but you have a lot of control over the hotel and we shouldn't have personal relations jeopardize our jobs. So, we should just forget that night ever happened."

"But I..."

"I just think we'd be better off by starting anew." My words are bitter in my mouth. I can't help but continue to think about how much I want my life to go back to that moment in the club where it felt like we were the only two people in the world, where his touch on my shoulder electrified my entire body. Imagine if his hand trailed down my back and made its way down...

"So there's no weird feelings." I rush to finish. Maybe I'm the one whose only feeling weird about this, and my babbling is only making it worse.

"Um, sure." He nods. "If that's what you want."

"Yup!" I force a grin out and immediately try to wiggle my way to the door. "Anyway, I really need to be going home now to feed my...fish. Good night!" I swerve out of his reach and speed walk out of the employee area and to my car. Once I'm inside, I take a deep breath and exhale out my mouth so the tears don't well up as much in my eyes. Of course, I just had to find love in the most inopportune times, with the person that is the most out of reach. Why did fate have to bring us together?

Chapter Four

Kellen

Marissa Renee Jung Waters.

I stare at her name in the hotel's employee database. Twenty-eight years old, born and raised in San Mateo, California. Years worked at the Blossom: four. First three years spent as a sales coordinator until she was promoted to group sales manager last year. I smile back at the wide grin she's giving in her employee ID photo, eager to make her smile like that again someday.

I keep scrolling down to see that there's another job listing on her profile. Casino Floor Server? For a few months now too. Those cocktail waitresses that wear the body-hugging, sparkling dresses that are tight on a woman for obvious reasons. I let out a deep scowl at my computer and flinch for a second. I hope no one heard that and wondered what I was staring at. Damn, I have to assume that Marissa does waitressing as a means to get some extra pocket money but I know how some people on the casino floor get, and I hate that other men get to ogle at her wearing that dress. I wish I could just claim her as mine so I can beg her to stop working that job only because I don't want anyone else to fantasize about her body like that. Like it's for my eyes only.

Our first real encounter post-club night yesterday was strange to say the least. I was geared up, ready to apologize for the moment we shared and how it was tainted by a drunk girl I immediately regretted kissing once I felt the taste of Marissa's lips, but she shut me down quickly. She blamed it all on being drunk and I didn't get the chance to tell her that the feelings I had for her weren't a side effect of my drunkenness.

I slump back in my office chair. Shit. Now if I have any chance to be with her, I have to convince her that it wouldn't jeopardize our jobs. I'd make sure of it. I don't know if I'd be able to convince her though, because she's worried that people will talk. With what I've heard people blabber about me, it sounds like they're a gossipy bunch.

I quickly sit straight up when I hear a succession of knocks at my office door.

"Come in!" I say once I've cleared my throat.

"Hi, Mr. Zhang, someone from the casino desk called and said they needed to speak to you," the person standing at the door says unenthusiastically to me. Look, I know it's a Monday but we can't have more pep in our step when we talk to our superiors? I guess as long as she's not talking to any guests like this.

"Thank you..." I trail on, trying to remember her name. I know it's a big ask of me, trying to remember anyone's name that works here, but I know that's the start I need to get the team to like me.

"Kayley," her voice clips with an annoyed tone. Oh yeah, she's the Front Office Manager. She was sitting next to Marissa at the assembly. She probably already got the 411 from Marissa about how to feel about me. And her lack of enthusiasm tells me I'm not on her favorites list.

"Kayley," I repeat back. "Thanks."

She turns and storms back to the desk and I slowly push myself up to walk over to the casino floor, which is on the complete opposite side of the hotel. It's only been a week since I started here and thus far, I can't complain much. No major fires that needed to be put out yet, and even though the hotel runs into their fair share of issues like guest complaints, room maintenance, and the like, I have yet to have a moment where everything feels like it's all crashing down on me. Despite the only conversations I have being work related, like meetings with managers or corporate, because no one wants to make small talk, I feel like I'm learning a lot. The Blossom is truly the well-oiled machine corporate always raves about. Everyone works really hard here. Positive reviews flood into our TripAdvisor and it immensely helps us edge out over our comp set. While we may not be the longest-standing hotel on the Strip, we're the one that everyone wants to make a reservation for.

As I'm making my way through our casino floor, which is huge at over a hundred thousand square feet of space dedicated to machines and tables, I almost trip when I see who's working.

Marissa is currently taking orders for an elderly man who's sitting at one of our many Lucky Dragon slots machines. He's eyeing her up and down and nodding a bunch, even though all she asked was if he wanted something to drink. I can see her mouth flatten as she really doesn't want to carry on a conversation with the man but he keeps speaking. I ball my fists at my sides. The struggle to not intervene right now is making my head throb. And seeing her wearing that dress is beginning to make my dick pulse. It's a light pink, sequined number that brightens her up in the casino's bright lights, and it looks oh so good against her light olive skin. I quickly turn my head and walk forward once I realize my work pants lean more on the tight side today and I don't really want anyone to be asking me why I'm hard right now at work.

"Shit, where was I supposed to go?" I murmur under my breath. Oh yeah, the casino desk. I don't interact with them much, so I'm not certain what reason they would need to speak to me. I ignore the long line of guests waiting for their turn and walk up to the left of the help desk, hoping my eye contact will get their attention.

I start to get annoyed when I see each of the attendants continue to ignore me and continue to yell "Next!" at the guests waiting in line. I was told they were the ones that needed to see me, so why are they making me wait? Before the next person walks up to the window, I swoop in right before them.

"Hey!" The guy in line yells. "No cutting the line."

I quickly turn around and swipe my hand across my name tag. "I work here."

He quickly mouths an "oh" and starts to back up from me. The casino attendant looks up expressionless at me and asks me, "Can I help you?"

"Yeah, I was told someone needed me from here?"

He blinks and his face transitions from blank to confused. "What's your name?"

I want to roll my eyes at him. So I guess it's not him that asked. "Kellen Zhang? I'm the new hotel Director of Operations?"

"Oh. Uh, yeah. Give me a sec." The guy turns around and disappears behind a wall. Minutes pass and people are being funneled to go up to the counter and the man helping me has yet to return. I can't even predict why anyone here might need me. Does it have something to do with a guest? Approval about ordering more chips? I groan. I should be back at my desk now and not spending so much time wandering around the hotel. I almost turn around to leave when I'm jerked back and a blindfold gets put around my eyes. The only sounds I hear are people's gasps as I try to squirm out of whatever tight grasp someone has me in.

"What the fuck is going on?! Someone let go of me!"

My hands are tied behind my back and I try to kick whatever is in front or behind me. My heartbeat accelerates. I'm being kidnapped. Why or from who, I don't have the faintest clue.

"Someone help!" I shout, but all I hear are murmurs from behind me and people screaming and running away. I try to wiggle out of my kidnapper's hold but whoever is grabbing on to me is strong. They hold me so tight that I'm not able to easily force myself out.

I try a little more to put up some kind of struggle so they wouldn't be able to move me very far but I don't think I'm getting very lucky. Now my feet are being dragged along the floor and I don't even know where I'm heading to.

Is this it? Is this just how I die? A week into my new job in Vegas and I'm already living the plot of a heist movie playing the role of the victim?

Before I call this a Hail Mary, I hear the grunt of one of the men, I assume by the deep voice, as he lets go of me and falls to the floor. Someone unties my blindfold and grabs onto my hand. I can't see who they are but their hands are soft and a lot smaller than mine.

"Come on!" The blindfold falls and I open my eyes to see Marissa running barefoot in front of me. She was the one that saved me?

"Wait, what's going on?" There are so many questions I want to ask: Who's trying to kidnap me? Why did no one offer to help me? And more importantly, why did Marissa?

"No time to ask questions now, we have to get you out of here! Come on, follow me." She's still grabbing my hand and starts to run along the casino floor to the hotel's ballroom area. It's quiet here when there's not a conference going on, so this is the perfect place to escape. I keep checking behind me if anyone is running after us, but thankfully it looks like we might have lost them.

Marissa fumbles for her keycard and uses it to unlock an unnamed door next to one of the ballrooms. She opens it and quickly closes the door behind her, careful that no one sees. She lets go of my hand and slumps against the bare wall as she works to catch her breath. She's breathing at a mile a minute while simultaneously trying to catch her breath. The gasps become louder and she's staring straight at the wall on the other side of the hall. I think she's having a panic attack and my thoughts race at what I can do to get her to calm herself down.

"Hey, Marissa," I whisper, stroking her bare arms. "You're okay. Just relax. Can you take a deep breath with me?" I lead her through breathing exercises that my mom taught me whenever I was scared.

Deep breath in...and hold for three seconds...and exhale out...

She starts to calm down a little bit and shuts her eyes.

"Better?" I ask.

She nods slowly and exhales a short breath again through her pursed lips. She slumps down to sit on the cold concrete floor and I kneel beside her.

"Yeah, thank you. Why aren't you worried?" is the first thing she asks me, still out of breath. Honestly, I am scared, but I see Marissa in a state of panic right now, and my mind immediately changes to ensuring she's okay before anything else.

"I...don't know. I should be. But you started having a panic attack. And I don't know, I went into some protective mode, I guess."

Her face softens a bit and she pouts. "Oh." She turns and her eyes avert to the floor. "Thanks. I don't get panic attacks a lot," she continues. "I hadn't felt something like that in a while. Doesn't help that I had to sprint on bare feet."

"But are you okay?" I ask.

"Yeah," she nods. "I'm good. Thanks."

Okay, now it's time to ask all the questions. "What...happened back there?"

"I don't really know the gist of it," Marissa says. "I was making my rounds and I turned to see you blindfolded and being held by a tall guy with a black hoodie and a face mask on. He was disguised really well. Anyway, I heard you shouting and people were running away from you but no one wanted to help. The people in the casino service area had all fled by that point. So I ran over and kicked him in the groin with my heel in the hopes that he'd let you go. Thankfully he did and fell to the floor in pain. That's when I grabbed you and tried to run as fast as I could before they found us. I was so scared that he'd try to chase after us, that he'd hurt us, so I just kept running until I was able to lead us somewhere where I know a stranger can't go."

"Someone's out to get me," I whisper. Not really in response to anything, just speaking my thoughts out loud. I quickly try to map out all the people who have me on a hit list. I guess it's a lot at this point. Maybe it's someone in the hotel, maybe it's someone who has an interest in The Fortune Group. My family's net worth is almost as high as a Hilton's; there must be someone who's out to wipe me of every dollar I have.

"It seems like it," Marissa whispers back. "And they didn't return with what they wanted yet, so who knows when they're going to strike back."

"Yeah," I nod. "Looks like I have a lot of explaining to do to my dad." I look across at Marissa and she seems to have calmed down a bit since our escape from the mystery napper. "Thank you," I tell her. "You saved my life just now."

"You're welcome," she returns with a soft smile back at me. "Um, I should probably get back to work. I'm still technically on the clock."

"Yeah, yeah you probably should. If you need to explain anything to your manager, just let him know that you pretty much just rescued me from an attempted kidnapping. I can personally endorse you if needed."

She lets out a gentle laugh and nods. "I will. Thank you. I'll see you around, I guess."

"Yeah."

She turns back to return down the corridor and out the door leading back to the ballroom. I can't really explain all what just happened, but my mind is anything but relaxed right now.

As I walk back to my office, my phone rings and buzzes in my pocket. The screen lights up and the contact name shines in my face.

"Dad."

Damn, word travels fast if he's calling about the incident.

"Hello," I answer in my usual monotone voice.

"Hello Kellen," my dad responds back. "I just got off the phone with Erick."

Joy, I wonder how Erick explained it to him. "I assume he told you about what just happened?"

"He did." A pause looms for a moment. "Are you okay?"

My dad isn't much for affection. I don't know the last time he's given me a hug, or said he was proud of me. When I would get hurt in sports growing up he just said that I have strong bones so I should heal quickly. If my body wasn't being put to use working, to him, it was deemed useless.

"I'm fine. Just took me by surprise."

"Okay good. You cannot afford to get injured with this happening now." Of course it's always about my productivity. "We will have a meeting with corporate on how we will proceed. For now, you are to not leave the hotel. Try not even to leave your office during work hours. We will look into funneling your correspondence through an assistant. We cannot risk anything happening while this kidnapper is still at large."

I slump against the wall and cover half my face with my free hand. Confined. No "Viva Las Vegas" moment for me any time in the future. I want to tell my dad he's overreacting, but I'd never thought I would be in a situation where I was blindfolded and bound against my will. So until we figure out who has it out for me, it looks like I'm about to discover every nook and cranny of the Blossom. At least we have almost every cuisine for food and access to a bar is on every corner.

I can't fight his demands, because I know that this is a big deal. I want to put my safety first, especially because I feel like shit for putting Marissa in danger, even though she offered to save me. "Yes, sir," I replied to my dad.

"Good. I need to leave for a meeting now. Send a calendar invite when you can meet about this. Do not forget to invite Erick and the Executive Team. Goodbye, Kellen."

He hangs up the phone before I can say "bye" back. I put my phone down on the cold, cement floor and tilt my head up to the ceiling. Shit. There's so much that I'm upset about: the kidnapping, the confinement, but I think most of all even though everything in my life seems like it's at its worst, I'm most upset that Marissa isn't next to me right now to comfort me.

Chapter Five

Marissa

We're sitting in the whirlwind that is a Las Vegas buffet and my mind just continues to spin.

I just saved Kellen Zhang from a kidnapper.

Someone's out to hurt Kellen.

And all I want to do is protect him, even though I've told myself time and time again I need to stop thinking about him.

Kayley returns back with a plate full of crab legs. We're here for Marcus, one of the banquet supervisor's birthdays. Why did he want to go to one of the most tourist trap places on the Strip? Probably because he likes food flowing aplenty, but I appreciate the company that surrounds me even if I think I never get my money's worth at buffets because I get full super quickly.

After I left Kellen to get back to work, I ended up getting greenlit to go home early that day because everyone thought I might have still been shaken up with what happened and needed to rest. I wished I could have argued against them because I only worked for two hours, but once I got home, all I could think about was fighting off Kellen's masked abductor and how if I hadn't acted sooner, he would have gotten hurt and I would've felt bad that I was too scared to do anything about it.

By now, word has spread far and wide about the incident. It was even broadcast on the news, and I don't know how it got to my parents, but it did and I got an earful of it from them driving home. Even though I felt terrified for my life, I had to grin and bear it and tell them that everything was okay with me, and that the hotel was going to work as hard as they could to make sure that this issue would be under control. I would rather have them not worry about me, even though I'm constantly worrying about myself.

After the call from my parents, my phone began to flood with texts from almost everyone in the hotel on whether or not I was okay. It feels weird, going from a nobody working two jobs to being the center of attention in the biggest thing to happen in Vegas in years. Forget money laundering or some underground casino ring, it's all about who has it out for the Blossom, and more specifically, Kellen Zhang.

"You were so badass," Amy in accounting says to me. "All it took was a heel to the balls and that guy keeled in seconds."

"Yeah Marissa!" Marcus exclaims. "You're like the hot topic in the hotel right now!"

"What did Kellen say when you rescued him?" Kayley asks.

I almost choke on my drink. Me playing superhero to Kellen had a different effect than what I could have imagined. I hadn't felt that panicked about anything in a while. Sure the incident with the drunk guy at the casino shook me up, but it didn't emit the same reaction as rescuing Kellen from a strong, disguised man that held him so tight it almost broke something. I've never run away from anything, only running for a race or to make it across a crosswalk, but the looming worry that someone was going to catch me made me gasp for air like I was drowning.

I wanted to be a hero to Kellen: complete with the confidence heroes bestowed, but that went out the door faster than I could rescue it back. Instead, I was the one that needed saving, and now all the feelings I suppressed about Kellen Zhang: those feelings of animosity, of making sure he was the bad guy, all went out the window. Because he saved me. He held me, helped me control my breathing, and I wanted to press my body onto his and have him hold me until it seemed like the monsters in my body went away. But I couldn't, because he's not mine to hold. And I forget that what he does to me, is all just him being a nice guy. He doesn't like me the way I want to be loved by him.

"Just thanks," I say. "He was kinda shaken up about everything."

"I bet." Marcus nods. "You know I don't love the guy, but no one deserves to be on some most-wanted list."

Everyone nods in unison. Kellen's first week as Director of Operations has been hard, at least from what I notice on the sidelines. Kayley tells me he tries to be approachable, but his execution fails. There are times when he tries to put up a front like he knows what he's talking about, taking care of guest issues that come up, but when they get executed, it all crumbles in front of him.

"Sometimes I think he has what's coming for him," Kayley interjects mid crack. The liquid from the crab leg spurts up and splashes around her. I hold my tongue. Jeez, I have to remind myself for future reference that I can't be making side comments on how nice his hair looks on any given day.

We finish up our dinner close to our two-hour time limit and as we exit the buffet, Marcus, who is leading our pack, turns around and grins as we walks through the casino floor.

"You know, we work in Las Vegas, but I don't know the last time I sat down at a table and just played."

Everyone chirps up in excitement. A murmur of voices starts to grow louder with the laughs filling the casino space.

"You know what, me neither!"

"It's been so long!"

"We should play!"

"So," Marcus begins. "Are we doing this? A good round of Texas hold 'em?"

Everyone claps in agreement and I'm beginning to feel sweat percolate across my forehead. I want to tell everyone no, I definitely do not want to do this. But then, everyone would pester me why, and spilling my secret was something I wasn't comfortable with doing to any of these people, even Kayley, someone I considered a close friend.

I wouldn't call myself a gambler, not anymore at least. But when I moved to Vegas for the first time, I dug myself into a deep hole. I learned how to play poker online on my own, and after hours dedicated to playing with strangers on the internet, I made my way up the ranks in the online poker world and thought I was good enough to enter a tournament. There was one slight problem: I didn't want anyone to know my true identity if I entered, because my name would be public on tournament websites.

Thus, my alias Janessa Frost was born. If you thought long and hard, you could put the pieces together that the name sounded eerily similar to Marissa Waters, but no one ever found out. I played my first tournament at MGM Grand with a hundred-dollar buy-in, and somehow made it pretty far, winning my buy-in back pretty easily. Pretty quickly, I started feeling confident. I, or Janessa, I should say, participated in tournaments every other week, and started garnering attention from the poker community. I wanted to enter the World Series of Poker tournament so badly, but I was nervous to bet ten-thousand dollars into a tournament where I didn't even know I would win. It was then I realized that there was only so much I could hide and continue to do before I would inevitably get caught. That plus the addiction of playing poker and the fear it'd get out of hand and I could potentially lose all the money I had over some game.

So, after I did not enter the World Series of Poker tournament, I decided Janessa would retire from the poker scene, and so would I. Since then, I got the job being a cocktail waitress so I could keep myself occupied with work instead of playing more, and have yet to play since. Well, apparently that is, until today.

I know I could just act like I don't know what I'm doing, play dumb, and just say I got unlucky, but that would go against my competitive spirit. Now, all my mind is racing to is the thought of just winning to feel good about playing again. And hope this doesn't start some trickle-down effect ending in Janessa announcing her return back to the scene.

"Sure, why not?" I say nonchalantly.

We make our way through the loud casino floor that I'm so familiar with, and walk into the hotel's poker room. There are some tables that are already occupied, and someone asks us how many of us would like to enter.

"There's five of us in total," Marcus tells them. "We all know how to play Texas hold 'em right?"

Everyone nods, including me, but I definitely look like I'm not as confident. Everyone else is beaming with excitement in hopes they'll come out victorious.

The employee working the poker room takes us to a table and we are seated with four others to make a complete table of nine. The buy in is pretty low for daily tournaments here, and there's a five-hundred dollar guaranteed prize pool. I have a feeling that my coworkers, especially those who haven't played in a long time, will soon be in for a rude awakening once they see the chips dwindling from their stack because they decided to take a gamble. We'll see who is the last to leave the table.

Our first six levels are through, and we reach the point where it gets more intense. Antes go up by a bit but I'm sitting comfortably with more chips than what I started with. I see the stress on Kayley's face as she wants to ask me how I'm doing so well, because I'm one of three people in our friend group who's still in the game. I'm multitasking in my head, not only trying to keep track of my hand, but how I'm going to answer if Kayley asks why I've kept these poker skills a secret for so long.

I should've let everyone know there might be a slim possibility that they might need to wait a while before they'd leave because I am the last one from our friend group standing, or sitting, at the poker table with the most chips. The other person left barely has enough for the next bet, but I'm certain that he won't be able to win much if he tries to go all in, which I have a feeling he's considering.

The cards are dealt to us and I don't raise anything before the flop, just to see if he would. He doesn't, which leads me to believe that he wants to play it safe and he's not confident his hands will carry him through.

I'll be honest, I'm not confident either. I want to raise enough to see if he'll go all in, but I have to hope I can get a better hand on the flop than what I have now, which is a queen of diamonds and a nine of clubs. I can be lucky and get a straight, or if I don't get that, hope my card is higher than his and bluff my way to a win.

The dealer puts down the flop: a king, a three, and a ten. I can't show any emotion but in my mind I'm yelling, "You've got to be kidding me." I don't know what to do. I can hope for a jack to get the straight and I'll know I'll be able to win. If I don't, then all I have on the table is a king, which will not be much of a benefit to me.

On the river, the dealer deals a two. Shit. The other player raises. Double shit. I call. The last card is dealt and I bunch my fists under the table. The last card is...a jack. Oh my god. The only way that he would beat me is if he has an ace, but I don't care. He raises, and I raise so he has to go all in. I watch if he does. He tells the table he's all in and he shows his cards first. A pair of kings. No freaking way. I show my cards. A straight. He has a pained look on his face and I slump back in my chair. I did it. I've still got it.

I feel the excitement seep back into my veins. Maybe it would be worth getting back into the game after all.

Chapter Six

Marissa

As I walk up to receive my payout, Kayley stops me in my tracks by running up to me and wraps me up in a giant hug. Her strength almost hoists me off the floor and I cling onto her so I don't fall.

"Holy shit, Marissa, you are so good at poker! When'd you learn to play?"

I hold my tongue. Kayley's one of my closest friends, and I feel as if I betray her trust if I don't tell her.

I've never told anyone my secret card game obsession for lots of valid reasons. Most of them have something to do with fear. Fear of judgment, fear of punishment, fear of friendship loss. You can't predict how you'll perform, and if word were to get out about my past, I fear it'll affect my ability to do well in the future. People would know me, versus thinking they knew a fake persona.

"I just played sometimes with my dad," I fib. "It's not a big deal."

"Not a big deal?" Kayley throws her hands up, frustrated. "It's the biggest deal! You're like a professional."

Professional, psh. That's a lofty word to use. Yes, in another, secret life, I was considered a pro. But I'm Marissa, an average person that might know a thing or three on how to play poker. I don't want to be anything beyond that.

"No, I think I just got lucky," I admit. I just need to deflect Kayley from thinking too much about my skill set.

"People who get lucky don't just win."

"Well, maybe I just have a really good bluffing face."

"Oh, you definitely do," Kayley nods. "I'll never know if you ever had those cards when you tried to raise me and knock me out of the game."

"You won't," I laugh. "That's like, the golden rule of poker. Never share your hand if you're the last one standing."

"Not even if it's to your bestest bestie?" she pleads with blinking eyes.

"Absolutely not." I grin as I feel the surge of relief fill me inside. Cool, I think I've avoided any secret tellings for now. At least when it comes to poker. The Director of Operations asking me to be his partner in crime to take down a potentially dangerous group of people set out to take the Blossom down, that still replays in my head.

Kayley turns to me. "Well, I thought this was fun. So, if you ever want to play another tournament, then I'll join you. I probably can't beat you, but watching you play was fun in and of itself."

"It was fun," I admit. Even though there was a valid reason why I took a break from playing poker, I did enjoy getting back into the game again. It was equal parts nerve wracking and exhilarating. Sort of like saving Kellen. Even though I wish I didn't find myself in such strange situations, I couldn't help but appreciate that they tested me and got me to step outside my comfort zone. "I think I would do it again." I grin at Kayley. Maybe if I kept myself under control, I could try making this a monthly event to fall back in love with it again.

Kayley and I say goodbye to everyone after I pick up my winnings, and we make our way back to the Blossom to pick up our cars. Everyone else is going straight to the employee parking garage, but I decide to tell everyone that I forgot something at my cubicle to go back into the hotel. I actually hadn't forgotten anything, but I'm still riding this weird high from winning so I feel the need to continue pressing my luck. Fifty bucks, I tell myself. I had won more than that tonight, so I feel somewhat comfortable risking that much right now, probably on some online blackjack game, just because I don't feel like going home yet.

Once I step up to the entrance that opens up into the casino, I pause for a moment to survey the floor. It is busy, almost every slot chair occupied by a guest and the tables are chock full of people cheering.

I walk over to the area where the video card games are and stop in my tracks for a moment before taking a seat. I look across from me to see Kellen intently looking at the screen, possibly pondering if he should hit or stand. As he reaches over to take a sip of his beer from his cup holder, he looks up at me and waves while pressing his lips to the rim of the glass. Now I have no other choice but to make my way over to him to say something.

"Hi." I walk up, taking the seat next to him.

"Hey yourself." Kellen smirks at me, with his dimples in full view. My heart melts at the sight of them. "What are you doing here so late?"

"We came from another casino," I tell him. "Marcus, one of the banquet servers, had his birthday dinner at a buffet. And then we decided after that we'd all play some games of poker and then we spent the rest of the night doing that."

"Poker, huh? You know how to play?"

I nod. "It had been a while since I played though."

"How'd that go?"

"Well, I won," I chuckle. "So you can say it went pretty well."

"Nice, good job!" Kellen raises his hand and I excitedly high-five it. My palm lingers on his for longer than a beat and then I quickly recoil. Any longer than that I would have wanted to intertwine my fingers with his so I could feel a layer of safety envelop my hands.

"Thanks. I have to admit it was pretty fun. Do you know how to play any card games? Well, obviously," I stammer. I can't believe I freaking asked him that while he was sitting behind a machine where you could play online card games. "You're playing Blackjack right now."

"I am," he laughs. "But I'll let you in on a little secret." He leans closer to me, almost enough for our faces to touch. Almost enough for us to kiss again and for me to remember just how much I loved how his lips tasted, even if I still questioned his intentions when it came to relationships.

"I don't actually know how to play any other card games," he whispers. "Never learned to play poker, baccarat, none of that. Just blackjack. Which doesn't even require much. Just maybe counting, if you know how to do it."

"That still takes strategy! I always try to press my luck too much in blackjack and I always bust."

He keeps the distance between us and raises his eyebrows at me. "Well, maybe I can teach you a few tricks sometime."

I let out a small "oh," not loud enough for his ears to listen, and then quickly increase the distance between us so I can calm myself down in case he hears my heart beating out of my chest.

"Maybe." I just shrug to brush it off.

"So, what are you doing at the Blossom this late?"

My chest hums and I hold my stomach tight for a second. He deserves to know. I have to tell myself that I need to build this trust with him, especially when there's a lot more stakes we'll soon be dealing with.

"Do you want to know the truth?" I laugh, slightly thinking how pathetic I am to choose playing more than going home and not thinking about my place of employment.

"Of course I do. I want to know everything about you."

I gulp. I'd share it with him too...knowing damn well that it could go wrong.

"I still felt this energy after playing tonight. Like I wasn't done trying to press my luck." I shake my head. "That makes me sound like such a gambler. I stopped playing because I didn't want to fall too deep into being one."

"Hey," he says looking at me. "If you were afraid of telling me because you thought it would make me think you have a gambling problem, then don't be."

"Thanks," I murmur. "It wasn't that really. I just...I used to play a lot. And my friends don't really know that. They think I'm Marissa who doesn't get herself into trouble and I know people might think differently of me once I tell them I like to gamble."

"Well, do you think that's necessarily a bad thing?"

I shrug. "I guess not. Maybe I just don't want people to think I'm doing something bad. You know, because it's gambling."

Kellen bursts up laughing and it feels like it shakes the room. "I'm sorry," he says mid-laugh. "I shouldn't be laughing. It's just, you're in Las Vegas. Sure they promote responsible gaming everywhere, but this city thrives off of all the money it makes from gambling. So, technically you still have a good heart because you're feeding into Vegas' profit."

"Look at you with all your business talk." I smirk. It was lowkey sexy, and I can't even imagine how my insides would feel if he started to add numbers into the mix. Revenue strategies and STAR reports did this weird number on me.

"That's not even really business talk. Don't even get me started on stock trading." Kellen continues to fixate his eyes on the video screen in front of him. He's contemplating if he should hit or stand, and when he clicks "Hit," a face card is dealt to him and the screen tells him, "You bust!"

"Dammit," he mutters. "I hate when I get fifteen. I never know what my next card is. So," he says, turning back to me. "You're here, why not play a few? Do you want something to drink?"

I purse my lips together. Of course I want to stay, or else I could have bypassed entering the hotel and just gone straight to the parking lot. I look over at my watch. It's past one in the morning. I can't drink now, or else I won't even get home until past two. Then again, I don't even feel tired. It's clear that everyone sitting in these casino chairs has no desire to sleep anytime soon, and I don't know if I will either.

"I don't know if I should," I admit. "It's late. I don't even know what made me think I should be spending time here." I quickly stand up and sling my purse over my head. "I think I should head home."

"Wait, Marissa, it's late, let me..."

"No, it's fine," I put my hands out and do a stopping motion. "It won't take me long to get home. Promise."

"Are you sure? You didn't even get a chance to play."

"Yeah," I nod quickly. Feelings have changed and honestly, I need to keep my distance. "I'm sure. I shouldn't be staying out too late anyway."

I quickly turn to head back toward the front, when I feel Kellen's hand grip my arm. What the fuck? I think. Then my thoughts soften. I'd want him to grip me like that any time. Like he wants to hold me close and never let me go.

"Just...can I see if there's a room available? It's late, you really shouldn't be driving home right now. I'm just looking out for your safety."

"Here?" Last I checked we were sold out. It doesn't happen often, but there's some big convention happening and our hotel's close to see that traction.

"Kellen, I'm pretty sure the hotel's sold out."

"Shit, you're right. From that convention. Okay then, you can stay in my spare bedroom."

"What?" Where did that idea come from? Why he was so adamant on me staying here, I don't know. Well, maybe I do. It could be a few reasons. Yes, it's late, and yes, I do live somewhat far from the Strip, and there are reckless drivers out this time at night. But, offering up a spare room? In his own living quarters?

Am I that important that he would open his home up to me to stay at the hotel? I guess so, but do I want to be?

"I have an unused bedroom, you're more than welcome to stay there if you don't want to drive back tonight."

"You don't think that's weird?" I know that we're better than we were when we first met, but I'm still thinking about how we met in the first place, and how we were alone for a moment and almost, just almost, kissed. That is, until I realized that I couldn't be with someone who was just going to use me for a good time and then move back to the next girl in line that can give him the same thing.

"No…" Kellen gives me a look like I was the weird one. "If it makes you feel better, there's also two bathrooms."

"Sure," I laugh. "That is a plus."

"I just want to make sure you get home safe. Time isn't stopping, you know."

"I appreciate it, thank you," I say, smiling and nodding to him. Maybe it's because I haven't had a lot of kind gestures thrown my way, especially from guys where I've felt something more than just a platonic friendship. And come to think of it, I actually don't think I've ever even slept over at some guy's place in high school. My parents were always so weary about that. When it came to sleepovers, they only trusted a few certain people, like my best friend Alisha and this one girl in my class that had a huge mansion in Palo Alto that was forced to invite the entire class to her place for a sleepover after Senior Ball. She just needed to invite everyone so she could lose her virginity to Matthew Alward, the star basketball player. Alisha and I were just there to dig through her family's dark secrets and swim in the pool at midnight.

"I, uh, haven't slept over at a guy's place before." Or even a guy's bed to add. I can count on one hand the number of times I've had sex. I think it's because I don't like hooking up. I want to establish a connection before opening my body to someone. Wait things through before being that vulnerable.

His eyes widen and he leans away from the casino screen. "Oh," he says after taking a deep breath. "Yeah I can see how this can be weird."

"I'm not a virgin," I rush to defend myself. But it seems now I've unearthed Pandora's Box with that confession. "Not that I want anything sexual right now. With you. Sorry, that makes it sound like you're not attractive. Okay, I'm going to stop before I dig a deeper hole." I take a deep breath and my sigh is almost as loud as the people screaming at the roulette table. "What I'm trying to get at is that I was never allowed to sleep at a boy's house growing up, and I never had a steady boyfriend, so this whole 'sleeping at a guy's place' is kind of weird for me."

"Hey," Kellen says, holding his hands up in a surrender kind of pose. "Don't have to be sorry. I get it. I haven't shown myself to be the most trustworthy guy since we met."

"Yeah, but in all fairness you've gone from being extremely untrustworthy to slightly trustworthy, so that's something to be proud of."

"I'll take it," Kellen smiles and those freaking dimples come out to play again. "So, how does my offer sound?"

Well, considering how I came into the hotel after a long night of playing, proof that I wasn't thinking about tucking in for the night yet, I'd say the offer sounds pretty nice. For once I didn't need to worry about being home too late or driving at all if I still wanted to have a drink or few.

"It sounds like a good opportunity not to pass up," I nod.

"There you go," Kellen smiles. "How about a drink?"

Chapter Seven

Kellen

Who the hell have I become?

Opening the place where I eat, sleep, and bathe to someone I barely know but can't stop thinking about?

Did I even put away the clothes I had dry cleaned off the dining room chairs? How much trash is on the kitchen counter?

Well, too late to go back on that offer now that she's accepted.

Marissa walking into the casino at one in the morning definitely was not on my bingo card for things I'd witness, and I definitely didn't expect her to come back from a poker tournament that she'd won, eager to play some more. But I guess there's a lot of things I didn't really know yet about Marissa that I found myself itching to inquire about.

I turn my head and look at her sitting next to me, playing blackjack and sipping on a Fat Tuesday yardlong. Her wavy brown hair is perfectly nestled atop her shoulders and she looks intently at the screen, debating if she is going to hit or stand. I could look at her all day, even if she was doing absolutely nothing. She captivates me, even though I know I can't act upon it.

We were in this weird limbo of we kissed as strangers, found out we're colleagues, and now she knows I've got more tasks on my to-do list, like searching for the people who are out to hurt me. Now, we're in this weird chasm of "friends", except I'm the weird friend that opens their house up for the night because I'd rather her sleep next to me than drive late or under the influence. We're really spending a lot of time with one another, and I can't help but think of every way I want to touch her body. Throw her on the floor, wrestle her around, god stop it, Mariah Carey voice in my head!

"Fuck!" she murmurs and slams the boozy slushee into the cupholder.

"Everything okay?"

"Yeah." She pouts through her straw as she reaches to take another sip. "I stood on sixteen thinking that the dealer would bust but he freaking pulls up with a twenty! This is like the fourth time this has happened."

"I mean, you can't really predict what card is going to come next, even if you try and count them. Poker's similar, isn't it?"

"I guess," she shrugs, resting her elbows on the screen. "At least with poker it's not just you and the dealer. It's strangely rewarding to see if you can make other players crack even if you know your hand is shit. If you can convince someone and still come out successful, you're doing something right."

"Yeah, I have no idea how to do that well. You're going to have to teach me that one."

She opens her mouth to speak and then promptly shuts it. "Nevermind. I had an idea but I don't know how well it's going to work."

"What idea was that?"

"Well, you're not going to get any experience in it unless you actually play. But, there's no way I'm risking you playing poker here. Wait...are you even supposed to be out right now?"

If we're really trying to cover our asses, no. I shouldn't be out right now. If I wanted to follow my dad's orders, I would be in my room, tucked deep in the corner of the hotel that only the elite can access. But he only said I can't leave the hotel. Within the premises, I was free to do whatever I want. And I couldn't fall asleep, so I left my room to walk around and find a snack. I'm dressed in a beanie, T-shirt and joggers. People usually see me in a business suit, so hopefully they think I'm just a guest with my more casual fare.

"Not technically," I answer. "But I couldn't take it anymore being confined to one room. And, I was hungry. I look disguised enough that no one would recognize me right?"

"Sure you do," Marissa jokes as she leans back in the chair. "You're really going to make this a challenge for me to protect you, huh?" I can see a hint of worry spread across her face soon after she speaks, like it's dawned on her how surreal this assignment truly is.

"Hey, don't worry, it's going to be fine," I rush to tell her. "I'm not going to let you take this on alone."

I almost reach my hand out to touch hers, but I quickly ball it up into a fist. I can't let my feelings get in the way. Especially after the way I ruined any chance of a relationship my first night in Vegas by being too drunk and too set in my ways of wanting to put my hands on every woman I saw.

"Okay," she nods. "Thank you. I just...have this pressure on myself to be the best all the time, no matter what I do. My mom was kind of strict on me growing up. She wasn't like a stereotypical Asian parent by any way, but she always made sure to tell me 'Do good in school so you'll get into a good college and later a well paying job!' Like that was the end goal: success. I didn't place in my school's science fair and she got all mad at me because she knew I loved science and wanted me to place first to show that hard work pays off."

"Yeah," I laugh, relating all too well. "My dad's the same way. Except he didn't give a shit about me growing up, he just waited until I was old enough to make sure I could take over one of his hotels to tell me I had to ensure this place was in top shape or else I'm moving back home."

"Really? But how is he going to measure that?"

"The usual. TripAdvisor rating, how high our occupancy is, employee turnover, how well we're doing against comp set, all those metrics ownership likes to care about."

"Oh yes, comp set," she rolls her eyes. "My favorite word in the hotel dictionary."

I shoot her a puzzled look. "Really?"

"No," she says, chuckling. "Just another way for leadership to tell us what we need to fix by comparing ourselves to others. Like why didn't we quote a higher rate for this group, but all I care about is making sure business is coming through the door."

"Yeah." I sit in on these meetings with other directors and the Fortune Executive team, where for the first time in my life I have to carry this confidence to explain to everyone that I'm doing a good job running my department. But, the collective stare of twenty execs does nothing compared to the one stare from my father, secretly critiquing me and my work ethic. When he speaks, everything he says makes me feel so small.

"Kellen, why did we wash these rooms?"

"Kellen, why do our reviews say we're not providing a good service?"

He might as well just say, "Kellen, why do you suck?" because he never wants to tell me anything good about what I've done.

"It was kind of destined to be my life once my mom birthed me," I said. "As the first born and only son of Lawrence Zhang, my sole purpose is to continue Fortune's legacy and help it grow. If I don't, then my dad will want nothing to do with me."

"God, that's awful. I'm assuming you didn't want to always go into the hotel business then."

"You'd be correct. Growing up I actually wanted to be a teacher."

Marissa's eyes grow wide, ready to pop out. "Really?"

"Yup." I don't even know the last time I told anyone that. Maybe it was when I had to write a report in elementary school about what I wanted to be when I grew up. A teacher isn't what screams out to people when they see me, but there was just something about the close connection my teachers had with me, the wealth of knowledge I thought they had, like they were a walking encyclopedia, that ignited this desire to be in a role where I felt like I could help shape the leaders of our future. Ten year old me was definitely not screaming, "I want to be just like my dad!" A cold, stone-faced businessman who only cared about the money.

"I don't really talk about it," I tell her. "Because there's no way that it's ever happening. I mean, I don't regret being in hotels. When I got to college I really grew to appreciate it. My professors were really supportive. I entered these case competitions and did really well. It was then I realized, maybe I was meant to be in the industry. I guess if I ever was tired of doing this, I'd teach hospitality at a collegiate level. That'd be like taking my dream I had when I was a kid and doing it with content I actually care about."

"That would be cool. Maybe I'd enjoy being a teacher. Definitely not to elementary school kids though. I decided that after I pulled my hair out so many times from babysitting as a teen."

"Oh no, I would not teach elementary school. High school seemed more like my forte. I've had to watch my nephew a few times and I felt just as tired watching him as I do after a workout. He's a workout."

I watch as she tries to stifle a laugh but fails and just laughs straight in my face. Might have felt a trickle of spit land on my face, but I can't say it really bothered me much.

"That really made you chuckle, huh?"

"Sorry," she says. "Maybe it's because I'm imagining you trying to chase after a toddler and all I can see is you out of breath from it. How many siblings do you have?"

"Just an older sister. She works for Fortune too. As the Vice President of Marketing. You know those New York moms who send their kids to some fancy day camp and buy designer clothes for them so they can look chic? That's my sister."

"She sounds like someone that I would judge by the way they look, but I'm sure she's a good person, if she acts similarly to how you do."

I feel my face getting warm, like I'm about to blush and turn into a tomato. I can't believe she almost alluded to me being a good person. A lot can change over the course of mere days.

"She is," I nod. "She pretty much raised me, because we're six years apart. Picked me up from school, took me to get ice cream and dinner when my parents had to go to some gala, which felt like it happened almost every weekend. Of course, as I got older, I kind of went through this rebellious phase where I didn't feel like I needed my parents or my sister, so we grew apart when we were both adults and moved out for college. But, I know if I was in trouble, she'd still take care of me, no matter what my age. This all makes me think I should probably give her a call. Catch her up on things not work related."

"Good," she nods. "You should."

"How about you? Any siblings?"

She shakes her head quickly back and forth. "Nope. Only child, now and forever."

"How's that?"

She shrugs. "It is what it is. The pros were I always got my parents' full attention, but cons are I didn't really have that person that took care of me when my parents weren't there. Like I had a best friend from back home, and we'd hang out almost to the point where it felt like we lived together. But, I think I ended up being okay with living with just my parents. No fighting, no favoritism, that kind of stuff."

That made sense. I know there were points in my life where I wish Kiera wasn't born, and times where she thought the same way about me. We fought a lot, and now that we don't live in the same area anymore, I am feeling distant from my family. Before I could just rant to her in the comfort of her condo, and now I'm left thinking when I can even make time in my schedule to talk to my own family. Especially because with them, it's all work and hardly any play.

"Sometimes I wish my life were like that. I love my sister, but she is definitely the favorite amongst my parents. Especially my dad. She can do no wrong in his eyes. And now that she has a big VP job with the Executive Office, she'll sometimes have this 'her way or the highway' mentality and it steers other properties the wrong way, but my dad always sides with her."

"Well, hopefully you'll get to a point where your dad can finally respect you," Marissa says. I smile at her. I know that she might say all these things because she has this instinct in her mind that she wants to ensure that everyone that's around her is feeling good, but I can safely say I don't remember the last time someone has ever said something so genuine and caring toward me. Something that isn't nitpicking my flaws or harping on ways I can do better.

"Thank you," I say. "That's one of the most genuine things someone's ever said to me. I'm starting to realize that this job, hell this industry, doesn't really come with a lot of kindness."

"It will, eventually. People will warm up, get comfortable with you. I'm sure you'll make someone smile soon enough."

I think the fact that I've already made Marissa smile more times than what I was even anticipating should be sufficient enough for me. Now, I'm only thinking about how I want it to be a sort of life goal to just make her smile all the time.

As time ticks on, we continue to talk, occasionally betting on each other to see who will win at the game of craps that's in the center of the video machines, and let the night pass us.

Talking to her fills me with so much energy I hardly even feel tired. Past me would be spending my Saturdays out at a bar late with friends, trying to make friendly competitions about who could pick up a woman faster, and then drunkenly taking one home for a one night stand. I thought that I would keep the same routines here, since the scene is just as vibrant, but the moment I set my eyes on Marissa, I can't even picture being that person. I'm having more fun betting on some dice than dancing the night away and making out with a bunch of strangers.

If only my room had one bed, and then we could live out that "one bed" fantasy I'm thinking about having with her right now.

Chapter Eight

Marissa

For someone who hates it when her friends force her to stay up late past her usual eleven o'clock bedtime, I sure feel like a hypocrite right now.

After one yard long Fat Tuesday and a few free cocktails from Collin, the bartender working at the casino bar, I start to feel the warm fuzzies kick into my system. It's currently three in the morning and while the Blossom casino floor didn't have nearly as many people as it usually does when I work an evening shift at 10 PM, there were still more chairs occupied than I was expecting of people pressing buttons aimlessly on the slot machine.

Kellen and I have yet to leave each other's side once I made the decision to sit down next to him and play a few more games. It felt like we had made it all around the casino at this point. Starting at the video blackjack area, moving onto a slot machine that also doubled as Monopoly, and now, we're at a roulette table where I've channeled that Game Grumps episode where they bet it all on twenty-three and even though I've yet to win the pot, I can sense it coming.

"Are you sure you don't want to...scatter your bets a bit?" Kellen asks quizzically. "You're really...confident that it's going to be twenty-three."

"I'm sure," I rush out. I know it's a big gamble, much like the last four hours of my life have been. But, I'm currently too inebriated beyond my usual amount to really care if the decisions I made will have some affect later on.

Even though I'm supposed to be the one tasked with protecting Kellen, he's doing a pretty good job of making me feel like I'm safe, even if he's yet to realize it. I know that if he hadn't been here, I would have probably just played twenty dollars worth of games and then called it a night. But, he's put his best hospitality face forward and decided that he was not only going to ensure I was safe and tell me to not risk driving home late at night, but he's also encouraged me to live a little, do those things outside of my comfort zone. Besides Kayley, no one in Vegas was successful in making me feel that way.

Reigniting a past life of mine tonight made me remember that I was good at something, after having the mindset that I wasn't for so long. I never got awarded anything for my merits growing up. I was just simply, average. I guess it was okay because no one had any expectations for me and thus, gossiped behind my back the moment I failed. Like, maybe if I had been valedictorian, like Emma Liang, who went to Stanford and then eventually dropped out because she didn't want to be a doctor and now makes influencer videos on how there are so many better ways to earn money than not being in a STEM-related field, I would have more people talking about my decisions behind my back, much like what Emma's facing now. But, I don't. And my mental health thanks me for it.

I watch eagerly as the ball bounces between each of the sections of the roulette wheel, hoping that one of them lands on twenty-three. As it slows down, I cross my fingers and keep my eyes glued on the ball, bouncing ever so lightly in each of the divots, until the wheel eventually slows down on fifteen.

"Dammit," I murmur.

Kellen claps because he played it safe and just bet it all on black, but the payout isn't as big as if it had landed on twenty-three.

"See, you could've won something if you had played it safe." Kellen smirks.

I throw my hands up. "But where's the fun?! If it had landed on twenty-three, I'd be screaming like I'd won the lottery." Maybe I needed to show him the video.

"Well, there's always a next time." Kellen lets out a huge yawn and then shakes his body back awake. "Shoot, what time is it?"

"Three-twenty," I said, pulling up my phone from my pocket. "I don't even remember the last time I was awake this late." Never, actually. I always woke up when the sun would rise, and couldn't fall asleep after that initial eye opening and stretch.

"Me neither," he says. "But I should probably call it a night. In case I get a call the next morning that I need to put out a fire here."

I slump my shoulders and pout. "Ugh, really? But I haven't even won on roulette yet!" That was definitely some of the Fat Tuesday doing the talking.

"Well, it's not going anywhere," Kellen smiles. "Come on, twenty-three. Let me show you your sleeping quarters for the night."

"Hmm, twenty-three. I kind of like it. Just call me Marissa Jordan." I do some poor excuse of a Jumpman while walking away from the casino floor and almost don't land on both my feet. Something snaps in Kellen and he tries to grab onto my elbow to keep me from falling. His touch sends a million little sparks down my arm.

"Okay, maybe not Jordan status yet," I say, standing back up and regaining my footing.

He smirks. "Maybe when you actually win on twenty-three."

Kellen leads me to the escalator, where we walk past the conference room area to a long corridor that points us to the villas straight ahead. We walk past the pool that's empty but still illuminated by light pink so the water has a glow to it, and the bright LEDs that draw an animated blossom tree on the face of the hotel.

"Wow, I never realized that the villas were so far away," I say.

"My dad wanted them to be secluded on purpose. You know, if some celebrities wanted to stay here and didn't want to be near anyone. There's also a private entrance on the left side of the hotel."

"I don't think I'll ever be able to relate," I say.

"What? To stay in a villa?" Kellen asks. "Never say never."

"Yeah true." I shrug. "Maybe it's my frugality coming out." I would much rather spend that $5,000 on a down payment for a car. Or rent. Something I actually can save and have it benefit me later. My mother would look down on me with disappointment spread across her face because she would think something like this is a waste of money.

"Just get a standard room, you only use it to sleep anyway." I could hear her commanding voice in my head.

"I don't blame you." Kellen nods. "There are better things to spend your money on. Besides, I think Revenue is told to jack up the prices on these anyway because it's like an exclusive thing. There are only so many suites in Vegas, specifically those that are bigger than some people's homes."

"Definitely bigger than my parent's house."

We walk up to the door of the villa and Kellen pulls out a key to unlock the room. The key isn't like one of those plastic ones we give to everyone else in the hotel. It's a fob encased in a leather pouch with the Blossom logo on it, and a blossom key chain attached to it.

The lock blinks green once he puts the fob up to it and opens the door.

"Holy shit," I whisper once he beckons me to step inside.

We're only in the foyer, but it's breathtakingly beautiful. The lights automatically brighten once we step into the room from motion sensors and the marble floor with gold specks in it shines at my feet. Large canvases hang on the walls: one of a huge blossom tree reflected on a body of water, and another of a palace. There are potted flowers lining both sides of the walkway, and as he leads me deeper into the room, there's a subtle yet sophisticated touch of elegance in the common area. Plush, leather couches surrounding a rustic, wooden coffee table. The wallpapers ares decorated with, as you can guess, more blossom flowers. Not to mention, a backyard area complete with an in-ground pool and waterfall flowing into it.

"So maybe I have been missing out."

"It's pretty cool, don't you think?"

"Pretty cool? It's like a mansion. Straight out of Architectural Digest."

It sinks in just how different our lives must have been growing up. Kellen acting nonchalant, shrugging like it's really nothing new, or else he wouldn't have just said it was pretty cool. Meanwhile, I am here trying to stop myself from holding my breath because I'm in awe of every minuscule yet grand detail in this room. I wonder what his place in New York is like. I'm sure it was very similar to this.

I turn to see him chuckling to himself watching me.

"What's so funny?" I ask.

"Nothing," he shakes his head. "It's just fun, I guess, to see someone in awe over something that seemed so normal for me growing up. It makes me happy to see someone excited over this."

He continues to lead me through a few more hallways, decorated with more paintings and floral arrangements, until he opens up the door to one of the two bedrooms in the villa. The bedroom, much like the living room, has lush greenery, a fireplace, paintings that are probably worth more than my car, and a plush king sized bed with a huge tinted ceiling mirror above it. Imagine it: having sex and seeing someone's ass reflected on the ceiling as they go down on you.

"So." He smirks. "What do you think? This is good for tonight?"

"This will suffice." I shrug nonchalantly. The problem in the morning will be whether or not anyone will be able to remove me from that bed that I know wrap me up like a bear hug.

"Glad to hear. Let me know if you need anything. Do you want breakfast in the morning? I can have stuff delivered."

Knowing that there's probably not a chance I will be sleeping much anyway, I nod. "That sounds great. Oh! Sorry, I did just remember something. Can I borrow like...a shirt? Just a t-shirt is okay. I...didn't really plan for this, so I don't have a change of clothes on me."

"Oh," Kellen's eyebrows rise up and he quickly nods. "Yeah, let me go grab you something. One sec."

After he disappears down the hall to his room, I slump back-first onto the bed. Yeah, good luck trying to get me out of this. Maybe it was weird of me to ask for a shirt. But I didn't want to sleep with my clothes on, and I'm definitely not sleeping with nothing but underwear on. Not whilst someone I imagined looked amazing with nothing but underwear on was sleeping in the room next to me.

"Here you go." He reappears with a large T-shirt that has the New York Knicks logo on it and mesh basketball shorts to pair.

"I know you didn't ask for the basketball shorts," he says. "But I figured you'd appreciate it anyway."

"Thanks," I reply. "I think I appreciate them more than this Knicks shirt."

"I figured as much," he says with a laugh. "Warriors?"

I nod. I don't keep up with it much, but my dad enjoys having it on during the season.

"I guess I'll just suffer for tonight though," I tell him as I toss the shirt and shorts onto the bed. "I do appreciate that you've given me something to wear at least."

"Good," he nods. "You're welcome." He does a wink with his eyes and I'm just about to melt in place. "I'm off to bed now," he says, making his way back to the bedroom. "Goodnight, Marissa."

"Night." I smile back. "Thanks again. For being so generous. I'm glad I didn't need to worry about driving home late."

"You're welcome. Comes with the job," he laughs.

Once he disappears from the doorway to my guest room, I close the door and lie down onto the plush bed. I slowly take my pants and shirt off, still partially glued to the bed, and take a deep breath in with Kellen's shirt covering my face. It has his scent on it. That scent that smells like the fresh air of a forest. I slide the shirt over my head and pull the shorts up my legs. Even though this isn't my home, I feel safe here. I feel like this place gives me a wall of protection, and I wish I could walk up to Kellen's room next door and slide myself into his bed with him, but for now, I feel comfortable that we're in a place now where I feel like I can lean on him to help me, be there for me. The only thing I have to worry about now is not letting myself fall too deep down a hole that I can't dig myself out of.

Chapter Nine

Kellen

I rest my head on my arm as my finger hovers over the mouse scroll. I tried my hardest to fall asleep in bed, even going so far as to count sheep, but my eyes shot open every five minutes and at one point refused to shut.

The time? 4:45 A.M.

Marissa's probably fast asleep and here I am thinking about all these what ifs. What if she's dreaming of me? What if she thinks about me the same way I think of her? Tonight turned into one of those nights where you spend so much time talking, laughing, reaching this sort of high where your body tells you it wants more, and it refuses to keep still. I feel like running a marathon right now, I'm that jumpy and excited.

I just finished playing a game of Gallant, which is the newest MOBA to come alive since League of Legends, before realizing that playing an online game isn't very fun if you don't know the people you're playing with. Taylor has asked if I wanted to play it before, but I doubt he's awake right now, and if he is, he might have someone he just met at the club snuggled up in his bed next to him.

Instead, I exit out of the game and continue my search on who's out to get me. It sucks that these people are actually decently good at covering their tracks. The masked faces, black hoodies, baggy clothing that has no way of detecting body shape. I hate how I can't place a figure or a name. I scroll through Google after searching, "Las Vegas Blossom Hotel Kidnapping," and find a Reddit thread that seems to have the information I need.

Kellen Zhang, Director of Operations and son to Fortune Group founder and CEO, Lawrence Zhang, escapes kidnapping on the casino floor of the Blossom Hotel. The kidnapper was wearing a black hoodie and black cargo pants. As of today, LVPD has not made any arrests and no leads have been confirmed on who tried to kidnap Mr. Zhang. Mr. Zhang narrowly escaped captivity when a woman wearing one of the Blossom's casino waitress outfits, later confirmed to be Blossom employee Marissa Waters, rescued Zhang after kicking the kidnapper in what witnesses believe is in the lower pelvic area. But the question still remains: who tried to kidnap Kellen Zhang, and are other Vegas hotels at risk?

I quickly read line by line the comments on this thread. Over a thousand of them. Shoot, I know we were on the news for a moment, but the number of interactions I'm causing shocks me. I don't have much of a social media presence, but somehow people find their way to learn everything they can about me. And tell me they wish I could have their babies, which I wish would stop.

"Wow, what did pretty boy do to piss off the mafia?"

"Something's happening in Vegas. There's been a surge in robberies on the casino floor in the past year. It seems like they've just found their next target."

A reply begins below the comment: "You're absolutely right. I live in Vegas and this is just another unfortunate event in the long occurring "take down" of Vegas moguls. Ocean's Eleven is very much real, y'all."

I slump back in my gaming chair. It settles in how real all of this is. When I was back living in New York, I thought I could just live my life. Sure, there would be people who might feel jealous of me, who might despise me because I'm rich, or because I am a part of a company that has to make decisions that others might not agree with. But, never did I think I needed to always watch who was on my back or treat life as if it was a chase. I may have strength to fend away others with the few years of kung fu I took, pretending that I'm a badass like Jackie Chan, but I don't know how long I could live my life always anxious of what's to come next.

I hit the reply button on the comment talking about Ocean's Eleven. I don't rush to give out my identity, but I need to try whatever I can to gain more intel.

"Do you know if anyone has caught any of these bad guys? Or if they've been busted in some failed attempt before? Curious what kind of group they are tied to." I debate whether I should say I'm close to or work directly with myself, if that would be helpful in someone giving me any information they have. But I leave it be, if anyone does want to share more information with me, we can take it to a DM and then maybe I'll reveal myself then. I walk over to my couch and put on an episode of an anime I was watching and toss a blanket over me. My eyes begin to slowly close because they are so heavy, and soon enough, the sound of the anime warbles in my ears.

I slowly blink my eyes awake and my ears tingle at the sound of coffee being dispensed. Initially I almost scream that there's an intruder in my house, especially after everything that I was reading last night. But then, my eyes blink open some more and then it's like I see an angel.

Marissa is standing in front of the coffee maker, wearing the Knicks shirt and mesh shorts I gave her last night. The shirt drops down to a little before her knees and the shorts spill a little bit past that. Her hair is loosely tied up in a half ponytail and some of her baby hairs jut out from the arms of her glasses. I've never seen her look so casual. For work, she's either in that cocktail dress or in business wear. This is my favorite outfit

I've seen her wear though. It's what she'd wear if I woke up next to her in the morning. It's what she'd wear if we were spending time at our home on the weekend. It's her, in her most comfortable and beautiful form.

I feel a sneeze creep up in my nose suddenly and I curse to myself before letting out a large "ah-CHOO!" God, so much for being subtle. And now Marissa knows I have the most ugly sneeze that simultaneously almost makes my intestines blow.

"Oh!" she yelps and quickly sets down the coffee mug she almost drops in fear.

"Sorry!" I sniff, getting up from the sofa. "Didn't mean to scare you."

"How long have you been awake for?" She asks, walking over to the refrigerator to find what I assume is creamer for her freshly brewed cup.

"Not very long. Maybe a minute or two."

"Oh okay." She finds my peppermint-mocha flavored coffee creamer and pours some into her mug. "Sorry, I kind of just made a cup of coffee without asking. I woke up and I figured I would make myself a cup instead of buying one."

"That's fine. I don't pay for coffee anyway. I take it you're the kind of person that needs coffee like a car needs gasoline?"

Her nod is confident. "It kind of only started when I moved away for college, but I don't get a lot of sleep no matter how hard I try, so coffee kind of acts like a medicine. It also helps me concentrate, which I don't do very well either."

"Same here." It's been difficult to reach a point where I'm fully able to concentrate on something, and even then, I lose that focus in about half an hour. Sometimes I think about seeking help for it, thinking it might be ADHD, but I was afraid to under the guise of my father, who refuses to think that something could be wrong with me.

"Do you have ADHD?" Marissa asks.

"Oh. I might. I don't know, I've actually never been diagnosed. I do have a big issue with focusing. It's kind of why I like being in Operations. I'm constantly moving around. I actually hate being behind a desk sometimes because my mind can wander easily when it's in front of a computer. But I also don't know how to keep an organized task list. I have like a bunch of Post-It notes on my desk every time I need to remember to do something."

"Good to know," she laughs. "I talk out loud a lot. I kind of feel bad that the other sales managers have to put up with it, but if you're not even going to be in your office half the time, it looks like I might be off the hook."

Jokes on her, I couldn't get tired of hearing her voice. And I know for a fact when she talks to clients her voice raises in pitch a little, like she was some magical fairy that was going to sprinkle pixie dust over everything. It makes my heart smile just a bit.

"Marissa, you're a Sales Manager. I can't stop you from talking. And you shouldn't be afraid of talking either. Your voice doesn't sound bad."

Her lips are glued to the rim of the mug and she takes an extra long sip of coffee before swallowing a huge gulp that I could hear from the other side of the table.

"Oh. Thank you. Still, I'll try my best to keep it to myself. Be respectful of your workspace and all that."

"Speaking of," I butt in. "We need to figure out a lie to tell Erick about why you're moving into my office."

I decided to ask Marissa if she'd be down to be my unofficial official bodyguard. Do some work on top of our own to investigate these masked people chasing me down. But we work in different departments, so working together is very out of the ordinary.

"Oh yeah. Shoot, I knew I was supposed to be drumming up ideas for something. What can we tell him that won't make him assume we're not plotting to take over some Vegas heist group? Or...whatever they are?"

"Something that we could just write off as a project for work that requires us to collaborate together..."

Before I can finish my thoughts, my phone vibrates loudly on the table. I peer over and see my dad's name as the contact.

"Shit," I whisper. "Sorry, I'll just go take this in my room. Feel free to look around for something to eat if you'd like, or watch tv. Hopefully this doesn't take too long."

I quickly eye Marissa nodding and rush to my room where I answer my dad's call.

"Hello?"

"Kellen," he says in his usual monotone greeting. Never a hello followed by a nickname. Nicknames weren't professional enough for him. My mom had to ensure he was out of plain sight before she called us by a nickname. I was always Kel and Kiera was Kiki when she'd tuck us in bed at night or in the house when dad was away on business.

"Yes, Ba?"

"There is a VIP who will be arriving at the hotel in a few weeks. A very important person that Fortune is partnering with. Given the recent events that have unfurled at the hotel with your kidnapping, we need to make sure this guest is well taken care of. Because if they like Fortune, they are going to help us immensely in securing our position amongst the other big name management companies."

VIP? All this shit is going on and he wants to bring in a VIP?

"Do I get to know their name?" I ask innocently.

I hear him sigh through the phone. Less of a sigh and more of a groan, in fact. He groans whenever I do something stupid. That he thinks is stupid. Like ask too many questions, because if he was really acting the way he normally does, then he would refuse to tell me who he's working with, not because he's afraid to blab about it to their people, but because he thinks if he utters anything out loud to anyone that it'll ruin its chances of coming to life. My dad is into superstitions like that.

"Fine. You cannot tell anyone yet okay? Not until I say so. The only people that know are Brandon Suk Suk and Kiera."

Of course the two people that already know are my uncle, aka the Executive VP, and Kiera...the Zhang family royalty.

"Why do I not get to tell anyone? I'm Director of Operations, shouldn't I have, oh I don't know, more power to direct?"

"Don't sass me, Kellen. Or else I'm just going to surprise you with the VIP."

"Fine, sorry for the comment. Can you please tell me so we can be equipped for their stay?"

"Yes, and remember, do not tell anyone yet. I'm planning on telling Erick tomorrow but that's it. We cannot lose this VIP if he does not enjoy his stay at the Blossom."

I sigh a bit myself. He's making it seem like this guy is just as important as the President or something.

"Okay, Ba. I promise."

"Okay. It's Andrew Tseng."

"Woah," I whisper. Okay, fair enough. That is an important VIP that we can't screw up on. "Wait. Are you meaning to tell me..."

"Yes," my dad cuts in. "We are in talks to have Andrew Tseng be our next resident at the Blossom. Extended resident. We're talking at least a two year contract."

Andrew Tseng is one of the biggest Asian music stars at the moment. A trilingual pop star who releases music in English, Mandarin, and Cantonese, he's like the Chinese Harry Styles. I know it's easy to automatically compare big name pop stars to Harry Styles, but Andrew Tseng is really all that eccentric pop and sexiness that people would say about Harry Styles. He even has the disheveled hair that somehow looks well kept.

I've followed Andrew Tseng since his days before being signed to a label. He'd post videos of himself singing on Youtube, just like Bieber had before he was discovered. A boy, not too far from my age, who wanted to do nothing more but to sing in front of people. He's definitely at the height of his career with multiple charted albums and just fresh off a sold out American tour, so my dad's not exaggerating when he says this is a big deal.

"Got it." I nod. "So this is huge."

"It's the biggest resident we will have in Vegas. Not that Dua Lipa wasn't big, but everyone will be lining up to get tickets to see Andrew. And this will be perfect for the Blossom's imprint on Vegas. If we can secure this, then we will drive up everything: occupancy, ADR, all of it. This will make us one of the most exclusive hotels on the Strip."

"Yeah, it will." And I'll get to take credit for leading the team that makes it happen. "So, my mission is to make sure Andrew wants to do his residency with us?"

"Yes. Well, there isn't much on the competition front. Wynn, Caesar's, they all have artists on the brink of retirement. They're catering to a different group of people. Whereas we're marketing a young, fresh voice, someone who has a lot of potential and is ready to rise on the Vegas scene. Of course, where we're fighting is to keep Andrew in Vegas. He can choose to tour anywhere, especially on an international front. He hasn't made too many moves into Europe yet, but Kiera says he's huge there. So convince him to make Vegas his home. And that includes convincing him that there is absolutely nothing to worry about, especially someone who wants to kidnap him. Speaking of, have you obtained any new leads on who these people are?"

I can already feel the disappointment sink in. My dad works fast, so telling him I've yet to find any new information will cast a dark spell over me. One that is filled with disapproving remarks like "I'm not working hard enough" or "I'm useless as a person to him."

"I've only looked at what others are saying from the news. I don't know what the name of this organization is or who's behind it."

"Well, keep working on it. This is your priority now. Andrew is coming the week of Chinese New Year and will be performing a show, one night only. You have until then to catch this group or you're coming back to New York."

"But Ba!"

"I don't want to hear 'but.' This is very important to us, Kellen, and you should take it seriously too. If you don't, you show me you're not a hard worker. Bye."

He hangs up before I can do it before him.

"Fuck," I mutter, tugging the door handle so hard, the door almost hits me before I open it. On a plus side, I should be happy. One of the biggest Asian pop stars is coming to stay at our hotel, and, if I keep a positive mindset about everything, it will bring in more business and I will get recognition for it amongst the major hotels on the Strip. But, of course now there holds a great weight with this responsibility. In a perfect world, I wouldn't even need to worry about the looming possibility of a mass kidnapper, and maybe other hotels don't need to, if this person's total focus is on me and only me. And now, if I don't catch this person or group of people, I have no other choice but to leave the Blossom. Leave Vegas, a place that I'm beginning to love, and leave Marissa, before I even get the chance to tell her how I feel. So, maybe my dad was right. I need to take this seriously. If I don't, not only does it mean that I'm not a hard worker, for the job and the hotel that I've grown to love, but for the one woman who's made me feel butterflies in my stomach.

I head back out into the living room, where Marissa hasn't moved since I left. She's still drinking her coffee and now scrolling through her phone.

"Everything okay?" she asks.

I take a huge swallow of my own spit and nod. Honestly, seeing her face makes this whole situation better in an instant. "It's going to be," I admit. "Looks like I got something for us to tell Erick if he asks why we're working in the same office."

Chapter Ten

Marissa

"This Reddit thread is really...something," I say, with my eyes glued to the computer screen. Kellen walked me through everything he had gathered about who could be behind all of this, and it's really as "straight out of a movie" as you can get. The mafia may or may not be involved; whoever the Chinese mafia is. I always had a sneaking suspicion that Vegas was riddled with people who worked "underground" to try and take back what they thought was rightfully theirs from the rich, but until I had to pry Kellen from a hooded man's grasp, I thought it was just what existed as plot for a good action drama starring George Clooney.

"I know it's not much," he says, pacing around his office. We had a late start because both of us had our actual jobs to handle before this. Kellen was dealing with a guest who trashed their room and refused to pay the deep cleaning fee, and I had to talk some sense into a group that had dropped a lot of rooms over what they contracted and didn't want to owe anything because of it.

"But it's a start." He's back to his desk now rubbing his hands over his face. "I don't know if I'm the only one who is dealing with this, but I haven't had the chance to get a hold of any other hotels, or haven't heard of anything on the news about new developments yet."

"Seems like they're trying to plot their next move."

"It's agonizing," he says from his desk, covering his face in his hands. "I have a big problem with being in control, and the fact that someone has control over me makes me feel...nervous all the time. Like, it makes my hands shake."

"Welcome to life with anxiety." I cautiously laugh, but I've grown comfortable with my life at this point, including the aspect of it where I panic about things that test my limits, or have trouble sleeping at night over things people say I should "just get over." If anyone tells me "get over it," I want to punch them in their throat so they can try getting over that.

"Sorry." He pouts and slumps a bit in his chair while still keeping a comforting gaze over at me. "I know it's scary, the whole panic attack thing. I didn't know how to react when it happened to you, I just wished it could go away."

"Me too," I murmur. There was that pang in my chest again over the words that come out of his mouth. You definitely don't tell that to someone who you just think is a workplace acquaintance. If you did, my heart would be too worn from thumping out of its chest too much. Maybe I just wasn't used to people looking after me when I would get anxious or panic attacks, because my immediate response is to just mask it so no one worries about me.

"It just takes a lot of deep breathing exercises. Something that I always have to work on. What doesn't kill you makes you stronger, that whole thing."

"The song they always like to play at the gym?" Kellen laughs.

"You know, they really do like to play it at the gym a lot. I mean, it does do a good job of motivating."

"So what's our plan?" I ask.

"Well, I need to start by gathering more information," Kellen says. "I can't imagine that these people are beginners at this. They didn't act like they were, so I will go in and find any record of a robbery that happened in a hotel in the past five years. If they haven't figured out who it is, then that might be better for us, then we can deduce it's the same group. And then hope they've left a trail that we can use as clues."

"That's a good start." I nod. "We can look into police reports, news headlines, something to get us more information."

"Exactly, and figure out who these fuckers are once and for all."

Kellen's voice suddenly goes deep and menacing. I jump a little bit. Seeing Kellen angry makes me soften a bit. I would hate to be the person that upsets him. He turns into someone that I don't want to mess with when he's angry.

"Yup." I nod, resisting the urge to shrink into the wall.

"It's getting late," he says, his tone softening. "Are you hungry?"

It's like he's a magician, because as soon as he says that, my stomach begins growling. "I guess I am," I laugh. "What do you have cooking?"

"Me? Oh, absolutely nothing. But, I can get food at one of the Blossom's many on site restaurants complimentary."

"Oh yeah." I sarcastically roll my eyes. "I forgot. Everything in the hotel is yours to take."

"Well, most. Obviously they can't give me any big casino winnings."

"Not that you need it anyway," I say without thinking. "Sorry, I shouldn't have said that. I really am trying to not think of you as some spoiled brat. I mean, you work as a hotel executive, you're proving yourself in that regard. Kayley just thinks 'CEO's Son' and wants me to believe the worst about you. I'm trying not to do that as much."

"It's okay," he reassures me. "I grew up a huge, spoiled brat. I went to private boarding school and Ivy Leagues for both undergrad and graduate. On my sixteenth birthday do you want to know what I got as my first car?"

"Tell me." I smirked.

"An Audi R8. You know that same car that Christian Grey has?"

"Yes…wait, why do you know that?" Maybe it was because he had a girlfriend who forced him to watch each Fifty Shades movie at opening release.

"Sister. She read all those books and watched the movies. When she had to watch me when my parents were out, she forced me to watch those movies. Which, at the time, newly adult me was cringing at how much they were having sex."

"That's the point," I laugh. "They're like fantasies." Like maybe us having sex might pan out.

"Do you…" He bites his tongue before finishing that sentence. "Nevermind. Live your life how you want to, I will not judge. My sister loves those romance novels. But they're definitely not my kind of read. Anyway, yeah, I had that car for my sixteenth birthday. I've been to every continent, save Antarctica, of course. Without hesitation, my parents gave us everything we wanted. But, once I was old enough to work, my dad spared no expense to put me on the hotel floor. I started out as a busboy during banquets, and then when I was in college, I worked part time as a front desk agent. Did that until I was twenty-one, and then I moved back into banquets and was a banquet supervisor until I left for grad school. Then I kind of got into that spoiled brat phase again, just because I was hanging out with people with similar upbringings to me, and didn't help around the hotel as much. Once I graduated, then my dad was kind of fed up with my bullshit and said I had to work for Fortune or else he'd cut me from getting my trust fund. So yeah, I am kind of here mending that wound that I had dredged up from my own decisions, but I really mean it when I say I want to be a good boss and a good employee. That just because I'm a Zhang doesn't mean I don't care about working just as hard as everyone else for this hotel. There's just...yeah. I recognize I've been handed life on a silver platter."

It was comforting to hear Kellen talk about his life to me, especially recognizing that he did come from a point in his life where he embodied that rich boy stereotype. I kind of wish I could have recorded his speech, so then I can prove to everyone else in the hotel that he's not as bad as everyone wants to make him out to be, but I was savoring this moment. The looming intimacy that was in the air, the rush of warmth that I was feeling that he was being vulnerable with me.

"I...appreciate that. Thank you for telling all that to me. It helps me better understand how much catching these guys mean to you. Well, besides for your own safety of course. That you're starting to carve a spot in your heart for us Blossoms here."

"I may not know everyone by name yet, but I do think that the Blossom has some good people that actually care about their jobs and the hotel they're working for."

"Yeah, there's some good people here. You should see about setting up lunch with them sometime. Like, get to know your staff."

"You think so?" He gets up out of his chair and walks around to the front of the desk, leaning back on it. "People actually will come to some lunch with me if I ask them?"

"Well, I couldn't speak on their behalf, but I would hope they'd at least come for the free food, and then stick around to get to know you."

"I'll definitely consider it. I think the staff should be rewarded in some form anyway. Food's always an easy option. Speaking of food, weren't we supposed to go to dinner?"

"Yeah, but then I kind of prompted you to tell me your life's story so we took a slight detour from dinner. But let's go," I say, standing up and stuffing my purse with my laptop before slinging it over my shoulder. "I'm really starting to feel hungry now."

We walk out of Kellen's office and make way for the restaurant annex where many of the food spots live. One of my favorite selling points about the Blossom was that the restaurant choices were diverse and the food was delectable. Sure, we were an Asian family-owned hotel, and so a lot of the restaurants had Asian cuisine, but there were choices at every price point, and often the food was stuff that you can make fast, but wasn't often found in "fast food" types of places.

Sometimes, I get to take clients to one of our restaurants after a site tour, in hopes that they may be persuaded by the food. One of my go-to places is a place that isn't too expensive, but has food that dances on your tongue as you bite into it. It's called "Happy Noodle", which as the name hints, always makes me happy when I eat it. It's a build-your-own-noodle bowl fast-food style kind of place where you choose your noodles, meat, and any extra toppings. My go-to is one that they offer as a "try this if you're too indecisive" choice: a beef stew noodle soup with egg noodles. It's a Chinese comfort food I used to force my grandma to make for me almost every day. I was – well still am – a fiend when it comes to soup. Any weather, any occasion, soup is my go-to. I have to take a gamble sometimes whether my clients who book room blocks at higher rates if they would have the same thoughts about Happy Noodle as I would. Joelle, our Director of Sales, kind of points me in the direction of something more high end, like Lotus, which is our most expensive dining establishment, but I always get turned off by it because they want to charge over $50 for a steamed fish when in reality, I just get turned off that I've been spoiled with it at family dinners and the price tag will never persuade me from thinking it's just as good, if not better, than one my grandparents can make.

So, when Kellen offers to go to Lotus, I can't say I'm wholly enthused.

"You sure you don't want to go to Happy Noodle?" I ask, my voice laced with a hint of begging because I could go for some noodle soup right now.

"You can get Happy Noodle whenever you want. In fact I know you went to Happy Noodle the other week because Joelle was talking about sales team updates in our director meeting and she told me you signed a contract at Happy Noodle, so it's time for a change." Kellen shakes his head at me. "I know it's delicious, but I have the same issue as you. I go there all the time. And you said you've never been to Lotus. Why are you being so fussy? I have to turn away people who want to dine at Lotus because the waitlist gets full months in advance."

"Ugh." I don't want to say why it's making me "fussy" because then we're going to revisit this whole rich boy talk, and I already had to stop myself from getting too carried away when I imagined Kellen as the mixed Asian Christian Grey driving in his Audi R8.

"I don't know how to explain it."

"Don't know how to or don't want to?" he said with a dimpled smirk at me. "Come on, Marissa. I think we've reached a point where you can consider me your friend, right? And friends tell other friends what's really on their minds."

Sure, I consider you a friend, but I also fantasize about you in a way that makes me want to rip your clothes off, so to classify that? I don't think friend is the right word.

"Yeah," I play it nonchalantly. "I guess you're my friend...fine. I've never been to Lotus, and I always shied away from it because I thought it was just a ploy to make an exorbitant amount of money on Chinese food that probably tastes better if my grandma made it."

"Ah, so you're fussy because this is another example of the rich getting to eat places they can just drop all their cash on."

"In short, yeah." I shrug. "I know it's just me being stubborn. I'm not even paying for it, so I shouldn't be complaining."

"Yeah!" he said defiantly, leaning in so he's centimeters away from my face before drawing back. "Sorry, just teasing, I get it. You know my family isn't like old Chinese money. My grandma and dad butt heads all the time about wealth and social status. He's wanted to move her into some huge penthouse apartment near Central Park, but she won't budge from her little spot near Chinatown. I get it, she doesn't need much to make her content, and she grew up in a village in China with no plumbing so living in New York is a luxury for her. Sometimes I wish I maintained some level of frugality as she does. Then I wouldn't be going through the same routine of closet cleanouts every year. And to your point about the food, you're right. There's something that just hits when it's homemade by a loved one. That's one of the biggest things I miss about not being closer to my Yin Yin. She'd bug the hell out of me just to bring me a bowl of jook, but once I took a spoonful of it, I didn't even care. She knew exactly what I needed at that moment and it was a meal cooked by her. But, the food isn't bad at Lotus. It's actually really great, just yeah, the price tag is pretty hefty. And they don't give employee discounts here."

We reach the entrance of the restaurant and I peer at the menu on a lollipop stand next to the host. Lotus is decorated like an elegant Chinese palace. Red columns hold the restaurant up to its high ceilings, walls accented with hand-painted gold dragons, and large, crystal chandeliers draping from the top. It's not like those restaurant banquet halls that have those gold plastic Chinese characters nailed; it's extremely elegant.

"Hi," the host says, smiling at us. "Welcome to Lotus. Do we have a reservation?"

"Yes, I called earlier and spoke to Harry. Two for Kellen Zhang?"

"Oh, yes! Mr. Zhang, we are so honored you will be dining with us. And you brought your wife! What a nice treat."

"Oh, no!" I start to feel my face flush. "I'm not his wife..."

"We're just friends. Colleagues," Kellen says, toying with his collar as well. "She actually works here too."

"Marissa Waters, Group Sales Manager."

"Ohh!" The host begins to turn red like a tomato herself. "My apologies. You two just look happy together, if that makes sense. Like I'm sensing some connection."

"Oh." Kellen nods. "Well, I'll remember that when we have to work on something together."

The statement does something weird to me. I know it was just a meaningless sentence, but it makes me feel deflated in a way. I'm feeling all these emotions for him, but at the end of the day, we'll never be anything more than workplace associates. We have to be friends, because our workplace relationship forbids us from being anything more."

"Of course," the host laughs awkwardly. "Well, let me lead you to your table. And let Harry know you've arrived. He's excited to see you."

The host walks into the restaurant and as we walk deeper inside, the more the ambience feels surreal. The lighting is slightly dim, to create some kind of dark mood, which has been proven to create a relaxing atmosphere, but it's so different from most Chinese restaurants I've been to. When I've attended banquets before, the lighting was so bright it lit every wrinkle on my face and every vein on the leaf of a bok choy. It was all energy all the time, but here, everyone is quietly chatting amongst themselves at each table while grazing at their food or sipping on a cocktail.

Every table we pass is occupied, and most of the guests eating are dressed wearing at least semi-formal attire. We fit in just fine, thankfully, because I'm wearing the same clothes I have to wear for work, but I can't help but glance at all the women in here who are wearing dresses that tightly hug their bodies and remember that iconic night when Kellen and I first met.

"Here you are," she smiles at us after placing the menus down on each of our plates. Our table is nestled in a semi-private area near the back of the restaurant, near the wall where there is a waterfall draping down into a koi pond.

Wow, talk about an immersive dining experience.

"I'll go tell Harry you have been seated. What may I get you to start with? Champagne? Wine?"

"We'll actually both start with the Yuzutini."

"Two Yuzutinis," she says, smiling. "Coming right up."

"Is tonight going to be you making all the decisions and me trusting you'll make good ones?"

"Pretty much." He smiles. "It's like Aladdin, when he holds his hand out for Jasmine before A Whole New World starts to play. He's standing on the magic carpet and says, 'Do you trust me?' with that charismatic look on his face. Pretend this is your magic carpet ride."

My cheeks flush. God, all I'm going to be focusing on is how in the world Kellen seems to wiggle his way into my heart with this knowledge of all things Disney on a whim. Pretty soon I might need to run over to that koi pond to splash myself in the face to snap the hell out of it or else I'm going to melt.

This isn't a date, Marissa. And you two are just friends. That's how it needs to be anyway. So you can both keep your job and focus on the mission at hand.

"Mr. Kellen!" A booming voice calls out to us. "So happy you are joining us tonight." A shorter Chinese bald man comes to join us. "What's the special occasion?"

"Nothing too special, Mr. Harry. I am just showing one of our sales managers the wonderful food here at Lotus."

"Ah, wonderful!" He looks at me and grins. "Welcome to Lotus! Have we met before?"

"Maybe," I say, unsure. I feel like someone like him I would remember super easily. Especially because his smile is one that sticks with you. "I've never dined here before so, I can't say I have. Marissa," I hold my hand out. "Good to meet you."

"Great to meet you as well, Marissa. How long have you been working here?"

I nod. "A few years. But only a sales manager for one."

"Harry is the general manager of Lotus. And also knows how to make an amazing tomato beef. Chef taking you under his wing yet? You might need to think about adding it to the menu."

"I did tell him we should consider it, but you know Chef, he's so to a 't' about everything. I can't even get him to admit that it's delicious. I saw that smile try and break through when he ate it, he can't fool me! But enough about me!" He claps. "What can I get for you? Did you get drinks in yet?"

"Yes, I ordered a yuzutini for both of us."

"Excellent place to start. Why don't I just tell Chef you're here and we'll just bring out what he thinks will be good for you. Don't even look at these." He pulls away the menus from our table. "Are there any allergies that we need to be aware of?"

We both shake our heads.

"Perfect. I will let Chef know and your first course will be coming out momentarily. And let me check on your drinks. It was great to meet you, Marissa!"

"So, safe to say you're just...royalty everywhere you go at the Blossom huh?" I laugh.

"I think that's a fair assumption," he laughs back.

Now I just needed to figure out how to be glued with him while also telling myself we need to keep things strictly platonic.

Chapter Eleven

Kellen

Harry wasn't lying when he said not to worry about it, because looking at all the food on our table, it looks like the entire menu is in front of us to feast on.

For our first course, we begin with an array of dumplings from their dim sum menu (which they don't even promote at dinner), including some very delicious Xiao Long Bao that are so chock full of soup it's like an explosion in your mouth, followed by every land and sea creature the restaurant probably has: Hainan chicken, a whole Dungeoness crab covered in fried garlic and butter, roasted duck, and a plate of abalone that they don't even put the price on the menu because it's the legit stuff that kind of became a "you only asked for it if you knew you could afford it" dish.

Not to mention: a bowl of my favorite, sizzling rice soup, for us to share, and some Singapore curry noodles. I don't even know where to begin, and neither does Marissa, whose eyes are glued to the array of dishes laid out before her.

"Overwhelmed?" I laugh.

"You could say that." Her eyes refuse to blink as she glosses over each dish. "I feel like I'm at a wedding banquet, except I have to share the same amount of food with eight people rather than two."

"I really didn't know what to expect when Harry said they'll take care of it, but now that I'm looking at everything, I can't even be shocked." My mouth starts watering at everything that's in front of me, and I don't know if it's from the food or Marissa or both.

"Here." I reach over to grab her plate. "What can I get for you?"

"Obviously a little bit of everything, but a double serving of the noodles. Those are a favorite. It's like Chef can read my mind from the kitchen."

"I get these every time I come here. They're one of my favorites too."

I hand the plate back to her and begin scooping some for myself. I had this plan set up the moment Marissa walked through my door. She was a little sluggish getting to my office this morning because her best friend became her office neighbor and refused to let her go off and do her own thing. Freaking Kayley. She's an amazing front office manager, but a pain in my side. I have to keep reminding myself that she knows how to get the job done well, despite her constant cold shoulder at me, and so I have to stop trying so hard to be nice to her in order to get closer to Marissa, because maybe that might screw up her work ethic. I couldn't make out what Marissa said after Kayley's tirade about rich guys, specifically me, but I need to figure out a way to stop her from persuading Marissa that I'm a part of the dark side, or something. Maybe the food will help.

"So, how is everything?"

Marissa is working her mouth to chew anything she can stuff into it. Her eyes flutter and almost go back into her head, making me think she's having some food orgasm, but it makes me picture her having a sex orgasm. Shit. I feel my lower half go hard. Now, my head is filling with the fantasy that she'll do the same face as she rides me in bed. Whenever I can get that to happen.

"It's so good," she says, covering her mouth from the food still being processed in it. "I'm sorry if I ever doubted the rich before, this tastes like heaven."

I cackle as I watch her finish chewing. "Aren't you glad we came here over Happy Noodle?"

"Definitely. But I will say, now you've really spoiled me. I want this soup to be made on demand, for crab to always be made like this. And don't even get me started with the noodles."

"Chef really has a magic touch when it comes to cooking," I say. Even before I started at Blossom, I've always kept my tabs on it from headquarters. One of our most crowning achievements is Lotus. My father scoured around the world to find the best chef to cook Chinese cuisine that had luxurious ingredients but still felt comforting. He discovered Chef Peter Geng on a trip to

France as development of the Blossom began underway. He was young, newly finished at Le Cordon Bleu, and ready to pack his bags to work his next adventure in Hong Kong when my dad approached him, asking if he could make my dad a three-course, plated Chinese dinner, chef's choice.

"You are too good to work under someone," he said. "Even if they have Michelin stars. What are your thoughts about moving to Las Vegas?"

Peter laughed at my dad, like he was out of his mind to take such a gamble, but he didn't really want to take a gamble himself.

"What, you really have all the confidence in the world to take an amateur like me? And what makes you think I would take a risk on your hotel that's not even opened yet versus going to a reputable restaurant?"

"These things are valid," my dad told him. "But, I have tasted your food. Sure you are not an Executive Chef yet, but you make Chinese food with such a good mix of flavors. It is very tasty. I know that you can be creative enough to curate your own menu. And, if you are nervous that this whole thing might falter, then you do not realize how many people search for good Chinese food in Las Vegas. We don't have much yet, but the market is there. You know Chinese people have money, and now, we're going to give them a reason to spend it. So, what do you say? Will you join me?"

They shook on it, and the rest is history. Lotus opened with the hotel, and my dad was right, the market was there. People flocked from all over the world to stay at Blossom, because it was the new modern hotel that appeared on the Vegas Strip. And the theming was so well done it felt like it transported you right back to ancient China. I don't fully remember what China looked like though; the last time I had been there was when I was in high school, but the recreation of the architecture still felt realistic. That, plus all the flowers we put in the lobby when we opened almost put Bellagio's lobby out of the water. Sadly, we didn't have dancing fountains to beat though. That I can still admire about one of the most iconic hotels on the Strip.

"How is everything?" Harry asks when he approaches our table.

"So good," Marissa mouths through her mouth, still full of food. "Thank you for letting us try all this food. I really don't think there was a bad food I tried tonight."

"Well, thank you for your kind words. Chef really puts a lot of care and attention into every single dish. All prepared with love, and the freshest ingredients."

"I'm really blown away," Marissa continues. "I told this to Kellen when he mentioned to me that he would take me here, that I'd never try here because it always seemed so exclusive and for the people who could afford it, but it's worth every penny."

"So does that mean you want to pay for dinner tonight?" I joke. I don't know what our total for all the food we ate tonight would be, but maybe it might make Marissa walk back on her words.

"I don't know if I would go that far," Marissa laughs nervously. "If I did, then maybe I would've ordered less things. If I was able to make that decision."

"Well, no need to worry." Harry smiles. "It is always a pleasure to serve Mr. Zhang and his guests. And I will give your notes to Chef. He always appreciates the kind words on his cooking."

"Is there a chance that we could meet him? Chef Peter? He's like, an icon in Vegas since opening Lotus."

My face recoils a tinge. Since when did Marissa know about Chef? She was just talking about how she refused to eat here because she thought it costs too much for a dish her grandmother could make better. Now she's speaking like she's a part of his fan club.

"Let me ask," Harry says. "I'm sure he can come out for a little to say hello."

"That'd be amazing, thank you."

"So you know about Chef Peter?" I ask.

"Not really. I mean, I've never met him. I've only seen all the press that comes out about Lotus. Winning all these awards, being named hottest restaurant on the Strip, and like seeing his photo in articles and stuff. I have to read up on this information because clients ask about it all the time. The restaurant sells itself."

"Ah, okay," I nod. "But up until today, you didn't want to try a single dish from Lotus because you thought it was too rich for your blood."

"Pretty much. I recognize that he makes good food, my frugality just comes through every time that I want to try it."

"Well, you'll get the chance to meet him tonight, were you expecting that?"

"Not at all." Her face starts to beam. Like this is some celebrity crush she has or something. I don't think I'm looking forward to seeing her reaction when he...

"Kellen," a man dressed with a gray chef's shirt comes up to our table. "Good to see you again."

Chef Peter is definitely not bad looking. His hair is buzzed almost to baldness and he's got tattoos up his arm as well as on his head. Not someone you would typically think of as the Executive Chef of a high-end Chinese restaurant, but definitely looks better to me than Ramsay or Flay. He's slightly older than me, in his late thirties. Hard to believe he helped start Lotus when he was twenty-seven.

"You as well, Chef," I stand and shake his hand. "Amazing job on the dinner tonight, as usual."

"Thank you," he nods. "And you're Marissa," he says, looking intently at her. I watch as her cheeks flush, not trying to get all bothered by her pretty much in awe at his sight.

"So great to meet you," he clasps her hand with both of us.

"You...as well. Thank you, again. I fell in love. With the food. Your food is truly chef's kiss if you know what I mean." She makes that kissing motion with her hands and lips and he laughs, a deep sexy laugh. This fucker.

"Thank you," he says. "What was your favorite?"

"Oh, that's not fair of me to choose! I loved so much of it. Maybe the soup? I'm a really big fan of soup, and your sizzling rice soup was some of the best I've ever tried."

"Thank you. It's one of my favorite things to make. Reminds me of when my mother would make it for me after school. I don't think I've made it as well as her yet, but I do think I'm always getting better."

"Well, you definitely won me over. I've already made a note to return."

"Oh yes? Well, I should give you my phone number. That way, I can whip up some more things to try while you're here."

"That...that would be wonderful." She's practically grinning now, and I'm almost on the verge of ripping this seat cushion off. She's not even mine, we're not even dating, so I shouldn't be controlling over her, but I am. Because I want to be able to make her blush and smile that way, and all this guy had to do was make some food that tasted good."

"Actually," she starts ruffling through her purse. "Here's my business card. My cell phone number is on it. Let me know when you want to set something up."

"Amazing, sounds great." He leaves her with a wink and then nods to me before going back to the kitchen. So much for a wonderful meal, now all I'm left thinking about is how the head chef just waltzed his way into flirting with the woman I'd also happened to have a crush on.

Now do I also need to add "not get jealous of other men" to my list of things to do?

"It was nice of Chef to come and pay us a visit."

"It was," Marissa says, still smiling like she's met a celebrity. "Oh my gosh, I'm still smiling. He's even more dreamy in person. He looks just so...confident. Whoever he gets to make food for when he comes home is a lucky person."

"I don't think he's seeing anyone," I comment, quickly realizing that I'm only making Marissa feel better that she might have a chance with Chef. Oh good, he's single, so I have more of a chance of hanging out with him and not feeling guilty about catching feelings! Stupid, Kellen. You were better off just shrugging and saying you don't know.

"Oh!" Marissa looks surprised. "That's...interesting. I mean, live your life. I...just...he seems like he's such a catch. I'm surprised that no one has wanted to settle down with someone as successful as him yet."

"Or maybe he hasn't found the person he wants to spend the rest of his life with."

"Could be," Marissa says, taking a sip of her martini. "Well, that's good intel then."

"What? You're thinking of settling down with him?"

She looks at me, shocked. I think I said that a little more aggressively than what I was trying for.

"No," she retorts. "Obviously I just met the guy, I'm not gonna start drawing our initials in my notebook. He seems nice, and I'm excited to get to know him more. That's it."

"Sure," I murmur.

"What's it to you anyway, Kellen? You've made it painfully obvious that you're not the type to settle down with one girl."

Oh my god, she's going to bring up the first night we met at Omnia? I'd like to think I was a very different person then compared to who I am now. I'm definitely no longer the immature, playboy-esque, hookups-only guy that I was when I moved from New York to Las Vegas, and that is majorly because of Marissa. Sure I made a big mistake by kissing someone else that night, but I apologized to her about it multiple times, and I thought when we agreed we'd help each other out, she'd forget about everything, but I guess I was wrong.

"Are you serious? I apologized to you my first day of work about that. I know I made a mistake that night. I was drunk, I was infatuated with the thought of having whoever I wanted, but I immediately felt bad that I hurt you and I didn't want to make that same mistake again."

"Well, it doesn't matter anyway. We can't even be thinking about dating each other. We're working together on this big project. I don't want something to get in the way of that, if us dating were to...not work out."

I slump back in my chair. So much for a nice dinner. I hate that it's ended with us arguing with each other, and it seems like I won't be able to say anything that will make her feel any other way about me, especially since she said she still thinks I'm going to still be a playboy around anyone that I lay my eyes on, which is anything farther from the truth.

"Yeah," I narrow my eyes. "Can't have anything I do mess it up."

"Kellen," her voice softens. "I didn't say that."

"You didn't have to," I said. "You're still thinking it." I push my chair back and shift my gaze away from Marissa. "I need to use the restroom, please excuse me. If you need to go, go ahead. I'll see you tomorrow."

I get up and leave toward the front of the restaurant and leave Marissa stranded at the table with nothing else to say. I know I'll probably think of myself as a dick later on that I abandoned her. Fuck, I'm already regretting getting up right now, but I'm too sad to continue to try and defend myself around her right now.

Chapter Twelve

Marissa

I hope that no one bolts into the bathroom right now, because I can't have anyone see me like this. Mascara smeared all along my lower eyelid, my nose as red as Rudolph's and snot dripping down from it.

I'm such a jerk. I knew that when I brought up that first night we met, I'd eat my words. I really don't think that Kellen is that kind of person anymore. In fact, I know he is a nice person who has really changed a lot since he started working at the Blossom. He's no longer that guy who doesn't want to put in the work and wants to party instead. Even though he's trapped in this hotel for his own safety, he doesn't complain about it. But, I just needed to find an out to defend myself from talking about Chef Peter so much. I knew that Kellen had some tinge of jealousy when I started talking about him, and lo and behold, my findings proved true when he would only give that murmured "sure" response.

To be honest, I only really projected my feelings onto someone else because I can't be thinking about Kellen anymore. I meant most of what I said to him. If something were to not work out between us, then it'll jeopardize all the hard work we've put in for his own safety as well as the reputation of the hotel. What I didn't mean to imply was that he was the one that messed up everything. I didn't think that, and if, hypothetically, we were to date, then I know he would be faithful to me. But maybe that's why he hasn't dated someone in a long time, because commitment scares him.

I pat my face down with a damp paper towel and take a deep breath as I look at myself in the mirror again. I don't think once Kellen got up that he wanted me to come back, so if he's sitting there right now, I don't want to do anything to anger him if I were to return. We wouldn't have anything good to say to each other anyway.

I take a deep breath and turn to walk out the door of the bathroom. As I begin to turn to exit the restaurant, I bump into someone exiting from the men's restroom.

"Oh gosh, I am so sorry!" I look up to see who I crash into and suck in a breath. Just my luck, I'd bump into the nice man wearing a chef's shirt and sleeves rolled up to take a peek at those muscled, tatted arms.

"Oh, it's fine, I'm sorry. I just really needed to...pee." Chef Peter looks at my still somewhat swollen face and opens his mouth.

"Marissa," he starts. "Are you okay?"

"I'm...okay. Not really. I guess I could be better right now."

"What's wrong?"

I shake it away. "It's nothing that you should be worrying about. That I should be worrying about. Kellen and I just got in a little tiff, that's all. I'll be fine."

"You're sure? I don't need to beat someone up, do I? I might get fired if I did, but you would tell me if he did something to make you upset, right?"

I hesitate. Did I trust this person that I just met to spill all my feelings to him? Maybe, he almost has an imprint as strong enough as Kellen in my mind right now, and he's not a bad person. He's been truly generous with all the food he's prepared for us tonight. Even if I did have any hesitations, he's proved himself with his hospitality alone.

"Of course. He didn't do anything wrong. We...just butted heads about something and got into kind of a heated argument. It was the first one we had since we've met, and I just feel more sad than anything that I might have said something to make him upset. I'm sure by tomorrow we will be fine and friends again. But thank you, it did feel better to get that off my chest."

"You really are too good-hearted of a person to deserve anything bad to happen to you." He takes a hold of my shoulder. "You deserve someone that will make you feel like you're worthwhile."

I stand there with my heart pumping and mouth trying to spit any words out. Damn me and my conflicting feelings.

"Thank you," I whisper.

"I have to get back to the kitchen now, but I'd love to see you again soon."

"Um, yes, of course! You have my card. Feel free to text me whenever you'd like."

He retreats back to the kitchen and I quickly bolt out of the restaurant. I think he just flirted with me but I couldn't think about that right now. There was much more on my mind.

Without any direction, I speed walk to the one place I know can help take my mind off of things. I go to enter myself in a poker game that starts in a few minutes and take a seat at one of the tables gearing up for play.

"Hi there." An older Chinese man with gray hair and a face full of wrinkles smiles at me. "Here to play?"

"Yup," I nod. There's a few other spots being occupied, but the entire table isn't full. I haven't played since Marcus's birthday, save for a few times online where I stayed up way too late past my bedtime trying to earn back a bunch of fake money I bet over the night. Thankfully, I was able to redeem myself, but the time it took cost me a few hours of sleep.

The dealer gives me my chips and we start to play. I get absolutely horrendous hands in the first few deals, but so far, I try to be safe. My first time to try and bluff comes when someone goes all in, and I actually have a two pair, so I test my luck. I have more chips than he does, so when he says all in, I'm not also trying to bet all my chips as well.

"Wow, we are raising the stakes quite fast, aren't we?"

I smile at the dealer. I can't make any distinct facial expressions or else maybe it would give something away. It's not like I have a great hand. He could beat me with a three of a kind. But, I try anyway. This guy has been taking some risky bets the entire night; I have the feeling that he really likes to get a rise out of people to get them to bet more.

The last card is dealt and I end up with a three of a kind. Whew, okay, and it's a face card. So I feel like I have a good chance of beating him. He can't raise anymore so we're asked to show our hands. He has to go last since he went all in.

"Three of a kind, with the Jack," I say. His face pales.

"Three of a kind, with the eight."

I laugh. Of course, I just happened to be lucky enough to have a higher value card.

"Damn," he says. "I thought I'd scare someone away with my bet."

"Sometimes, you just get lucky. But, I'd definitely not try and bet high all the time, soon enough people will try and pick up on your shenanigans."

"Duly noted. Thank you." He leaves the table and the dealer flashes a smile to me.

"You play a lot?" he asks.

"I used to. Haven't really done much in a few years. But I'm looking to get back into it."

"You're pretty good. You know how to call a bluff."

"Thank you." Playing a lot does help with getting a grasp of the types of poker players that are out there. The ones who are good at hiding their bluffs, the ones who take gambles and succeed, and the ones who want to take gambles but fail. You also don't have many opportunities arise when you get good hands so in those cases your confidence will help ride you all the way through, but a majority of the time is when you have to learn to trust your not so great hand will get you far too.

Our game ends and again, I find myself with the most chips at the end of the game. The people at the table played a good game, but I somehow did have the rare hand of a flush that propelled me to take a risk and win a ton of chips that kept me safe for the majority of the game. Of course people were disappointed, but in my defense, I was stunned myself. I haven't been dealt a flush in a long time. So, again, I finish the night on top.

Everyone leaves the table but the dealer tells me to stay behind for a moment.

"Yes?" I ask.

"You play good," he says. "I know this is just the first time you are playing here, but you play like a professional. Have you considered entering into a tournament?"

"Not really." Yes. Since I figured out I could play well again. "I don't know if I like all the stakes that come with playing in a tournament. I'm more of a leisure poker player."

"Well, you could try. People make a lot of money from tournaments. If you're good enough, you could win a few millions."

I laugh. Wouldn't that be something. "I would probably have to quit my job to go professional though."

"Do you like your job that much to continue working instead of being a professional poker player?"

At this very moment? Not exactly. I'm kind of dreading going back to work tomorrow to share an office with Kellen while the remnants of last night loom over us awkwardly. We probably wouldn't have slept the rest of the night off our fight by tomorrow, so it'll just be a matter of time before someone breaks to apologize, and I wonder who is going to do it.

"A little bit. I mean, I do love my job. A lot. And even though there are days where I question what I'm doing with my life, I don't think I could see myself being anywhere else. And even if I were to be good enough to pursue poker professionally...there aren't that many people that know I gamble. I wouldn't want my family to be disappointed in me for pursuing a career with so much risk."

"Ah, yes. You're Asian right? Are your parents strict?"

I nod. "Well, my mom is. But my dad basically listens to anything that my mom says, so even if he's the more lax parent of the two, he's not really relaxed compared to some parents that tell their kids they could do anything their heart desires."

"Oh, yes. I know what that's like. I have two kids, who are both adults now, but one kid wanted to be a musician. He wasn't bad at it, the guitar, but we had to tell him if he wanted to pursue music, he'd have to put in a lot of practice and effort, and I think he just wanted to find a way where he could sing all the time, because being a nurse was really stressful for him."

"So, what did he do?"

"He's actually a project manager for Kaiser. So, no more nursing, but he still gets to work at the hospital, and then on the weekends, he and his band perform at local bars. They're starting to get more recognition for being a local band.

"All this to say..." he pauses, searching for my name.

"Marissa."

"Marissa. I'm Wing. All this to say, Marissa, maybe it is not a bad idea to find yourself a happy medium. In life, much like a poker game, there are many chances where you need to take a risk, even if it scares you. And then you'll find out, if the risk pays off or not. But you won't realize it unless you try."

"Thank you." The advice helps me beyond just my conundrum with pursuing my poker career. But I don't know if I want to delve that to Wing yet. I've toyed around with the word risk too often in the past few days, and it always seems like I'm finding myself in more situations where risks are required. And while I'm still feeling scared of doing anything that feels out of my comfort zone, I know that I have to try and do something, or else I'd be left looming in the realms of constant "what ifs."

"Will I see you again, Marissa?"

"Probably," I nod. "I spend a lot of time here. I, uh, actually work here. So, you'll see me roaming around the hotel a bit."

"What do you do here?"

"I'm a group sales manager, so I basically help bring business to the hotel. And then sometimes I work as a cocktail waitress on the casino floor. So more business, but I wear a dress in hopes people will give me more tips."

"Well, that's fun," he chuckles. "I think? I wish I could wear a dress so people can give me more tips."

"It has its ups and downs. You probably don't have people tell you they wish they can feel the sequins all across your chest."

"Nope, I have never had someone tell me that."

"Lucky," I laugh. "That's not the worst thing people tell me, but I get some kind of flirty comment made at me almost every shift."

"Yeah, the worst thing I think that happened to me was that I got chips tossed in my face when someone lost."

"Oh yeah, that is definitely not fun. Especially because these chips could definitely take out an eye." I pick one of them up and hold them close to my face to examine it. "Pesky little things."

"Well, if you are ever back here in the poker room for another game, you let me know. I work here Wednesday through Sunday, usually in the evenings."

"Well that works perfect for me, because I get off work at six."

"You'll have to come by then," he smiles. "Even if it's just you at the table, I'll try and help you on your poker skills. Get some other dealers to join in. Or maybe we'll set up something weekly at my house. There are lots of other employees here who like to play. We've been talking about getting a tournament set up just between us at Blossom forever, but no one's done anything yet."

"I think that sounds like a great idea." I definitely feel more comfortable playing with people I know by proxy instead of total strangers. We can all talk about our grievances we have toward the Blossom while also playing a low-stakes round of Texas hold 'em.

"Well, you have a good night, Marissa. And good luck." He gives me a quiet nod as I gather my chips to cash in.

I walk to the casino's guest services desk and get my winnings all sorted out when I see a familiar body when I'm ready to walk back to my car.

"Great." I mutter. Am I going to be the bigger person and relive my moments in hope they'll turn into something good? I guess this would be the time to figure that out.

Chapter Thirteen

Kellen

"**B**ust again? You piece of shit game," I murmur. I've spent too much of my own goddamn money to try and blow some steam from tonight, but everything I've tried has made me more stressed. I think people are staring at me, thinking to themselves that this guy must be going through a rough patch because he keeps murmuring expletives to himself every other minute.

I should have figured out that coming back here would possibly mean that I might lose it all, much like gambling always is, but I didn't want to go home angry. I thought if I won something big, I would be filled with enough excitement and my mind would be taken off of the fight that Marissa and I had at dinner, but since I have yet to hit a jackpot, then you can guess how my mood has shifted. Yup, I am still very much that grumpy, stressed-out person I was leaving Lotus. And now, all I'm thinking about is how Marissa might be off fucking the goddamn Executive Chef and I'm here wishing I could take back anything I said to get us to be friends again.

I don't know if Marissa said that because she meant it, or she was angry that I was being a jealous asshole, but the words still exited her mouth and left an imprint on my mind. Great to know that no matter what I do, if I try and be that better person that Marissa deserves, she will just think about me the same way. I'm not a person that stays committed. If we were talking to Kellen from two years ago, newly enrolled in grad school, and going out to New York every weekend to try and find girls at bars to hook up with, sure I would tell you that a girlfriend is a waste of energy, and that I don't want to settle with one when I could try my hands at all. But now that I've found the one, or the one who's made commitment sound a lot less scary, it's too late. I screwed up, I said some dumb shit, and now she's put all her focus into someone who is successful and doesn't need to worry about their job affecting their relationship. I guess it's better anyway; he took her away from me so I don't need to wallow anymore about what I can't have. It's like the Band-Aid was ripped for me.

"Hey," a whispered voice jolts me from my concentration in the game and I turn around to see who it is. My eyes go wide. Marissa's still here, in the same clothes she's been wearing all day. Meaning she hasn't left. My mind automatically assumes the worst, that she did fuck the chef and now she's on such a high note that she had to tell me all about it. Do I think I deserve it? Probably. Doesn't make the pill any easier to swallow.

"Hi," I reply. "You're still here?"

"Yeah," she nods. "I went to play a game of poker. You know, to help take my mind off of things."

I almost want to pound my fist in the air. Thank god she wasn't doing anything that my mind had retreated to. "Yeah, same reason why I'm here," I say, motioning to the screen waiting for me to make a move. "Did you win?"

"I did. I'd like to think it was because I was dealt a flush, and so I went all-in, but I'm usually not so lucky."

"Nice. That's cool, that you won. Now are you thinking you'll go pro?"

"Gosh, no." She playfully rolls her eyes. "The dealer at the table asked me the same thing. I'm like, look, I won one game. That hardly constitutes me as a pro."

"But you didn't just win one game. You won two, right?"

She nods, sitting down in the chair next to me. "Two hardly constitutes me as a pro also. I couldn't qualify for the World Series of Poker on two wins."

"Well, you technically could. Anyone can enter in the World Series of Poker as long as they pay the buy-in."

She rolls her eyes at me. "Okay, rich boy, let me rephrase that. I couldn't enter in the World Series of Poker and make it far enough where I'd win back the entire buy-in fee I spent entering. I would not spend ten grand on a buy-in fee just to play in the biggest poker tournament in the world anyway."

I've never seen Marissa play, but by the way she's talked about poker twice to me, she sounds so excited about it. The fact that she even was able to win a tournament and another game makes me think she's not inexperienced. I don't want to pry, but she's definitely hiding a part of her life where poker seemed to revolve around it and I'm curious what happened to make her so shy about her skillset. She must have had a pretty big loss that cost her a lot to take a hiatus, or even ever return. And now I'm wondering if there was a way that I could ignite the spark again.

"Hypothetically, would you enter if someone sponsored you? Like you just had ten-thousand dollars given to you and you had to use it to enter into the tournament?"

She pauses for a second. "I mean, I don't think I could say no at that point. I'd want to, but it seems like a waste of money to me though, and I think that person should save that money for other things like, I don't know, a car payment?"

"Of course, it is much more practical to spend that kind of money on a car payment," I chuckle. "It's just a hypothetical. We'll see if it happens or not."

"Oooookay," she drawls. "You can just let this person know that hypothetically, I'm probably not worth investing ten-thou-sand dollars in, so if they hypothetically have this money, then they can take it elsewhere."

"Noted. I will make sure to tell that to this hypothetical person," I wink.

We sit in silence for a bit, Marissa goes to swipe her card and load some money into the machine. I don't know if she's waiting to tell me that she's sorry, or if she expects me to say it first. I want to, but I'm so bad with apologies. The first time I tried to apologize, she just had it ingrained in her mind already that there was nothing I could say to make that situation better. Even though it did and we came around, I still get nervous that I'll mess up and say the wrong thing. I stare back at the screen asking what I want to do for my next move. I could hit, hope that I will get a good number that will poise me to be at a good number to win. Or I could stand, let the situation ride out and wonder if I made the right decision. Huh, life is a lot like Blackjack I'm realizing. I often hit when I feel like it's worth the risk, because I just have to try. Maybe I need to do the same thing with Marissa. Make the first move, or else I'd be kicking myself that I let something ride its own course and wonder if that was the right thing to do.

"I'm sorry," I say as soon as she finishes saying sorry herself.

I laugh. So maybe we were more on a mind meld than I originally thought. "Well that's awkward. You go first." I'm more interested to hear what she has to apologize for, because what she said was completely valid in many aspects.

Marissa sighs before taking a deep breath with her eyes closed. She opens them and stares at me, where I can definitely see the apology written in every part of her face. "I'm sorry for saying that you haven't changed since that night at the club. I didn't fully mean it. Sure, I was mad that you were being jealous, but you're not the same person when we first met. You're a lot more caring and kind, and you're a good friend. I don't even think I properly said thank you for taking me to dinner at Lotus. But thank you, it was one of the best meals I ever ate, and I think a lot of it has to do with because you got me to get out of my comfort zone. I've been telling a lot of people that the word of the day always seems to be risk for me, because I've been trying a lot of new things, and it's scary to take risks, but so far you've been by my side throughout all of this, and I can't thank you enough, for being a good friend to me. I don't want us to fight anymore; it really sucked when I just saw you walk up and leave. I didn't want to go back into work the next day and just have us sitting in the same office, hating each other."

"Hate's a strong word, Marissa. I don't think I could ever hate you." Because I know that I'll never be nearly as good hearted of a person as Marissa is, even on a bad day. I don't even think she has a bad bone in her body.

"Well, strongly despise. There, is that better?"

I laugh. "Much."

"Well, I don't think I get to be off scot free about this either," I chime in. "I'm sorry too. I shouldn't have been jealous. You're right, you're your own person and you can talk to whoever you want to. I'm not your guardian, your bodyguard, parent, whatever you want to call me. Point is, you're an adult that is allowed to talk to whoever you want, and I don't want to jeopardize what we have, which is a good friendship, so I promise I am going to be better at being a good friend, because that's what you deserve."

"Thank you," she whispers.

We sit silent, and it's like the sounds of the casino are drowned out and I only hear the beating of our hearts, mine pumping faster and faster. The urge to lean forward is eating at me, and I'm resisting to jump out of my body and lean closer to her. She hasn't moved yet either, her lips puckered like they're just asking to be kissed. I take a hard swallow. She talked so much about risks, am I going to be that person who is going to take the plunge as well?

I lean in closer to her until there's barely any space left to breathe. I'm practically panting now. "Marissa," I whisper.

"Yeah?" she asks back.

"Can I tell you a little secret?"

She looks puzzled. "What's that?"

"You know the whole reason why this whole fight started was because I was jealous."

"Jealous of what?" She asks, all innocent. I scoff and playfully roll my eyes at her. She knows that I'd do anything to make sure that no one else could lay their grubby hands on her. That I want to be the only person to rub my hands up and down her body, caress her with the affection that I think she deserves, which in my opinion, is bigger than any hotel on the Strip. Any hotel in the world.

"Don't act like you don't know," I say, smirking.

"Kellen," she breathes, saying my name with a raised pitch. "We can't..."

"Stop," I envelop her small hand with mine. It's the first time I've held it since she pulled me through the casino to evade the kidnappers. "I know what I can and can't do, but what I want right now, more than anything, is to kiss those perfect lips of yours. And I know there are consequences, that we might not be able to do this for much longer past tonight, but I want to taste you, for once in my goddamn life, to show you how much I want you, Marissa Waters."

"Well," she smiles. "What's life without taking some risks?"

I grin, losing anything that's tying me from exercising restraint and pull her into me. I start by lightly brushing my lips with hers, but once her lips pucker I guide her closer to me and stroke her back as I invite her into my mouth and brush my tongue with hers. She tastes even better than I remember, and this time it's without the booming bass from the nightclub or the fear my past will come back to haunt me. I tilt my head a bit to deepen the kiss and smile as she groans into my mouth.

She breaks off the kiss to catch some air. "Shit, Kellen, you taste so good."

"Wait until you get to taste more," I laugh. I go back to kissing her, and she finds her way onto my lap. She gasps when she sits down onto me, feeling how hard I am underneath my pants. I want her to feel how hard she makes me, even if it means I'll have to wait a little bit so we're somewhere more private. She sits there for a moment on top of me and I watch her lips pout slightly, and she tries to blink the tears streaming down from her face.

"Hey," I lift my hand to cup her cheek. "What's going on? Why are you crying?"

"It's stupid," she laughs and shakes her head. "I'm just sad that I love this so much."

I'm confused, I thought everything had been feeling good. Was I missing something? "Why are you sad?"

"Because, Kellen! I like you a lot and you like me too, obviously, but that doesn't change what's going on in our lives. We still work together, we still have to put work above anything else, and we sure as hell can't be dating when you've got a target on your back! Yes, we said we should be taking risks, but I don't want to take a risk and lose you, lose whatever we have."

"I know," I say, pulling her closer. "I know." I'm rubbing her back, and burying my head into her hair. "There's a lot that we need to talk about. But I don't want to talk about it now, please. Can we just say tonight, screw the rules, and get it out of our system? One night only, and then we'll go back to living our life, how we're supposed to?"

Marissa sighs. "You know that never works out in the long run."

"I do, but I can't get you out of my head. I want to do everything right by you, even if it seems wrong. I want to be able to call you mine, just once, and do things to you that I've dreamt of doing the moment I laid eyes on you."

"I want that too," she pleads. "So goddamn much."

"Then what do you say?" I look deep into her brown, glittering eyes. "Do you trust me?"

Chapter Fourteen

Marissa

I feel the adrenaline rush holding Kellen Zhang's hand though the hotel. I'm neglecting a key detail that this is also the hotel we both work in, and will continue to do so because I'm so enamored by his touch. As we kissed and I straddled him on the casino chair, there were definitely onlookers staring at us, thinking to themselves, they are probably way too drunk and just met a mere hour ago. What happens in Vegas, right? Little do they know that we've been building up these tensions for a while now, and finally had enough where we needed to just do something about it.

I know Kellen was jealous, and I always knew deep down, amidst all the tension and bickering, that we only did it because we were too afraid to act on feelings that we had stored deep down inside of each other. Did I think we were going to kiss? I can't say I was going into my apology preparing for it. In fact, I was hesitant at first. There's still a lot looming over our heads and after tonight, I can't say for certain if I'll leave feeling better or worse, but safe to say right now, while our hands are grasped in each other's and we're waltzing through the hallway back to Kellen's room, I feel happy.

Kellen opens the door into his room and as soon as it shuts, he grabs me by my waist and hoists me up so I'm eye level with him. I wrap my legs around his waist and grab his face with my hands.

"This is how I wished we could have ended up straight after dinner, but we had a few hiccups along the way."

"Oh so that's why you wanted to take me to a fancy dinner," I laugh. "So you can butter me up before you spill all your feelings on me."

"Pretty much." His chuckle is deep and sexy and I melt seeing his dimples come into full view, nearly as deep as craters on the moon.

"You're so lucky you have dimples," I caress his cheek and brush right past them. "They look so sexy on you."

"Oh yeah?" He gives me a quick peck. "That's why you saved me, huh? Was so I can show you my appreciation through these guys."

"It might have been a plus."

Kellen gently pushes me up the wall and tilts his head up so our lips meet again. I part my mouth open for him and he lets out a moan, as I grab onto the little bits of hair on the back of his head and give them a tug.

"Can I take you to my room?" He whispers in my ear.

I nod. I didn't think tonight would be complete unless we did, and the last time I got to stay here, I was feeling like something was missing, because I wanted to tear down the walls between us and climb into his bed so that I could wake up in his arms.

He sets me down and pulls me through his room. Down the familiar hallway, he opens a door to a much larger bedroom than the one that I was sleeping in last time. This one has similar ornate decorations, but definitely way more grand, similar to the decorations in Lotus, and artwork that was standard for many of the rooms. Some blossom tree with a lake in the back and the inside of the palace. The bed is different than the standard one, there's a large wooden backboard with red and gold lining the edges and columns holding it up with an enclosed mirror looking down on the bed. Well, this is really something if you're trying to get it on, you get a full back view of someone butt naked.

"Wow," I mouth. "This is like a palace."

"It's definitely a little extra," he laughs. "But the bed is the most comfortable you will sleep in."

"Even more comfortable than the one in the guest bedroom? Because that one was comfortable."

"They use a special type of memory foam for the master bedroom. Here." He effortlessly lifts me up by my legs and carries me in his arms. "See for yourself."

He gently tosses me onto the bed and I melt at how it feels so firm yet so soft. It hugs me in and I feel like it contours to my body shape so easily. Not to mention, it feels naturally cool when I press into it.

I crawl up to rest my head on the pillow and the pillow is perfectly firm and cool against my cheek.

"Oh my god, this pillow is so nice," I moan. "How do I get this bed in my house?"

"Probably by special order," Kellen says, crawling up next to me. "But you can come and stay here whenever you want." He pulls me and rubs my back, resting one finger in the groove of my spine, and I go in and rest my head on his chest.

"If you're wondering where I am during lunch, it'll be taking a nap here." I flutter my eyes closed and almost fall asleep right there. Kellen kisses my forehead and laughs.

"Mar," I love how he says my nickname. "Can you take your clothes off for me?"

I hold my breath. It had been so long since someone saw me completely unclothed. Did I feel ready for this? My insides, as they started to feel more wet, felt like they knew what the answer to that question was, but there was a part of my mind that still told me maybe we were moving too fast.

"Marissa," he nudges me a little back to reality. "Are you okay?"

"Oh, yeah, sorry. I...no one has seen me like that in a long time."

"We don't have to do anything if you're not ready," he says. "I'm sorry. I shouldn't have moved so quickly. I want to make sure you're ready for this."

Ugh, curse my hesitations. "No, don't be sorry. I...I'm sorry. Believe me, I want you to touch me, feel me, give me all the love I know you have for me, but I know that if we were to have sex, then I'd start feeling scared about us and how this is all going to end up. I really like you, Kellen, and I don't want something to happen where I won't be able to do this around you anymore."

"I know," he whispers. "Believe me, baby, there is so much that is at stake. But, I just want you to know that if you want me, when you want me, I will be here. I will wait ten years if I have to if it means I'll get to be with you."

"No you wouldn't," I laugh. "I wouldn't even wait that long for anyone."

"Then you don't know how much you're worth it to me." He leans down to touch his lips back on mine. My panties are damn near soaked. Shit, I don't know when I'll get the chance to pleasure myself, and the urge to come is eating away at me, especially when he's telling me these things like how much I'm worth the wait.

I couldn't just beat around the bush any longer. "Kellen," I swallow, letting myself take control. "Can you...feel inside me?"

The desire in his eyes flames and he grins down at me. "Shit, Mar, yes. Of course I will."

I pull down my pants and unbutton my shirt, and then reach back to unclasp my bra, tossing it aside once I feel the elastic retract.

"Fuck, Marissa," he pants. "You have the most beautiful body I've ever laid eyes on."

I tilt my body closer to him and pull down the hem of my underwear. Kellen caresses my body down my stomach to my pussy and starts with one finger inside me.

I breathe, letting out an "oh" as he shoves a second finger in there.

"You weren't kidding when you said you were wet," he chuckles.

"All thanks to you," I urge out, gasping in between.

He tilts his head down and starts kissing me, moving his lips to the rhythm of his thrusts. I sigh into him as he feels around my clit and starts to rub it.

"Kellen," I breathe. "You're...doing....so good."

"Yeah?" He says, taking my breast in his hand and moving to pinch my nipple between his fingers. "It's a good thing I don't want to stop then."

He repositions himself so he's kneeling right above me. He grabs the bottom of his shirt and rips it off, revealing a beauti-fully sculpted body and a large tattoo of a red Chinese dragon on the right side of his body with the Chinese character "口" drawn right above his right pec.

"I didn't know you had a tattoo."

"I got it when I graduated from undergrad. The dragon I've wanted all my life. The Fu I got kind of as a weird homage to my family when I knew I was going to be tied to it forever. Reminds me that a lot of my life might have been hard, but like the name entails, we've been blessed with a lot of good fortune."

"That's really sweet," I say, reaching up to stroke the character. "That you have a part of your family imprinted on you."

"They're a lot, but I love them. But, enough talking about me. That wasn't the point of me taking off my shirt."

He scoots down and buries his head into my pussy. Oh my god. I had only thought he was going to do a couple fingers in and out. But his mouth, his tongue, the way he's sucking me down there, it sends my heart racing.

"Oh fuck. That feels so good, Kellen," I pant. "You...I'm going to come soon."

"Do it baby," he says looking back into my eyes, "I'm the only man that gets to make you come now and forever, do you understand?"

"Yes," I nod. His mouth returns and I buckle at his tongue licking my folds. He comes up and sticks his fingers back again, curling them up and out. I feel my heartbeat quicken and I arch my back up. Kellen reaches and grabs my waist to pull me closer to him. He sucks at my nipple and I push myself into him. My body groans as I come, every muscle relaxing once I finish.

"Oh god," I say with my mouth still open. "I...That was...something."

"Yeah it was," he whispers into my neck. "You're amazing, Marissa."

"Thanks," I breathe. If that was him pleasuring me, I can't even imagine the sensations we'll feel when we both feel each other inside of me.

"Sorry I didn't really pleasure you as much as you did to me."

He goes back to resting at the head of the bed and sets his arms out to wrap me in them. "You don't need to be sorry," he says, giving me a peck on the top of my head. "My whole focus was making sure you were having a good time."

I rest my head on his bare chest and he wraps me closer into him. There's so much that I want to say, all these feelings that I want to spill out to him, that after that euphoric high I just experienced, that I too, don't want anyone to be with him, but there's a lot going on in both our lives right now, and a relationship will just sour everything before we would be able to taste anything sweet.

"Now what happens?" I ask.

"I don't want to think about what happens next," he says, pulling the covers of the bed over us. "I just want to be happy with what I have now, and that's you."

"Okay," I sigh. "I want that too."

"Well, then let's just spend the rest of the night being happy." He reaches over to his nightstand and turns on the television in front of us until I feel utterly pooped from the orgasm he just gave me and I fall asleep with his arm wrapped around my bare body.

Chapter Fifteen

Kellen

"We need to get out of here," I calmly tell Marissa as we see people ducking into stores and finding any escape route. Just our luck that the one time we explore Las Vegas, we're stuck in a mall with an armed robber.

"Come in here," someone working in the Chanel store whispers to us. "Hide before someone sees you!"

We bolt into the store and someone begins to lock it up once we're told to hide behind the register.

Marissa takes a deep breath in and slumps her back against the wall.

"Are you okay?" I ask, grabbing onto her thigh.

"Yeah, for now. I'm just happy we're safe inside somewhere."

A man wearing a suit and tie comes over to us. "Just got off the phone with mall security. Apparently these people have been led here on a tip that someone they've been looking for would be shopping here."

Oh fuck. There has to be someone else high profile they're looking for, right? "Would you happen to know the name of the person they're looking for?"

He gives me a stern look into my eyes. "Yes, someone by the name of Kellen Zhang."

Of course. How are these people able to find me? We even made sure that we'd disguise ourselves so that people don't recognize me. I mean, it was mostly just covering my hair using a beanie, but I thought it would be sufficient.

"Oh," I gulp. "He better watch his back then."

The man looks me dead in the eyes. "Mr. Zhang, I know who you are."

"Well then," I nod. "That was awkward of me to say."

"We're sorry," Marissa chimes in. "We don't want to put you in danger. Tell us to get out of your hair and we'll do it."

"And where would we go? In the belly of the beast?" I cannot have Marissa go out there. I don't want anything to happen to us, but I especially don't want anything to happen to her.

I turn and look her deep in her frantic eyes. "I have to make sure you're protected at all costs."

"Okay," she nods. "I just feel bad we're making these innocent people a target now because they've offered to hold us hostage."

"Don't feel bad," the man in the suit says. "We want you to be safe."

A store employee crouches down, breathing hard. "Some-one's at the door. They want to inspect the store to see if we have him. They're armed."

"I'll go," I tell them. "If they want to see me, then so be it. I don't want you to risk anyone's lives for me." I turn to the man in the suit. "Please make sure she's safe. If I can't make it back in time, can you take her back to the Blossom Hotel?"

The man nods. "You have my word."

"Kellen," Marissa grabs onto my arm. "Please don't go."

I wrap both my hands in hers. "I'll be okay. I promise." I give her a quick kiss before standing up. "I'm going to try and get some answers."

I walk to the front of the store with my hands held up in a surrender pose. The man at the front of the store is wearing the same thing the person who tried to kidnap me at the hotel was: a black hoodie, black sunglasses, and a mask.

"Is this what you wanted?" I ask. "To finally take me hostage? Whoever you are?"

He chuckles and pulls the gun, pointing it straight at me. "Well, aren't we one smart cookie. Where's your bodyguard huh? Your little side piece? Little shit knows how to kick some-one in the groin. I wish you could've brought her with you so you can watch me take her out for myself. Oh, but you did, didn't you? At least that's what we were told."

"What if she isn't here anymore?" I gritted.

"Then I'll just pull the trigger right..."

"No!" Marissa's voice comes booming out from the back and she's running to shield me. "If you want me, just take me. But please don't hurt him. He's just trying to protect me."

"I think someone needs to do a better job of protecting," he says to her. "You know, it is a lot easier to find you when you don't have your little Blossom bodyguards parading around the hotel. You should know better than to escape your safe zone."

I clench my fists and map out in my mind a way to get the gun out of his hand. I don't know how much of his crew is on the mall premises; we need a way out. And I thought I would just be okay by sacrificing myself, but Marissa had to open her mouth and expose herself, and now my job becomes more than just defending myself.

He puts the gun in his pocket and grabs a hold of Marissa's arm. Hard. She jerks towards him and he begins to tie her arms behind her back. She starts kicking his legs.

"Stop! What are you going to do with me?"

"We're going to make sure you can't do anything to protect your boyfriend here from us. And that means taking you for ourselves. If...you...could...just...stop moving..."

I bolt from my position and kick him from behind when he's not looking. He probably should have tied me up if he really wanted to be that smart, but once he had his focus on Marissa, I became a nobody. He falls to the floor, on top of Marissa and I've got him right where I want him. In a place where I'm so filled with rage that he even laid a hand on her and I put him in a headlock from behind and pull the gun out from his pocket and point it to his head.

"Let her go, now." I'm practically shouting through my teeth.

"Or what? You'll shoot? If I even move my head just a bit, you'll be shooting the love of your life right in the head. As long as you got me in a lock, I've got her."

"Kellen," she starts gasping for air. Shit, he's cutting off circulation in her throat. "Do something!"

I try and roll him over so that he gets off her and onto his back. With enough momentum, I might be able to scare him into falling back. I plant my foot on the ground and silently count to three. On three I pull him up from his neck and he lets go of the rope he was using to tie Marissa up. He grunts and is now on my front. I sit up, and find another piece of rope he had on his belt. I'm pulling his arms back and tying them quickly while I have him lying down.

"We called the cops," the store employee runs over to tell me. "They should be over soon. Good work."

"Thank you." Sure enough, the cops show just minutes after I finish tying him up and they take care of the rest for me. I run over to Marissa, who the store employees are comforting after she almost loses consciousness for a brief moment.

"Are you okay?" I sit down next to her and wrap my arm around her shoulder.

She nods. "I'm fine now. Just still trying to get my breathing right."

"Mar," I look deeply into her eyes. "You almost got hurt. You can't expose yourself when I tell you to stay where you are."

"I'm sorry." Her eyes start watering now. "I got scared. I just kept hearing him say he was going to kill you. I saw the gun pointed toward you, and I thought if I gave them what they wanted, which was me, I'd keep you safe."

"I know, baby," I pull in close to my chest. "And you are such a strong woman. But, my purpose in life now is putting you first. Even if you've been tasked to save me. I can't have anything happen to you. I'd never forgive myself."

"I know," she whispers against my chest. "I feel the same about you."

We waited for the cops to talk to us about everything, so they could get our statements in to file a report with.

"We have a name of the man who we arrested," one of the officers tells us. "Jameson Yang. Tied to a group of Chinese men who call themselves the Fortune Hunters. Their purpose since their founding is to..."

"Find and destroy The Fortune Group," I finish. The name couldn't be any more obvious.

"They have tried hard to devise a perfect time to strike. But now is the best time with Kellen working full time in Vegas. So, they've worked around the clock to take down Kellen in hopes they can take down your father."

"I see. Well, looks like they may have done a good job," I say. "Somehow they knew I was here."

"Yes, we figured out that someone who works at the Gucci store that you bought an item from earlier today had close ties to the Fortune Hunters and told them you were at this mall. We arrested him shortly after arresting Yang."

"Fuck," I murmur. "So, I did get us into this mess." I didn't even think anyone would be able to trace us, but there's no escaping my purchases so long that they're under my name.

"It's okay," Marissa says, putting her hand on my shaking thigh. "What matters is that we're alive."

"We're instructed to take you back to the Blossom Hotel, and have notified your father of the incident."

"Wonderful," I sigh. He's going to have a field day with this one. Especially because I went back on his specific instructions. I can only hope he doesn't cut off my stay starting today.

We head back to the Blossom and to my office. I look at my phone for multiple missed calls from my father and texts.

CALL ME NOW.

"I have to call my dad back," I tell Marissa. "I'm sorry. You're welcome to stay here, but I'm going to probably work from my room the rest of the day. Making phone calls and working through reports and stuff."

"Okay," she nods. "Let me know if there's anything you need from me."

"I will," I bend down and give her a kiss, wishing I could grab onto her forever when she starts to wrap her arms around my neck. I break apart suddenly before getting myself in too deep.

"I'll text you when I'm done, maybe we can hang out."

She nods and I turn to head out of the office and start to dial my dad's phone number as I'm walking through the casino floor.

"Kellen," my dad answers.

"Hi, Ba."

"Don't 'Hi, Ba' me. Do you know how angry I am with you right now?"

"Ba..." Fuck, that's how you know he's intensely angry with me. "Father, I can explain."

"What else is there to explain? You disobey my rules to leave the hotel, and because of that, you get yourself in trouble with the exact person that is after you. After our family! And for what? A girl? Dating should be at the bottom of your priority list after everything you have put this family into. And a hotel employee? We have a strict rule against dating colleagues. You know this."

"Technically it is only in direct departments and between managers and subordinates, the employee handbook states."

I hear him sigh. "Yes that is true, but you are a director; you have a corporate responsibility to not let your feelings get in the way of your work ethic, which means no fraternizing with any hotel employee."

"...Okay fine. I recognize that. And I apologize."

"This is strike one, Kellen. I'm not going to ask you to move back to New York immediately just yet, because I want you to find out who these people are and take them down. Despite your bad decisions, we were still able to get a name of the group who is trying to come after us. Fortune Hunters. The name clearly explains their motives. Now, because of your reckless-ness, you are under no circumstances allowed to leave the hotel. If someone catches you again, that's strike two. And I might not be as forgiving. And no more hanging out with this woman unless it is for work-related purposes. You also put her in grave danger because of your decisions. What if she died under your watch? What would you do about that then, huh?"

I feel tears starting to form in my eyes, and I rarely cry. But, my dad asked a question that throws me off my element. A picture flashes in the back of my head of Marissa being crushed by that man, and lying still with her eyes closed. I keep shaking her but she doesn't budge. She doesn't wake up. And I cry out in anger that I wasn't able to save her.

I blink out of it and take a big sniff. "I don't know, Ba. I would never be able to forgive myself."

He sighs again and his tone grows softer. The last time I cried in front of my dad might have been when I was a baby and I didn't know any better. "My Xiao Qiang. You are so strong. But you need to make the right decision. And sometimes the right decision doesn't equal the best one. If you love this woman as much as I think you do, you need to be careful. Please."

"Yes, Ba." I don't even know when the last time he called me Xiao Qiang was. It's a nickname from a movie, translated to Little Toughie. It's what he used to call me when I was a kid, because I always wanted to mimic those actors that I would watch fight in the movies. Or the last time he had a begging tone in his voice. To ask me please for something, because most of the time, everything just felt like it was a demand.

"Do you know, one time, you weren't even born yet, Kiera was just a baby. I had to save her from a burglary attempt we had at the Grand Fortune. Maybe it is the same people that tried to hurt you and Marissa, but this was thirty years ago. We just assumed someone was just trying to attack someone who's newly rich in the city. But your mom had to go to the hospital, because she was so bruised and beaten up from trying to protect Kiera. I wasn't even on property. I was off at an investor meeting near Wall Street. I was so distraught with myself I took a week off work. So upset that I put the two most important people at that time in danger."

"I didn't know that, Ba. Why did you never tell me?"

"It's a time that I don't like to remember, Kellen. To this day, I still don't know the people who hurt your mother. But, I have a strong feeling that they might be the same people who are trying to hurt you."

I clench my chest as I lay in bed, only looking up at the ceiling while my phone rested right below my chin. I'm thinking about a lot - obviously about Marissa right now, and wanting to ask if she's okay, but also about my mom. I know that she is a strong person, she rarely talked back to my dad, which I knew was difficult because when he got angry, he would yell as loud as his lungs allowed him. But, maybe the reason why she rarely yelled was because there was a time that her life was on the line, and she wanted to make sure she did anything to make herself as well as my father feel protected.

"Okay, Ba." I say. "I'm sorry. For talking back about this with you. I had no idea that you and mom went through that. I know now it is safer to not take any chances. I don't want anything to happen to Marissa, the same way that it happened to mom."

"It's okay, son. I know what it's like to love someone too." He laughs for a moment, a genuine giggle that I don't even think I've heard my father make since maybe I was a baby. "Just be careful. Do not leave the hotel and do not be seen out with this woman. I'm telling you now, I'm not saying that you can't see her, but just watch out for who's on your back."

"I will. Thank you, Ba Ba."

"I love you, son."

I almost choke back a sob again. "I love you too."

"Call your mom sometime. She'd be happy to hear you've started seeing someone. You know how long she's waited for you to bring someone home."

"Well, if all goes well, then maybe we'll get to come home soon. I'll bring Marissa too. I know she'd love to visit the city."

"Sounds like a plan. Bye Kel."

"Bye Dad."

I throw the phone onto the bed and sigh. There was a lot on my mind that needed to be processed. I get up and walk to grab a beer from my fridge and hop onto my computer, typing the phrase Las Vegas Fortune Hunters in my Google search bar. And once the search results come up, I can't believe the things that are staring back at me.

Chapter Sixteen

Marissa

Yesterday was a much needed day to shut myself off from the rest of the world, relax at home, and not communicate with anyone unless it was for work. I decided I was going to only answer work emails from home because business still operated as usual, but I shut my phone off from any texts from anyone so I didn't need to immediately recount the events that had occurred at the mall.

I feel bad that I didn't answer any of Kellen's calls or texts, because he was at the scene of the crime. He understood how scary it was to be in that store yesterday, and he saw me wince in pain from the weight of the man sitting on me, crushing every bone in my body. I almost felt like I was going to lose consciousness for a moment, that's how much oxygen had left me. But, Kellen had come to my rescue and got the guy off me and eventually arrested, but it still didn't change the fact that it happened and I can see the bruises.

I take a deep breath in as I try and sit myself up in bed to get ready for work. My body still feels sore from what happened, but overall I'm feeling in less pain than yesterday. As I look at myself in the mirror of my bathroom, I can't bring myself to show off a happy, smiling face yet, because my mind still floods with the nightmares of being crushed, helpless, and on the verge of losing everything, especially after I felt like my life was actually headed in a good direction.

I make myself a coffee to go and head to the Strip for another day of work. Kellen hasn't texted me how he's doing, or asked how I'm doing. I don't know how the conversation with his dad went. Knowing all that he's told me about his dad, it couldn't have gone well. We knew the rules and we broke them. And if there's something that Kellen's dad despises more than anything, it's when Kellen goes against his father's wishes and breaks the rules. I dread the moment that I step into the office and see his gloomy face and he tells me right there that we need to stop seeing each other because his dad is going to forbid us like some Romeo and Juliet plotline. Hopefully we don't end up dead at the end of it.

I press my key fob to get into the building from the employee entrance and turn red when Kayley meets my gaze in the employee break room. I wince, scared for once in my life to talk to her, because I know she's pissed. She found out what happened and texted me multiple times, asking why I was with Kellen yesterday at an upscale mall in Las Vegas and if I was ever going to tell her that Kellen and I might be more than just friends, considering he bought me a four-thousand dollar dress. Now that she and I have locked eye contact, then I can't just ignore her and explain what's going on.

"Hi." I solemnly walk up to her at the table with some of our other coworker friends. The moment I sit down they sense the tension and awkwardly tell Kayley they need to report to their desk for work.

She gives me a sour look and then goes back to scrolling through her phone and sipping on her coffee. Rude, even though it's partially justified. But, there is a lot that I need to think about, for myself and what I needed to protect, that Kayley was so stubborn to try and understand.

I sigh loud enough so she could hear me. "Sorry I didn't respond to your texts."

She sighs back and looks at me with her "over it" face.

"It's not okay," she says. "You know that, right? Especially after what happened yesterday. Do you think I like seeing on my phone 'Breaking News' headlines and then being ghosted after them?"

"No."

"Exactly. And you were with Kellen? What is your relationship with him? It must be pretty special if you two were shopping at Crystals on a work day."

"We're not together. But, we like each other. As more than just friends. I can honestly say I did try really hard to keep a distance from him so we could stay strictly friends, but it was hard. He didn't deny that he's had feelings for me since we met, and we've talked a lot since working together. We're...I haven't felt this attached to a guy in a long time. Yes, we've kissed, and I've slept with him the night before the incident at the mall. The entire reason we went to the mall was because he thought it would be good if I got a change of clothes, because I didn't bring any of my own. I didn't think we were going to be at the one mall where there are a bunch of luxury stores filled with things I can't afford, but he offered and I couldn't say no.

He bought me this really beautiful silk dress from Gucci that I feel like I should wear but I'm also terrified of wearing because it brings back harsh memories of what happened that day. We weren't robbed of anything, but Kellen had sacrificed himself in hopes that's what the guy wanted. He didn't. He just wanted to kidnap me and watch Kellen suffer that he couldn't do anything to save me. He had said if Kellen didn't tell them where I was...they were going to shoot him."

My eyes started to water. "I had no other choice, Kayley," I breathe. "They were going to shoot him right there. And I felt so helpless. My whole job is to be protective of him and I felt like such a coward."

She doesn't say anything as I let out a quiet, yet gut wrenching sob, but gets up from her seat and crouches down, reaching her arms around me. "It's okay," she says, rubbing my back. "I'm so sorry that you had to go through that. That is super scary, and I wouldn't wish that onto anyone, especially you. And I'm sorry. I know that you have been going through a lot and I haven't been able to be a good friend and supportive. Instead I've been extremely rude about Kellen. He's not really a bad guy. I think I was just too stubborn to give him any chances. But someone who is willing to risk their life for you is someone that I support a hundred percent. Even if they're rich and entitled and don't work as hard as I wished they did."

A laughter bubbles up in my mouth and I'm feeling relieved. We hold each other for a moment more until Kayley runs over to grab me a tissue.

"So, you two aren't dating? What's up with that?"

"Well, after the incident happened, he had to talk to his dad about us and I've never met his dad before, but I don't think they really get along. If you think Kellen is that stuck-up entitled rich guy, his dad is that and more. Everything is all work and no play with him, and he was the one who told Kellen at first he couldn't even be leaving the hotel for fear he was going to get caught. I mean, I understand it, but they don't really have that loving relationship that I have with my parents, or you with yours. I don't think Kellen's dad can really love him if he's not doing a good enough job with work. I mean, he was basically forced into doing this job so he can continue running the Fortune Group after his dad retires."

"Yeah, that's rough," Kayley says. We get up and make our way over to our offices once I feel like I don't look like a tomato anymore and could actually show face around others. "Did he say he would rather be doing something else than working for the hotel?"

"He said at one point he wanted to be a teacher. I know it's kind of hard to see him in that kind of position, but maybe he would be good at it."

"I will admit he did need to teach us about different rate codes and I think he did a good job of that. He knows how to articulate everything in a way that people are able to understand. Which helped my job a lot because I had my patience up to here with people who were not understanding what the different promotions were and what amenities came with it."

We wave hello to the front desk agents working at the time and head back to our offices. As I walk through to Kellen's office, I see the door is closed. I thought that he wasn't in yet, but the light is on inside.

"See? Pretty soon you two will be besties. And you have to be besties if and when we start dating. Because I am not going to have the two most important people in my life at each other's throats because of some spat."

"Fine, fine." Kayley says while opening up her office door. "But just know I'm higher on the pole than he is because we've known each other longer. I don't care if he's saved your life. You've definitely saved mine. More than once."

"Thanks," I give her a hug in the middle of her office. It's been a while since we both had a heart to heart moment like this. "I promise I will be honest with you going forward about stuff that is going on in my life. Especially when it's milestone events like these."

"You better. Jeez, someone is actually able to win Marissa Jung Waters' heart over? I need to know about this stuff!"

"Trust me, I will give you all the intel about all things love life as soon as it happens. Well, the stuff that I feel comfortable about sharing."

"Eh, I'll take it." She pushes me from my shoulders into the hallway. "Let me know what you're doing about lunch!"

"Okay!" I wave goodbye to her and then take a walk the short distance to Kellen's office. I don't know whether or not I should knock. Because the door is closed, I should be respectful and do it. But, it's my office too temporarily. I can't just knock and wait if he's not there, I have to answer all the emails for my actual job too.

I take a deep breath and gently knock on the door. There. There's that one hint of respect I was going to give him. I wait a moment before he answers, and when he doesn't, I groan and just whisper a "fuck it" to myself before going inside.

The door is unlocked and I notice that he isn't behind his desk. Great, the guy wasn't even here and I waited for a brief second out of respect for him before opening the door. In this aspect, a text would have been nice letting me know that he wasn't going to be here around the time that I was.

I plop down on my seat and almost slam my face to the ground when I see my inbox is flooded with at least a hundred emails over the last twenty four hours. Thankfully the winter is a slow time for us, not too many groups will be staying here and the ones that do are small social ones who may be traveling for the holidays or planning a winter wedding. Once I comb through and respond to everything, it's nearly almost noon and he still hasn't shown up yet. I don't ask where he is, because I don't know if he's been asked to not talk to me. What if he's also not even allowed to be in this office? Then why would he give this office to me? I could have just decided to go back to the Sales office.

I almost reach my phone up to ask him when the door opens and he walks in. Dressed in a full suit and tie. With the suit jacket unbuttoned.

Hot damn, that little peek of his chest is making my mouth salivate.

"Hi," I croak. "Where have you been?"

His hair's not gelled anymore and is flying in all different directions. What kind of meeting is this he's been in? "Budget meeting. For the past three hours. God, I want to rip my hair out. I do not need more stress added onto my life. And apparently we are performing way under the forecast amount, which I think is completely justified because it's not our busy season yet. But, they're trying to egg us on for promos to push because apparently people are saying they do not want to come to a hotel that is the center of a kidnapping scandal."

He closes the door behind him and sets his laptop on his desk before walking over to me and lifting me up into his arms.

"How are you?" he asks, while burying his head in my hair.

"Well, I'd say I'm a lot better now, thanks to this." I return the hug and wrap my arms around his waist. "I thought you wouldn't be allowed to see me anymore. Your dad didn't seem like he was all that happy with what happened."

"He wasn't," Kellen shrugs. "But, something weird happened. We had a very intimate conversation. And, he kind of opened up to me about some things. Things that I had never known about my parent's lives growing up. Like…just some really surreal stuff. Apparently, before I was born my mom had something similar happen to us, except she was all by herself and my dad wasn't there to help her when someone almost beat her to death in our hotel in New York."

"Oh my god." My jaw drops. "Kellen, that is awful, I am so sorry."

"It's okay. Well, my dad told me it was. I can only hope my mom is okay because of it, but I'm sure she gets nightmares of the day it happened thirty years later. But, he told me that because I had a moment with him where I told him that I had never felt so helpless in my life than yesterday. I realized in that moment that I had never cared about anyone more than how much I care about you, Marissa."

"Really?" I tilt my neck up and take a look into his eyes. His baggy, weary eyes that look like they've barely had any time to sleep and recharge.

"Really," he says, leaning into me and giving me a soft, tender kiss. "You mean the world to me. I don't want to lose you before I get to call you mine."

"I don't want that either," I whispers into his chest. "So your dad knows? About us?"

He nods. "At first he was angry that I would make such a careless decision, taking you out and everything. Which I know it is. But, he told me about that incident with my mom, and he said that's why he doesn't like that I take risks like this. Because he doesn't want the same thing to happen to my mom to happen to someone I care about. Someone like you."

"I care about you a lot too," I say while tugging onto his shirt. "I want nothing more to be done with this whole situation so we can both move on with our lives." I roll my eyes playfully. "These bad guys are really putting a wretch in my plans to post all that sappy shit newly made couples do on social media."

His eyes go wide for a moment and he leans back while still gripping onto my waist. I burst up laughing. I can't believe he'd think I would be that kind of person to blast my relationship in hopes that I would get some attention. Or that I even had many people on my socials to have something like this be worth discussing.

"I'm just kidding," I lean back into him with just enough force so he loses his footing a bit. "Don't you know by now I'm not very big into social media? Or that I don't really have enough followers to make a big scene of it?"

"I thought I did," he laughs. "But you kind of caught me off guard for a second. I don't know, maybe people change. I know people aren't going to be very happy about us if I post you on my social media."

Kellen has a much wider social media following than I do, and I don't think anyone would be enthused to see a picture of a smiling couple when they go to his social media to see him shirtless at the beach or perched behind a nice steak at some upscale restaurant. I might be liable for some people's phone replacement bills if and when we go public.

"Absolutely not," I shake my head. "I'll be getting death threats on mine for being the one person who was able to hold you down."

He lowers his head and presses his forehead so it's touching mine. "Well anyone that tries to send you a death threat they can go fuck themselves. Because label or not, you belong to me now. And I want you to be screaming my name when I'm entering into that sweet, sweet pussy for you." He reaches his hand over my waist and unbuttons the top, reaching into my panties and sticking one finger in me. He begins rubbing my clit and my knees buckle while I'm still standing in his arms. I go weak for a moment. This, now? This was actually happening, and I was ready to savor every moment of it, the moment where we make our feelings known to one another, by opening every part of our body up to one another.

"Kellen," I breathe. "You're...such a tease..."

"Good." He lets out a deep sexy laugh and I let out a moan. I want more than just one finger feeling me up and down my clit right now. I swipe my hand down from his waist and onto the outline his hard dick gives against his pants. He sucks in a breath and I return the same evil laugh.

"Who's the tease now?" I grit.

I rub my hand up and down the lining of his zipper. Oh my god, I haven't even touched his dick skin to skin and yet I'm already feeling like I'm going to burst.

"Take...it...off..." he grits. "Now, Marissa."

I laugh, my voice going deep. "Really?"

"I can't take the waiting any longer. Let me come inside of you."

He quickly runs behind his desk and grabs something from his drawer. He returns in front of me, holding up a condom resting between two of his fingers.

"Gotta come prepared," he laughs.

I know that you can have sex anywhere: against the wall, in a bed, on the floor. If you can position yourself in such a way that makes it work, then do it. But, something about being naked on an office floor in the same vicinity where my work life exists makes me shudder.

"Is it bad that I'm absolutely dreading having sex on the bare carpet floor? Like what kind of scraps are hidden in the crevices?"

"Do you want to lay on my jacket?" Kellen asks.

"You'd be okay with my bare ass on your jacket while you fuck me?" This jacket had to be designer. And probably worth somewhere in the thousands.

He laughs, like I just asked a rhetorical question about sex on the floor. "If it means I get to fuck you, then by all means."

I shake my head, but start to kneel down on the drab-colored floor, letting each piece of clothing drop from my body one by one. They say you need a work/life balance, but I don't think I could enjoy both in the same place.

Chapter Seventeen

Kellen

Marissa begins taking off her clothes, right in front of me. She unbuttons her shirt, letting it fall behind her and steps out of her pants one leg each. I watch as bits of her skin appear before my eyes, that soft, sweet skin that I loved to touch.

"Here," I walk up to her, fixating my gaze on her bra. "May I?"

She nods, and I reach my arms around her and unclasp her bra, letting it drop delicately onto the floor with her other clothes. I push up one of her breasts, and pinch her nipple between my thumb and pointer finger, rubbing it gently in my fingertips.

"Oh," she whispers.

"You like that?" I smile, watching her mouth form an "o" and exhale a wisp of air.

"Uh huh," she nods, and I tilt my head down and kiss her. At first, it was a gentle touch of our lips, but she opens up for me and brushes her tongue against mine, and all inhibitions break loose. I grab onto her, pulling her up to me and invite myself in, moaning when she grabs onto my bottom lip.

"Kellen," she groans, and I sinisterly look at her, how disheveled she looks, and how I'm going to make her fall apart in my arms. I lift her up and place her down on the carpet floor. She touches her ass onto my suit jacket and it ignites a flame in me. I sprinkle kisses down from her mouth to her breast, sucking the nipple I was playing with earlier.

"Oh fuck." Her head tilts back and her back arches up, pushing her breast closer to me. I can't tease her anymore, because teasing her is making me want to burst.

"Are you ready for me, Marissa?"

"I've never been more ready for anything in my life."

I kneel up from her and take off my briefs, tossing them aside with the rest of the clothes. She lets her underwear down, and I reach to put the condom on.

"I love every time that I get to see your body."

"Just wait until I'm inside," I forewarn her. Gently, I find my way inside her and once I do, I start slowly thrusting. It's the most sensational feeling in the world. No other time before has made me feel the way I do right now. Not just the pleasure I'm getting from having sex with someone, but looking at the most beautiful woman I've ever met meet my gaze and flush at how good I'm making her feel.

"God, Marissa, you're so tight for me." I whisper into her neck, keeping my pace steady, but as I thrust in her, I sigh at how good we feel together. "I don't know how long I can last."

"Don't worry," she pants. "You're doing so good. I..." Her eyes roll back and her breaths become more rapid. Her quiet groans start to amplify, making my pace quicken. I fixate on her breasts bobbing up and down. Those beautiful, full breasts, that I grab onto for support.

As she cries out, I yell and spill into the condom. I finish, panting inches from her.

"Good job," she praises. "That might have been the best sex I've ever had."

Ditto to that. The way we fit so well together, makes me dance inside. "I think so too." I reach down and kiss her. "Let's do it again sometime?"

"Gladly."

We clean up and take turns making ourselves up like nothing happened to go to the bathroom. It probably wasn't the best idea to have sex in my office because we needed to walk down the hall to where the restrooms were to clean up and hope no one suspects anything, but my first time with Marissa was a dream come true.

I come back, almost about to slide on my pants and hear my phone ring. I look over if there's anyone saved in my contacts that's calling.

"MOM."

"Oh. This was not the time that I wanted to talk to her. It's like she's a freaking mind reader." I walk over to grab my phone off my desk and slide it to answer. "Hi Mom," I answer.

"Hi Kel! Sorry, are you busy? Your dad said you were in a meeting earlier but you should have been out by now."

"Yeah, I finished it. No, I'm not busy right now." If she had called two minutes earlier than I would have had to let her call go to voicemail.

"Oh good. How's everything going with work?"

"It's fine. Well, better than it was before. I'm guessing Ba Ba told you about...what happened."

"Yes," she pauses. "He told me what happened. Do you want to tell me how you're really feeling about that?"

"Well, I'm feeling better." That was the truth, especially given the circumstances. "I'm just happy that we're safe and Marissa didn't get seriously hurt."

"Oh yes, this Marissa girl. I'm so happy you've found someone, Kell. Do you know how long I've waited for my baby to settle down with someone?"

"Well," I brace myself on the desk, still only in my boxers. "We're not really labeling it yet. Ba doesn't want us to until we've figured out everything with the investigation. And I don't even know what Erick is going to say yet. I can't let her lose her job over this if he condemns this whole relationship thing."

"Well if he does he can bring it up with me. I don't care if you happened to fall in love with a work colleague. You're still professional at work and you know how to separate work and pleasure. Right?"

"Yes." I stare at my suit jacket still on the floor. Definitely a separation between work and pleasure. We're all entitled to lunch breaks, right?

"Good. Your father would not be happy to see the hotel under performing because of your distractions."

"I've already disappointed him enough," I laugh. "I don't try and always do it but you know how much he loves his hotels."

"Of course I do," she laughs and pauses for a second. "Sometimes too much. I know he wishes that he was there more for you two growing up."

"He told me about the robbery at Grand Fortune. Just after Kiera was born."

"I know," her tone changed all of a sudden. Not the chipper, happy person that always presented a smile wherever we go. "It's scary, isn't it?"

I nod to myself. It was already scary being there. What if I wasn't?

"I'm not mad at your father. For not being there when it happened. Grand Fortune just opened up, and he needed to make investors happy, which meant constantly meeting with them, because we didn't know where this would go. He was...is...an ambitious man who took a big gamble to bridge Asian luxury in the American hotel industry. And he had to work much harder because he's an Asian immigrant. It was also a time when we were at odds with Yin Yin and Ye Ye. They didn't even really want to see Kiera when she was born."

"What? Why?"

"Your grandparents really could not stand that your father was marrying me. They pushed him so hard to marry a Chinese woman. I met them for the first time, and they were disgusted with me. They thought I was too privileged and wouldn't understand all the stress they went through to make it in America. Which, I'm not saying they're wrong, but when your sister was born...they said she didn't look Asian enough to be their grandchild."

"Wow, Mom. I'm so sorry. I couldn't imagine. I know people used to tell me that in school, but to hear it from my own grandparents, I'd be so much more hurt."

We only have our Yin Yin now; my Ye Ye passed right before I graduated onto high school. She doesn't do much anymore since she's older, just walks a lot around Chinatown and forces my dad and uncle to take her out for lunch occasionally. But, there were a few times where she had to take care of me and my sister, and she'd tried her best to make sure we were fed and watch all the cartoons we liked on tv. Her English isn't fluent, but she talked as much as she could to us. I don't even think I noticed if she felt some animosity toward us, because she didn't show it. She beamed whenever she had to introduce us to her friend at Mahjong or the bakery by her apartment.

"Your dad had to do a lot of convincing that I, or our children, weren't going to be going anywhere." My mom chuckles. "I learned to freaking make doongs to try and get her and I to have a conversation."

"Did it work?"

"Oh yeah! That was when she told me what she really felt: when she came to America, she was bullied by her white coworkers because of her thick accent. Then they would say things about animal eating or how her eyes looked small. It made her think that all white people were going to treat her and her family like that, so she wasn't very happy that your dad fell in love with someone who looked like all the women that bullied her. I understood her anger. I know that even though I didn't grow up rich by any means, I never had the same struggles that she did moving to a new country with a different colored skin tone. But, somehow I was able to win her over."

"What'd you say?"

"I told her that your sister was going to grow up and want to learn about where her family came from, and that even if she didn't like me, she owed it to her grandchildren to teach them about her culture. And then when the robbery happened, your father was so upset about everything: losing me, putting me in danger, that he told them that this couldn't happen any longer. Either they tried to be a part of our lives, or we moved far enough away to never be a part of theirs."

I slump back in my chair. I thought I knew my parents, knew enough about their lives and struggles. Obviously the struggles my dad faced being an Asian hotel owner, but my heart broke for my mom, who just wanted to love my dad and be a good mother to her kids, and that the two people my dad had cared for the most before her, thought she was going to hurt my dad.

I trace the tattoo on my chest. □. Good fortune, which I thought I had for years. Turns out, I only had it good because my parents had so many struggles.

"Well, I'm happy everything seems to be back to a good place. I'm sorry that it took so much to get there."

"Oh it's okay, Kelly. I knew the moment I said 'I love you' I was not going to leave because life got hard. Almost forty years later, I think we're still doing good."

I agree. My parents still survived through marriage, while some of their high society friends got divorced for mutual reasons, or for a few, it was because they were having affairs with their admins that just graduated college. My parents stopped seeing those people for good reason.

"I think so," I laugh. "I think you two could also use a vacation. It's the holiday season."

"Oh, we'll see. I'm assuming you're not coming here for Christmas?"

I hadn't thought too much about it, because work preoccupied my thoughts of leisure, except when it came to getting Marissa to take her clothes off. It'd be my first Christmas not in

New York, which also meant it was my first without snow. As much as I'd like to take the time to fly there, for once I felt like it'd be too much of a gamble to leave.

"I don't think I can. Ba probably wouldn't let me anyway, leave the hotel to go to the airport. What if someone figures it out and they follow me to the airport?"

"I know, it's very risky," her voice starts to sound anxious. "Well, figure out who's behind this so you can come home. And bring your girlfriend! I would love to meet her."

"Okay, Mom," I say, biting my lip. She would, but I know my father still has his apprehensions.

"Are you in your office? I realized I should have clicked Face-time. I haven't seen your face in months!"

"Uh mom," I hesitate. "I don't know..."

"Why do you sound unsure? Kellen Lawrence Zhang, what are you not telling me?"

"Ugh," I groan, hitting the accept button. My shirtless body, leaning back on my chair fills my moms screen and I see her mouth gasp when she sees mine on hers.

"You're naked," she says. "In your office. Why? You know I was never a fan of that tattoo you wanted to get on your chest. Even with the 'Fu' it's so much ink."

"Well, it's kind of too late to get it removed."

"Don't deflect!" Her voice raises as I hear the door knob turn. Just wonderful.

"Hey, I'm back!" Marissa yells and stops when she looks at me holding my phone behind the desk. She quickly shuts the door and mouths: "Why are you still naked?"

"Mom, I have to go. I'll call and explain later. Okay love you bye!" I press hang up before she gets to let out a peep.

"Did I interrupt something?" Marissa asks.

I set my phone down on my desk and waltz over to gather my clothes and quickly shuffle my feet to put one pant leg on at a time and a white shirt at a minimum over my chest.

"My mom decided to call me at the most convenient time," I say with a touch of sarcasm lining my tongue.

"Ah," she nods, still carefully analyzing every part of my now-clothed body. "How'd that go?"

"Fine, until she realized that she wanted to FaceTime me and soon picked up on why I wasn't very fond of the idea."

"Because you were naked."

I nod. After I told her I'm separating work from pleasure. What a load of BS that ended up being.

"I'm hoping she doesn't tell my dad. Because if he finds out, he'll definitely tell Erick that I fucked in my office and we'd get in trouble."

"Is your mom like one of those people who keep your secrets for your own benefit?"

"Kinda," I sit down on my desk. "She's kept a lot from my dad when I got in trouble. To save me from possible punishment."

"Well then, we don't have anything to worry about right?"

"Yep." I smile at her and turn my head once I hear my phone vibrate.

> Kiera: Mom texted me & told me you had sex in your office. Nice job Dai Dai. You're such a horndog.

I slump my shoulders and drop my phone on my desk, reaching to cover my face. Of course she wouldn't tattle to my dad, but she'd need to blab about it so my sister is the one hearing about it.

"Everything okay?" Marissa asks.

"Yeah, I'm fine. My mom just told my sister and now I'm never going to hear the end of it."

"Oh my god," she laughs. "I'm sorry, but I think that's probably going to be just as bad as if your dad found out."

"I know," I murmur. "She's nothing if not a button pusher."

I reach over and grab my phone to send her a text back.

> :P Can't believe she fucking told you. Hey, at least it's with someone I think might stick."

> WHAT? Kellen ACTUALLY in love?? What has Vegas done to you?

> Don't even get me started. I've been almost kidnapped, held at gunpoint, and a Chinese mafia out to get me. Vegas is more wild than anything I could have thought.

> Yeah I know. I'm sorry. I wish I could just make all these people disappear so you can actually live a normal life.

> It's ok. Everything happens for a reason. And I wouldn't have gotten close to Marissa if it wasn't for all this.

I set the phone down and peer up at Marissa, who's still standing with her hands folded in front of me. I smile warmly at her.

"Why are you smiling at me like that?"

I grab onto her hand and pull her close into me. "I'm just happy at how everything's turned out. How all the bad things that happened somehow led me to you."

Chapter Eighteen

Marissa

The entire sales team is sitting in one of our many conference rooms for our month-end meeting right before everyone begins to take off for the holiday season. The sad part about working in hotels, as compared to other corporations, is that we barely get any time off. We get eight holidays a year as managers, one of which includes Christmas, but only Christmas is paid. Not Christmas Eve, not the days in between Christmas and New Year's Day, just one day to celebrate family and indulge in lots of food.

This year, I wanted to go home for Christmas, but since it was in the middle of the week and because we had Andrew Tseng's show to prepare for in a few weeks for the hotel's Lunar New Year Celebration, I couldn't take time off. My parents were sad, but they understood. I would be flying home in March anyway for my cousin's wedding, so they'd see me then. By then, everything we'd be working for would be over and I'd hopefully leave Vegas and not feel scared doing it. The hotel had to stay open for Christmas anyway, because of all the tourists that wanted to spend the holidays behind a slot machine, so there were still festivities to be had.

Kellen and I had been spending a lot more time together, cautiously of course. Spending more time away from him made me feel worse than spending time with him, so we've agreed that for now, we'd spend nights together only on the weekends. Staying in the hotel was worth the wait. His villa had a jacuzzi in the backyard we'd lounge in, which was perfect during the cold, crisp nights.

Of course, because our robbery caught citywide attention, Erick had to call us in and question our relationship. Kellen rehearsed exactly what we'd say so he wouldn't raise suspicions.

"We've both been working on this together, and I went to buy Marissa a gift as a token of my appreciation. We're not dating and understand the consequences if we were in the scope of our jobs." With that, he seemed to be understanding. Thank god, or else I don't know how we'd be able to wiggle our way out of that one. So far, the only person that knew our intentions behind the scenes was Kayley, who's aware we like each other but we can't label it anything. She hasn't really warmed up to Kellen, but she is trying to be more amicable to him for my sake. Somehow they were able to have lunch together and not yell at each other, which made me almost tear up a little.

"Obviously, we are poised to begin Quarter 1 strong," our Director of Sales, Joelle, says. We're all looking at this PowerPoint with future groups on the books, and today was the day that I was approved by Erick to talk about Andrew Tseng visiting. I had to hide this from the team since I heard the news, and everyone still asked me why I was working so close to Kellen, so I'm glad I finally didn't have to lie.

"We've got a few conferences to look forward to, as well as some social blocks that are looking to bring in more revenues than what we were hoping. Marissa also has a special project she would like to talk about." Joelle motions to me, and I get up and walk over to the front of our conference table, with my laptop in hand. I reach to grab the cord to plug in my laptop from her and the screen pops up with the slides I was working on yesterday with Kellen's help.

"Hi everyone." I wave. "I know I have been MIA for the past few weeks from the office, and that is because I have been working on a project that I have had to keep hidden from you all until I was allowed to share more information about it.January is our Lunar New Year celebration month, and in true Blossom fashion, we go all out. Decorations, lion dancing, food galore. I'm happy to announce that we will be doing this again, but with a special guest."

I press the right arrow on my keyboard to bring up a graphic I tried to conjure up myself of Andrew Tseng with clip-art Chinese lanterns along the top border of the graphic.

"Andrew Tseng will be visiting our hotel and doing a special show for one night. Him and his crew will be staying with us for the week in preparation. A total of 32 rooms per night, and it is imperative that this goes off without a hitch. Because if he likes it here, he will be the Blossom's newest residency."

Everyone murmurs a "wow" or a "no way!" once I break the news. I feel the surge of excitement coursing through my bones. That, coupled with relief. I'm bad at keeping secrets, but somehow I was good enough to keep quiet about this one until now.

"That's so cool, Marissa!" Leo shouts. Everyone else nods their head in agreement.

"So, that's why you've been sneaking off with Kellen," Lina nods. "I thought you were fucking the owner's son."

Everyone snickers in laughter and I have to work my face muscles to ensure I'm not blushing too hard.

"Of course not," I say with any ounce of confidence that I have. "We've just been working together. We're keeping things strictly business." My stomach sours at how far from the truth that sounds.

"He can be mine," Leo says with his eyebrows raised. Everyone shoots him a weird look and he throws his hands up. "What? The man is beautiful." That gets everyone to chuckle. I can't nod my head in agreement or else I'd be eating my own damn words with what I just said.

"Okay okay," Joelle pipes up to quiet us all down. "Enough fawning over our superiors. I can't be sending you all to HR before one of the biggest artists this year is set to arrive. Was there anything else you needed to share with us, Marissa?"

"Not really." I shake my head, then press my finger on the right arrow to go to the next slide. "Here are some VIPs and room assignments. Please note, we will need to have him enter through a separate entrance and Operations will pre-key, pre-check all reservations. For us, his team is planning to have a meeting space set so people can work out of, and Kellen, Erick, and I are dining with his tour manager at Lotus the night of arrival. As you all do, just make sure you put your biggest smile forward and do everything you can to make him feel welcome. We can't have anything we do mess up his chances of coming back semi-permanently."

"What about the gang that's trying to kidnap Kellen?" Luke, our Director of Events, asks.

I bite the inside of my cheek. I thought I could ride the wave of excitement for the entire time and people wouldn't be needing to ask hard hitting questions. But, Luke is known to ask questions about worst case scenarios that interrupt my positive thoughts and I wish he'd stop.

"We're working on it," I answer him respectfully. "We get new information every day and the police have been working hard to trace any members near us so we can locate the source." I wish that we were further along in the process, but gangs who know what they're doing make it harder to locate their whereabouts.

"Okay," he says cautiously. "You know there are clients that have expressed concerns to me about booking an event with us because of this, right? It's very disappointing to hear we are losing business because of some hooligans."

This is just something else. I slam my hands against the table, and death stare directly into his bleak, blue eyes. "For your information, Luke, these hooligans have tried to kidnap one of our employees, and also have physically hurt me almost to the point where I couldn't breathe. Don't think for a second that I don't want these people gone and out of my life just as much as anyone else."

There begins an eeriness that fills the room after my confession and Luke's mouth stays stuck wide open. I pause, looking around the room for just a moment, before telling everyone that my portion of the presentation had ended and I walk back to my seat.

The corner of my laptop lights up with a notification.

NEW TEAMS GROUP CHAT: LINA ROBLES & LEO HOWARD

LINA: Girl that was fucking awesome

LEO: Yeah you tell that bitch who's boss

MARISSA: Omg stop

But thanks — dude is really fucking annoying

LINA: Like how dare he??

LEO: Yeah, he should try almost dying from an armed robber.

MARISSA: Lmao love you guys

Joelle dismisses everyone once the presentation ends, but asks me if I can stay behind. Luke still looks like he regretted anything he said, but I was over it to accept his apology right now. He clearly had his frustrations, but taking it out on me, who was still trying to recover what happened, was something I didn't need to listen to.

"Sit, sit!" Joelle says cheerfully once the door shut. I take the seat across from her, a little nervous. I don't think I did anything wrong, so I shouldn't be anticipating this as a bad conversation.

"How are you doing?" she asks.

"Okay, I guess." I shrug. Normally I think I would have just grin and bear it and tell her I was okay, but I was still feeling the effects of my tirade at Luke.

"I'm sorry about Luke. I am planning on having a chat with him tomorrow about that. He...that was uncalled for."

"Yeah," I nod. Not surprising, given he's always the one to comment on everyone else's mistakes before calling out his own. "I understand that everyone is frustrated because of what's going on. I try to push through when groups are telling me the same thing. But...it's just, when you live through it and see just how much these people can do, it's scary. I never thought I'd have to watch my back as much as I had to since they tried to kidnap Kellen. I definitely feel like I'm stronger, but I still feel so scared."

"I get it. Or, I know that this is really tough for you. But you're really being very strong doing all you can to make sure the hotel is ready for this big group. You've grown a lot more since you were promoted to manager. I see your dedication every day and you've truly blossomed." She laughs for a moment. "Ha, get it? Blossomed? I make myself laugh."

I chuckle back. "Yeah, that is really funny. Good job." Except no one knows how badly I'm suffering inside at how I've been hooking up with the Director of Operations and forced to keep it a secret from my colleagues.

Chapter Nineteen

Kellen

I can't do much to decorate this year, but I hope that the small decorations I ordered online suffice for a not-white Christmas in Las Vegas. I bought a bunch of those fake trees from Target and sprinkled them around, some atop the fireplace, some on the dining room table. An elf on a shelf that's smiling down on us. And of course, a tree. I don't know how long I will be in Vegas for, but something I loved so much in our New York home was that we had tall ceilings. So, every Christmas we bought a nine-foot tree that stood in the corner of our living room. It was magical. There were big, bulbed lights, snow that was artificially sprinkled onto the tree, and large, glass ornaments. My favorite was the one that had a miniature Grand Fortune in it and fake snow sprinkled down it when you shook it. It was late to have that made for the Blossom, but eventually I wanted to make one because this was my home now. The tree I bought was smaller, but still had that fake snow on it and I bought some blue and silver ornaments that seemed to go well with the room's furniture.

I even went so far to buy us stockings. One that had the letter "K" on it and the other an "M." Marissa told me that she was staying here for the holidays because she didn't want to use up her paid time off until she was going to be leaving to go back home for a family wedding, and then she was going to spend two weeks at home. It wasn't until March, but two weeks felt like a long time being miles away from each other. Especially because the longest we've gone without talking now is three days.

When I Facetime my mom for advice, she can't help but smile that I was the one who was taking charge to plan the most magical holiday I could for someone I had only known for a few months.

"You did such a good job decorating Kelly!" she beams as I was walk with my phone camera pointed at my living room. "It looks nice. Maybe next Christmas if you come, I'm having you decorate the house. These bones don't work as well as they used to."

"Sure," I say, planting myself on the couch and wiping my forehead. "It's a lot of work, though. You always do a good job. I'm just surprised that I was able to find enough decorations. Target has some cute things."

While I have to say, the decorating part was fun, I don't know if I could also spend time cooking an entire feast. That was extra work that I didn't feel like tacking on. It won't nearly taste as well, and I thought Marissa deserved a feast. All we'd be feasting on if I made dinner was burnt food.

"I got this for Marissa," I say, taking a bag from under the table and showing Mom. "What do you think?"

She gasps and her face lights up like a Christmas tree. "Oh, Kell. That is beautiful! What made you want to get this?"

"It was kind of a special shared moment between us. I wanted to get something that was meaningful and I know she'd love."

"Oh my gosh, she will be over the moon! I kind of want to ask your father for one. You think he'd say yes?"

"It doesn't hurt to hint. You're the one person he likes to spoil." I got spoiled too, especially with how much I was able to get away with growing up. But he will buy my mom anything she wants because that's the way that he likes to show his love for her.

"Thanks Kell," she says, smiling through the screen. "Okay, I'm going to let you go so you can have some time with your lady. Let me know how everything goes!"

"I will, Mom. Tell everyone hi and Merry Christmas for me."

"I will, Kell." She blows me a kiss. "Love you."

"Love you too."

There's a knock at my door not too long after I press the end call button. Thankfully, the kitchen staff worked quickly to make everything for our early dinner. I walk up to the door and smile as I see Marissa, dressed in a red oversized sweater and holding a large gift bag with a Christmas tree on it. Big bag makes me wonder what goodies might be hiding under there. We didn't explicitly tell each other what we've been wanting for

Christmas. Honestly, I just want to spend a lot of time with her, naked in bed preferred. The presents are just another way for me to show her how I feel.

"Hi," I smile at her.

"Hey," she says, with a hint of blush coloring her face. "Merry Christmas."

I quickly pull her into my arms and let the door close behind us. "Merry Christmas." I whisper in her ear and give her a kiss on the cheek. "How have you been?"

"Fine," she nods. "Surprisingly busy, but I guess that's not really a surprise. The sales team had positive reception to the news about Andrew. Although one man: Luke, our Director of Events, was so fixated on the bad and only wanted answers about the Fortune Hunters and went on a rant about how they're making us lose business. Then I told him unless he knew what it was like being almost choked to death, he could shut the fuck up. Although I wish I could've said 'fuck' during the meeting."

"Wow," I beam. As if I was already in love with her, this badass move was just icing on the cake. "Good for you for taking a stand. Sorry you had to bring it back up."

"It's fine, I'm just glad I was just able to share how I really felt. I don't think he's wrong for thinking that way, it is an unfortunate situation, and I would wish it could disappear so we can have people stay here and not feel like they're at risk. But, everyone was doing so well with focusing on the good and praising me, or us in a way, for working hard to make sure this can happen, and he had to bring it all down. I think that's what makes me so upset about everything, that he wanted to focus on the bad way more than focusing on the good."

"Yeah, that kind of does suck." It reminds me of all the meetings I have to have with our staff about our TripAdvisor ratings, and even though we're one of the highest scoring hotels on the Strip, people often don't think to make reviews on the good things but will always make reviews on the bad.

"But I'm happy you stood up for yourself. What did Joelle have to say?"

"She was actually very understanding," she says, leading herself onto the couch, where I take a seat next to her. "She was sorry on Luke's behalf and told me that she was going to talk to him about what happened. And she was very proud of me for standing up for what I believed in. She said she's seen me grow a lot since I started here."

"That's great. Do you ever think that you would want to be like her one day? Or move up to being a Director?" Marissa was still young in hotel career standards. Most Directors were older, even close to my parent's age, and Marissa had just barely turned 30. There are exceptions to the rule, and people who work just as hard, if not harder, than a Director, but with great power comes great responsibility. Doesshe feel ready to tackle on that yet?

She pauses for a moment. "I don't know," she shrugs. "On one hand, I would feel so happy to be at a place where I have more responsibility and the 'Director' title. But, then you kind of have to do right by ownership, and that meant that you really couldn't be anyone's friend. You had to make some tough decisions that people weren't always so ecstatic about."

"Yup, you couldn't have said it better." I stretch out my arms and put one around her. In the beginning, I had felt kind of sad that I was coming into this role, in a new place, and didn't really have the chance to be the nice guy I wanted to be, in hopes of pleasing everyone. Instead, I had to come to terms that I was going to make some tough decisions that would cause people to turn against me, and now, even though I don't always see eye to eye with everyone, I can at least say I've done a good enough job making decisions that were beneficial for the hotel.

I reach to turn on the fireplace that we're sitting across from. I bring over mugs from the kitchen and fill them up with my favorite wintertime drink: a hot toddy.

Marissa grabs the mug from me and wraps her hands around it. "Thanks," she smiles. "The place looks so nice. Did you decorate it all yourself?"

I nod. "A lot of looking at Christmas decorations from Target, then asking if one of the concierge people could help me pick stuff up. I know I probably won't be in this room the same time next year, but I wanted it to be special because I'm spending it with you and you don't get the chance to spend it with your family."

"Thank you." She smiles and leans over to give me a quick peck. "I know I could've flown back for a day; it's not a far flight at all. But with the VIP group, and just all the uncertainty surrounding my life right now trying to catch the Fortune Hunters, I opted to just take a longer vacation when my cousin gets married next year. But I'm happy that you're here too, at least I'll be able to spend the holidays with someone. And you even did such a good job making everything look so festive!"

"It was hard work, but I'm glad it paid off. I didn't do the same for the food though," I chuckle. "That I had the restaurant concoct something for me."

We walk over to the kitchen island and I hand her a plate. She's smiling as she walks around the small space, looking at the plethora of food that I have lined up for our special day.

"Okay, but this is still amazing, Kellen. How did you know all these foods were my favorite?"

"Well, the beef stew noodle soup I knew was a for sure. But everything else, I kind of just assumed. The claypot rice is one of my favorites. They do a really good job of making the rice a perfect stickiness."

We gather our plates and sit down at the table. I can feel the drool forming in my mouth at how wonderful it smells, and I know it's going to taste just as good.

"How is Christmas like with your family?" Marissa asks. "Is this the first time you're on your own for the holiday?"

I nod. "Christmas is nice…I mean, it's very small. My parents, my sister, her husband, my nephew, and my grandma. We kind of do the traditional Christmas even though we're Chinese. It's the one time that my mom kind of gets excited that she can cook something that also happens to please my grandmother. We usually do a spiral ham, mashed potatoes, roasted veggies, and a rack of lamb or prime rib. The decorating is definitely on another level. My mom hires a professional crew of people to help her decorate my parent's place. From the ten-foot Christmas tree, the tinsel that drapes across the room, all these glass icicles that hang down from the ceiling. It's just as winter wonderland as the Macy's in Herald Square is. Just less of the mechanical figurines. But I wouldn't be surprised if she bought a holiday train set to circle around the tree next year for my nephew."

"So, you'd say Christmas is kind of a big deal."

"My mom tries to make it." I feel like it all started because she wanted to be in competition with the moms at our schools on who could have the best decorated house amongst the other Lower East Side kids I grew up with. I think people kind of underestimated her because they assumed Chinese families don't typically do anything special for Christmas, but she proves them all wrong. And since then, it's been the one time of the year where she's felt joy in putting in effort to make something feel magical.

She says it's because she never had that extravagant Christmas growing up, and neither did my dad, so if she was going to go all out for something it was that. Then my dad decided the same needed to be done for the Lunar New Year as well, which is why the hotel kind of goes all out for those two holidays."

The holiday decor at the Blossom, I would argue, wasn't the biggest and the best. Some of the other luxury hotels have grand Christmas trees that are at least fifty feet tall, and polar bears made out of flowers. Ours is just a Christmas tree with some giant pink light up presents surrounding it. But come Lunar New Year, we'll be doing everything in our power to make sure that we have the most grand decor that will blow everyone else out of the water, complete with lion dancing and Chinese instrument performances in the lobby every hour.

"It makes sense," Marissa says. "I like seeing all the decorations. It's like one of my favorite parts about the holiday. Everything is so picturesque, it's like you have the magic of winter without the snow."

"Maybe next year, I can take you to New York so you can see what a real winter wonderland looks like." Of course, if we were still together. If I spoke it into existence, maybe it'll come true. Forget the forbidden relationship that we have. I'm not going to wait around for a year to be with her. I'm going to defy whoever I need to be with her. Even if that might be my own father. If this time together is proving anything, it's that I've never felt more happy during a holiday than spending it intimately with her. But, until I could figure out what a relationship looked like: which meant giving her all the attention she deserved, I had to restrain myself. Commitment was a word that loomed over my head like a rain cloud, and I was more focused on the storm than the calm before it.

"I'd like that," she smiles. "You know, if and when we're together. I know there's still a lot up in the air about that."

Ah, so I guess it was weighing on her mind. "No matter what," I say, rubbing my thumb over her knuckles. "I'm just happy being here with you. This is one of the best Christmases I've ever had. Even better than the time my parents surprised me with that huge Lego Millennium Falcon set as a present."

"Really?" She bursts up laughing. "Well, don't want to burst your bubble, but I definitely didn't get you something as cool for a present."

"That's okay," I tell her. "You didn't even need to get me a present."

"I know, it's just one of those things where I wanted to. You were kind enough to host me for the holidays, and you've been nothing shy of amazing to me these past few months. I think it was finally time to tell you how much I appreciate you."

"Do you want to exchange presents now then?"

"Sure," she nods. She gets up and reaches for her present that she left by the doorway. When she walks back, she holds the somewhat large holiday themed bag in her hand and hands it over to me.

"It's nothing much, like I said, but I saw this the other day and I thought it would be something you'd look nice in."

I place the bag on the floor and rip off the layer of tissue paper covering the present. I pull it out: a tan-colored, cashmere button-down coat that's wonderfully soft to the touch.

"I know you probably are no stranger to coats like this, but when I saw it, and then I felt it, it was so nice that I couldn't not buy it. I hope it fits. I kind of had to guess your size, but if it doesn't fit you can exchange it. It won't hurt my feelings."

"This is amazing," I say, holding the soft coat in my hands. "Thank you." I pull her in for a hug and wrap my arms tightly around her shoulders. "This is such a thoughtful gift. Truly. I'm excited to wear it soon."

"Good, I'm glad. I know that we can't really be venturing outside much, but I'd like to hope that we'll be able to get one chance to see all the holiday decorations in the other hotels next year. It's so fun to see what everyone has planned."

"Definitely." I stand up and walk over to the armchair where I was sitting earlier to talk to my mom to give Marissa her gift. I had to get a different bag to hide what store I had bought it from, but it was also in a bigger bag, around the size that she had given to me, in hopes of trying to confuse her on what the size of the gift was.

"I bought this for you, well I actually had to give my card to someone to buy this for you, because I wanted to get something meaningful to you, and this gift I thought was meaningful for the both of us, so I raced as quick as I could to buy it before they didn't have any left."

"Okay," she says, giving me a confused look. "I have no idea what this could be."

"When you see it, I think you'll see what I mean." I hand her the bag. "Go ahead, open it."

She takes the bag and rips open some of the tissue paper I had stuffed in the bag. She peers her head over and gasps much louder than her own natural voice usually projects.

"Oh my god, Kellen." Her eyes begin to water and she quickly brushes her tears away. "You got this for me?" She takes out the dust bag for the black Chanel 19 bag that I bought her. This is definitely one of the most expensive gifts I have bought for someone. I mean, I haven't even bought my mom a Chanel purse. And neither has my dad, yet. When I was thinking about what gifts to buy her, I ultimately thought about this one, because she mentioned to me how she had wanted a Chanel bag her entire life, but could justify buying one. And if she had one, she'd rub it in everyone's face that she had owned one, and the thought of that made me smile. Maybe because it made me realize that it can be something that ties her back to me.

"Yeah," I nod. "Don't think you needed to get something just as expensive or anything. I just got it because I know you were eying that bag, and even though the brand itself has ties to memories of us in more unfortunate circumstances, I think that all your hard work leads itself to this kind of reward."

"Thank you," she whispers. She sets the bag down and cups both my cheeks with her hands. She leans forward and gives me a soft kiss on my lips. I can still feel the tears on hers, but I take her face in my hand and brush away her tears with my thumb. "This is the nicest thing anyone has ever given me," she says. "Probably the nicest thing anyone would get for me besides like, an engagement ring or something."

"You're welcome." I give her another kiss. "This is probably the best I can do for now, and I'm glad it's enough." I make a note to myself that I'll need to one-up myself when I buy her an engagement ring, but that's for future me to worry about.

"It's more than enough." She looks deeply into my eyes and rests her palms on my chest. "It's everything I could ask for."

She buries her head in the crevice of my shoulder and I feel my face harden. I breathe in a deep breath into her hair. I know that I got this for her because I care about Marissa a lot, going so far to say that I love her, but life is hurdling so many obstacles at us that I'm starting to ponder if my love is strong enough to hold onto her. Or I love her so much that I think she deserves so much more than my baggage and me.

Chapter Twenty

A fter another sales meeting with Joelle, I'm craving for something sweet to ease my anxiety about keeping my doings with Kellen private. There's a boba stand I frequent at least once a week, and today feels like another day to itch my craving.

I text Kellen to ask if he wanted anything.

> Marissa: Going to pick up boba before I come back. Want anything??

> Kellen: just oolong MT with boba — 50% sweet/ice. Thanks <3 strategy meeting probably only halfway over…dying rn.

> Marissa: ugh sounds awful — lmk if you want something to help with that later ;)

I stick my tongue out at my phone. Flirt talking was not in my wheelhouse, but I had no idea how else I was going to try and explain I wanted us to relieve our stresses over sex later. Even if

I was going to be doing it with a huge secret weighing on my chest.

Kellen: … now I can't get up from my seat because these pants don't do a great job of hiding my boner. Thx :P

I laugh, and react with a "ha ha" on his last text. I go to the app and order our drinks and pass by the poker room, where at the front there is a sign that says:

"Coming Soon! Blossom's Lunar New Year Classic Tournament. Guaranteed $750K Prize Pool. Sign Up Online Now!"

Dammit. Kellen didn't say anything about this poker tournament. Why would he though; he's not the one who makes the schedule on when tournaments are happening. This feels too good to be true though. The perfect thing that the Fortune Hunters can come and invade. It'd be a stupid idea to have a tournament with that kind of knowledge that they're still out there, but maybe it's the exact reason why they're doing it. Lure in the culprit using a bait. This time, the bait came in the form of a $750K prize-pool tournament. I could play and not have anyone find out, right? This is helping Kellen out, if anything. …As long as I can keep my identity a secret. I open my phone to the sign-up page and put my information in. Looks like we're reviving an old friend.

Kellen wasn't done with his strategy meeting until near the end of the day, so we just decided to order dinner and eat at his place since I'll be spending the night. It's a good thing I don't have many responsibilities at home, like taking care of any pets, because I spend more time in his room than at my own apartment. He even gave me a section of the closet to bring clothes for the week.

Today's dinner of choice was a surprising change from the Asian food we felt comfortable with, probably because I for once had a craving for something else, but I let Kellen make the decision on what. He decided on Italian and got us some pasta Bolognese to share which did just the trick.

As we were slurping up spaghetti with reruns of Bob's Burgers playing on the television, Kellen's phone beeps and he grabs it to see what notification pops up. His eyes go wide and he drops his fork on the table.

"What's up?" I ask.

"Holy shit."

"Kellen," I press him again. "Is everything okay?"

It takes him a moment to get out of the mindset he's originally planted in but he finally nods. "Sorry," he says, looking at me. "The Director of Casino Services just texted all the Directors. There's this poker tournament happening in a few weeks. They think it'll be a good way for us to lure in the Fortune Hunters."

"Oh. I actually saw the poster when I walked back from grabbing boba. Is that a safe option with everything going on?" I try to seem as nonchalant about it as possible to not stir any attention about it or about me.

"I know, it really doesn't feel like it," he says. "But, it might get us closer to who might be working for them and us. That's kind of why we set it up. To see if the money will draw in something like a raid or something similar. But, anyway, that's not why I was so shocked. Do you follow poker much? Like know who the pros are?"

I shake my head. I didn't like that I'm lying to him right now. It feels icky and honestly makes it hard to stomach my dinner.

"I don't follow it much, but I watch every once in a while, especially when the big tournaments are on. I know, I don't play myself, but it's interesting to watch others play. And the money involved is just on another level. Anyway, there's a really good poker player who kind of dropped off the face of the earth a while back and our Director of Casino Services just texted me that their name is in the pool."

I almost choke on the wine I'm drinking. "Oh. What's their name?"

"Janessa Frost. She was like, one of the top female poker players back in the day. I thought for a moment she'd try and win the WSOP tournament but she ghosted the community one day and no one knows why. But she's going to be in our tournament. Isn't that amazing?"

"Yeah," I shriek out. How was I supposed to know that Kellen would be so invested in the poker community that he knew who Janessa was? I didn't think I was that big in the community, but apparently I was wrong, because of all the people

I didn't want to know about Janessa, Kellen was at the top of that list.

"But now, it's like, we need to hope that we know this will attract a Fortune Hunter. And I feel bad but I don't want to use Janessa as bait, but because of how renowned she is in the poker community, we might not have any other choice."

"What do you mean?"

"Like, there is a very strong chance she is going to do well. Even though she's been out of the community for a while, people have seen her playing online again recently and she's done very well. She hasn't entered into an in-person tournament yet, but she must be feeling confident enough to do so if her name's on here. And we need to catch that person, so as much as we'll have security in that tournament, I'm afraid that Janessa is going to get hurt because they're going to target her during the tournament."

I started breathing faster. It started feeling like the onset of a panic attack, my pulse rushing and I couldn't talk. Kellen had seen me like this once before, and the way he had comforted me was one of the reasons why I had fallen for him so easily. Now, I was thinking a mix of different things. I had to tell him, right? But he would immediately tell me to pull out of the tournament, and I agreed, this might be the only chance we had to catch whoever was on the inside. And if I couldn't be that person, then who would? But, I already got hurt once, I don't think I could stomach that same thing happening again.

Especially when Janessa Frost wasn't even a real person; she and I had the same body. I was perfectly fine with crafting my own plan to take them down, but hearing that Kellen might be using Janessa as bait as well made me start to worry that maybe I won't be fully in control of my plan.

Kellen quickly looks at me sobbing and rushes over to grab my hand. "Marissa, what's wrong?"

I keep panting and shaking my head and he rushes over to pull me into him.

"Hey, you're okay." He starts rubbing my back. "Try and relax okay?" He lets me rest my head over his shoulder and buries his nose into my hair.

"I...can't..." I heave.

"What's wrong?" he asks. "Please, Marissa. Tell me what's bothering you."

We wait a few minutes until I can get my breathing square again and I break apart from him.

"You can't tell anyone this." I whisper. "Please. I need to trust you with my entire life right now, and I need you to keep this a secret."

"Okay," he nods.

I bite my lip and take a deep breath, exhaling with a loud sigh.

"I'm Janessa Frost."

He blinks, not saying anything but still kneeled next to me. His mouth opens slightly, ready to say something but the words are struggling to come out of his mouth.

"Um," he begins. "That...can't be possible. Janessa's hair is long and has blonde highlights. You two look nothing alike...well...maybe not identical." He leans in closer to me, trying to see what features we both share.

"You ever watch Hannah Montana?"

"That's a work of fiction, Marissa! This is real life."

"The same rules apply!" I shout. "I asked for you to trust me and you can't even do that right now!" I don't even realize how much I'm shaking right now. The last time Kellen and I fought was before we were even doing...whatever it is we were doing. Kissing and having sex a lot.

His face softens and he returns to having his arms around me and pulling me tight to him. "I'm sorry, baby," is what I assume he's saying into my hair, but it comes out kind of muffled. He takes a deep breath in and exhales on the top of my head.

"This is just really surreal right now," he says, looking right at me. He laughs a bit to himself. "I've fucked Janessa Frost."

I playfully roll my eyes at him. Of course I know he's saying this to be funny and lighten the mood, but Janessa only exists in the poker-verse.

"No, you've fucked Marissa Waters. Janessa Frost doesn't do hookups. Or dates for that matter. She's a lone wolf."

"You know, the more I think about it...Marissa...Janessa...Waters...Frost. You really did not make it hard to distinguish Janessa much farther from you."

I'm surprised he's even able to make the correlation. I've gone...how long? And no one has realized that I have a secret identity as a Vegas-famous poker player. Maybe it's the realization that he's fucked the body of a famous poker player that makes his senses light up and work harder.

"Well, you're the only one that figured it out thus far. I think people have just thought we were two separate people and didn't take the time to do some investigative sleuthing. You didn't even think we were the same person until I had to yell at you to trust me."

"I know," his lips downturn to a slight frown. I know he's genuinely upset that he didn't want to believe me at first, and I wonder if it was because he might have had some slight feelings for Janessa back when I was more active. Or that he just didn't want to believe I could be a good poker player. People gave Janessa scrutiny just because she was a woman in the ring. "I'm sorry, again. It's just...that's so crazy. And kind of cool. You did say you were good at poker, so I can't say I'm surprised much anymore."

"You can still be surprised, it's okay," I laugh, grabbing onto his hand. "I'm surprised that I've decided to make a comeback. I never thought I'd be bringing Janessa back from retirement."

"Why are you? And why did you leave in the first place? You probably would be making so much money that you wouldn't need to work here."

"Okay, well to answer the first question: I had the idea because I wanted to see if I could get any intel on who might be the mole working for the Fortune Hunters. That's kind of why I started freaking out a little when you were talking about your plans for Janessa and the tournament. I know that I'm risking a lot to be playing in person again, but I'm going to be careful. I can play observer from being on the floor, and that might be what we need! But, I don't know if I can play bait as you're hoping I can. I know I might get hurt, and I was willing to take that risk, but I'm terrified. What if my identity is revealed? That's the whole reason why I quit in the first place. I was afraid that I'd move up and the more bracelets I got, the harder it was to keep my identity a secret. If I went pro full time, I would have to reveal my true identity, which at the time wasn't a viable option. My parents would be so disappointed in me if they found out my career for the rest of my life involved gambling."

"No." Kellen lets go and shakes his head, moving to hover over me. "I can't let you participate, Marissa. You're absolutely right, you could get hurt. And, whoever you are, Marissa or Janessa, I can't risk it."

Damn, my anxiety is doing its work to try and block any ounce of confidence I have in my body. Now all I want to do is try and see if I was capable of bringing someone down.

"No," I stand up for myself, defiantly. "I'm sorry, but I have to. I know that I panicked about being hurt, but you're right first. Someone needs to take them down, and I need to be willing to take that risk. I need to play. And I need you to trust me. Please."

He purses his lips inside his mouth and sighs. I feel bad that I've subjected him to a lot tonight, mostly because I unearthed a secret that I never thought I would tell anyone. I mean, it's one that I wouldn't even dare to tell my parents. But, I didn't want him finding out in a different way. Like if I did this tournament and I got in trouble just as he said I was going to, then I don't want him finding out who I was when I possibly had the wig torn off my head and I was being dragged against my will.

"Okay," he relents. "I think you should, too. But I'm beefing up security. Double the amount of guards. And I'm watching you from the camera room. Should you have anything happen to you, press a call button immediately. Okay?"

I nod. I was scared, but I know that I have to do this for the better of the hotel. Let's just hope I'm as good as everyone hopes I am so there's more of a chance that people will pay attention to me. For once, I can't believe I want to attract attention. Although, I could just argue it was all Janessa doing the talking. She's everything Marissa isn't: sexy, confident, knows how to flirt with a man and have it serve as a distraction.

Kellen grabs a hold of my arms and grasps onto my muscles tightly. Oh my god, is his grip strong. I know the guy does a good workout, but I'm beginning to lose feeling in my arms.

"Please. Let me know if you feel in danger at any time you're playing. I will rush down immediately to help get you out of trouble. I don't want anything to happen to you."

"Okay," I nod. "I will."

He pulls me in for a quick hug and we kiss for a brief moment. "So, do you offer private poker lessons? Especially to men who you like fucking in bed?"

I laugh. "I guess some people I can make exceptions for. But I think it might need to come with a price."

"Name it."

"You did say I'd offer it to men I like fucking in bed." I take my arms and wrap it around his neck. "I think I might need a reminder on what I like."

He presses a finger to my lips to shush me and with no hesitation, lifts me up so that I'm cradled in his arms. "Say no more," he says while I'm laughing from all the ways he's tickling my body from his moving arms. "You're going to remember the moment I'm inside you."

"Can't wait," I smirk at him before he's hoisting me on him and we're making out so hard we forget where the bed even is.

Chapter Twenty-One

Kellen

I'm a ball of nerves, sitting in the casino's camera room with a perfect view of the poker area for this tournament. I was already a nervous wreck because this tournament was a huge risk that we kind of planned on the spur of the moment, but now that there are at least a hundred participants and one of them happened to be the woman I was in love with disguised as a professional poker player coming out of retirement, I needed to be more aware of what was happening more now than ever before.

Thus far, no signs of Fortune Hunters have made themselves known to us, but it is probably because they are keeping themselves hidden until the right time strikes. My guess is that it won't happen until the end of the tournament when there's the fewest amount of people left but the most amount of money at stake.

I frantically tap my leg under the desk, watching the screen as people are making their way into the room. The Director of Casino Services, Desmond, is next to me with bodyguards blockading the door behind us.

"Janessa just entered into the room," Desmond says. Obviously he doesn't know who Janessa is, but he told me the moment she enrolled in the tournament, so he's kept his tab on her because he knows this is a huge deal. I watch as the screen enlarges so the view of the poker room is the only one we have an eye on. Marissa is wearing her signature Janessa hairstyle and large-framed sunglasses to hide her eyes. It's like she's an entirely new person. If I was walking by her in passing, I wouldn't have even thought she was Marissa. I wished I could've planted a hidden microphone that I could listen in on what she was saying. All I could see is her talking to huge names in the poker world. I scowl to myself when she's hugging one man in particular: Rory Vinland, one of the youngest players in the Top 10. He's slightly younger than me but I hate how he's eying Janessa like she's a snack. He might as well be doing that to Marissa. I know that it's not Marissa doing the talking, that this guy is just smooth talking to someone who he thinks he knows, but it still rocks me to my core that someone is touching her like that and I can't swoop in to do anything to stop them.

And yet, if that was Marissa, without the disguise or anything, I couldn't do anything either. She's not bound to me like she would be if we were official. I haven't asked her yet to be my girlfriend, and I'm figuring out when would be the right moment to, but I haven't thought of a time yet that felt perfect.

I don't think that now's a perfect time, because we're both busy and I don't even know how to be in a relationship anymore. I think we're exclusive, I know we're exclusive, but we're not supposed to be official as long as there's a Fortune Hunter trying to seek me out.

"She just took a seat," Desmond recites. I see the table she's sitting at. Thankfully she's not at the same table as Rory.

The first few rounds go without anything happening. The player pool drops at a steady rate. Originally at a hundred, it dwindles down to sixty at the end of the half. Marissa is still in it. Hell, she is in like the Top 10 in total chip count. I wonder what happened for her to quit. I know she said she was afraid that people would find out who she is, but I would've tried to figure out a way to stick through it if I was going to be this good. She could probably make more money than I technically have in my bank account right now. She'd be like on Bilzerian level or something damn near it.

"Okay, last few rounds," Desmond says, after we've sat for hours watching the screen. The last round has ten people left, Marissa and Rory being two of them. Rory has edged Marissa out slightly on total chips in his possession, but she isn't very far behind. She's the only woman left on the table, and I think all the players want to try and get her out first.

I watch the dealer pass out cards to each of the players. Everyone calls, before Rory decides to raise. A few people fold, but Marissa decides to stick through it for the sake of seeing if he's bluffing. Rory smirks at her and I want to punch that face of his when he makes that damn smile. I wish I knew if Marissa was annoyed with him. She has to be right? She hates when guys overtly flirt with her. Guys who think they're all that and then some. It was how she felt for a long time with me, and somehow I was able to help change her mind. Feelings definitely had something to do with it.

She signals to check and the dealer flips up the last card. Rory nods and then raises more than triple the pot is at the moment. One guy decides to go in with him, risking all the chips he has in his possession, and Marissa sits there, debating for a moment. She has the chips to call, but that would put her a steep disadvantage if Rory has what he thinks he does. Marissa decides to play it safe and folds, and thank goodness she does, because Rory has a flush and wins the pot, meaning there's one more person out of contention.

"Oh my god, baby, you got this," I whisper as I lean in closer to the monitor.

"Who are you talking to?" Desmond asks. "You in love with Janessa Frost or something? Does she even know you?"

"She doesn't, but a guy can dream right?" I ask jokingly.

"Oh yeah," Desmond leans back in his chair and rests his clasped hands on the back of his neck. "Don't tell my wife this but Janessa Frost is hot. I'd let her deal me a hand any day."

Oh my god, not him too. I ball my fist as to not want to punch this guy. Desmond is a nice guy anyway, and very good at his job but is there someone that can just not tell me what they want Janessa to do to them? Take a deep breath, Kellen. Just remind yourself that Janessa isn't real and Marissa is. They're the same brain, even if they might don different hairstyles and personalities. You're going to bring Marissa home with you tonight, win or lose, and if she wants to live her dream out of being Janessa again, then we'll allow her, because deep down, we love her. Which scares us that we can even feel this way about someone.

"Weirdo," I murmur. I look back closer into the monitor as the game rages on. Shoot, when did the remaining number of players dwindle down to four? I take a deep breath and try to look at how many chips are in Marissa's possession. She has been playing really safe, so she hasn't racked up as many chips as Rory has. She still can remain in the game for long enough, but pretty soon, if Rory gets cocky again, he might keep on eliminating players and just win because he has enough chips to.

On the next round, he tries to raise again, and Marissa nods to raise. I forget that the longer this game goes on, the higher the ante becomes. So while the pot was already large to begin with, it just got a lot bigger. Rory raises after the flop, and Marissa calls. On the turn, the dealer pulls a king of diamonds.

"All in," Marissa says, pushing all her chips in. Desmond and I both gasp at the same time. I don't know her hand, so I can't say if she's making a good decision by doing this. I can only say I know Marissa well enough that even under the persona of someone else, she is never confident enough to bluff her way through a bet like that, so she's trying to get back some chips she lost to make sure she has an edge out from Rory. The question is, will we find out if he has the same confidence to let the river flow all the way through?

"Fold," Rory mumbles. Marissa takes the few chips on the table and slides them over to her.

"Coward," I say to the screen.

"Yeah!" Desmond chimes in. "You're too scared to lose all your chips because you know Janessa will kick your ass."

"Alright bud," I give him a pat on his back. "Let's not get too carried away now. At least they're both still in the game." I just don't want Rory to be the one who comes up on top. He's extremely cocky and even though he might be trying to sweet talk to Marissa and flirt her up after the game when he comes out victorious, it won't matter so long that he's making her feel like she's making a big mistake right now.

The end of the game comes close and the only two remaining players now are Rory and Marissa. Marissa has less chips, but if she goes all-in and wins, that will give her enough chips for Rory to barely skirt by with how high the ante is right now.

Neither of them risk anything right now. They've kept checking one another, which means Rory is starting to falter. He's had so much confidence going in, but he might feel now that Marissa has an upper hand on him so he's not bluffing as much. I get a closer look at Marissa, still with the Janessa wig on, but she's decided to take off the sunglasses. My heart almost skips a beat. In full Janessa beat, she has on thick false eyelashes and a face full of makeup, so it really doesn't look like Marissa, who wears maybe tinted moisturizer and lip gloss at the most. Janessa looks like she's ready for a red carpet. She still looks beautiful, even if her full face is caked on with layers of makeup. And I also know deep under she's beautiful too, because I want nothing more right now than the game to be over and for Marissa, not Janessa, to leap into my arms, a winner or not.

"I'll raise," Marissa says.

Rory returns with his usual smirk. "I'll go all in."

"He won't be able to afford the ante if he does that," Desmond says. Someone will be a winner now if Marissa calls.

All she does in response is nods and pushes her chips to the center of the table.

"Oh my god." My jaw feels like it's going to fall to the floor and my heart feels like it's going to fall out of my chest.

"Come on, baby," I whisper quietly to myself so Desmond doesn't interject in my anxious bubble right now. "You can do this."

The last card is shown and it's a six of spades. I watch Marissa go stoic. I can tell that she's shocked, but I can't tell if it's in a good or bad way.

"What does the bitch have?" Desmond seethes. I'm assuming he's talking about Rory, or else I think I'd have to throw punches to at least two people tonight.

"Straight," Rory says. I can see Marissa's face grow with worry. I bet she has a straight too. But, she can't see what his high card is, and she needs to have a higher card to win it all.

The dealer motions to Marissa to show her hand.

"Straight," she also tells the dealer. I lean in closer to see what her cards are and I gasp when I see the cards laid out on the table.

"Ms. Frost has a high 9 while Mr. Vinland has a high 7. Game goes to Ms. Frost."

I pump my fist in the air and everyone claps in unison when the game is called. Rory and Marissa shake hands and he doesn't say much, other than good job and she nods a thanks back to him. Rory goes to shake the hand of the dealer and Marissa then follows him.

That's when I see her being pulled hard toward the direction of the dealer and jump when I see her head slam down on the table.

"Don't move!" The dealer shouts, pressing his weight onto her head. "I want to see everyone crouched under the table." He takes a gun that he's taped under the table. "If you escape, you can kiss your reigning poker champion goodbye." He presses the gun to Marissa's temple and she whimpers in fear. No. This is my worst nightmare. That a Fortune Hunter has been working in my hotel and I didn't even know.

"Marissa!" I yell.

"Wait." Desmond sharply turns his head to me. "Who's Marissa?"

Oh no. "Did I say Marissa? I goofed. I don't know what prompted me to say that. That's not Marissa, obviously, it's Janessa." I try to brush it off by laughing, but my laugh comes out as more of an evil cackle and Desmond steps back with a fearful look on his face.

"Kellen," Desmond looks at me straight in the eyes. "Who has their head in a headlock right now and is holding on for dear life while one of our poker table dealers has a gun to her head?"

"Janessa Frost," I answer honestly. "...who is actually Marissa Waters' poker superstar persona."

"Kellen." He rapidly blinks. "You're telling me that Marissa Waters, someone who works at this hotel, is being held hostage while she is disguised as a professional poker player."

I nod slowly. "Now can we stop talking and go help them? Alert security to rush to the poker room, now!" I bolt out from the camera room and book it down to the poker room to hopefully save Marissa, because I promised myself I'd do anything to protect her.

Chapter Twenty-Two

Marissa

I can't believe this. Again, I'm stuck in a position where I feel helpless and all because I trusted my own judgment, but it's only backfired on me. I look up at the man pointing a gun to my cheek. Wing, the poker dealer that I was so happy to have at my table for my final round, is of course, working for the Fortune Hunters. And he's got me pressed against the table while everyone in the room has either fled or forced to crouch and hide. They have the entire poker room on lockdown, and their own guards barricading the doors.

"What do you want from me?" I cry out, trying to still play the narrative that I'm Janessa. "I did nothing wrong!"

"You're very smart, Janessa," he whispers into my ear. "Or should I say Marissa? There's no such thing as Janessa Frost. You can't fool me."

I try and swallow the lump stuck in my throat. "How do you know?" I ask.

"Your style is very distinct. I noticed it when you played as Marissa. You do this thing with your fingers when you're confident with your hand. This rubbing fingers gesture. I have never seen anyone else do it before, but I saw it every time you played a good hand. And just my luck you did it again. That's how I knew I got you right where I wanted you."

I can't believe it. My lucky finger gesture is the thing that got me in trouble. I knew if I was going to put myself in danger like this, I needed to hide my little "isms" so no one would notice. But, I didn't think I needed it, because I had only played poker in this room once before, but I guess people really pick on when someone is that good. And I got everyone in trouble because of it.

I can't reach into my phone and tell Kellen about this. I can only hope that he saw everything unfurl from the cameras to come rushing down and rescue me.

"What are you going to do with me?" I cry. I feel so helpless with my hands tied behind my back and if anyone tries to make a move, their lives are at risk.

"What we should have done a long time ago. You're not good for our mission to take down Kellen Zhang. You're too strong, and you're extremely smart. I mean, look at how you won this poker tournament. Reviving your professional poker persona to try and trick us? How foolish of you. And now every poker player in this tournament will know how much of a fraud you are, and soon, the entire world."

"Please..." I cry out. "I can't have this get out. I will never play poker again. Please."

"Stop begging!" He yells. "You fucked up, Marissa. And now your knight in shining armor boyfriend is nowhere to be found."

He will be, I think to myself. He has to be. He promised that he'd keep a close eye on me, and now I'm just waiting for him to come and help. Or maybe he's not here because he knows that they're going to hurt him if he does. I groan. I hate all this uncertainty and how I can't even know what's going on in Kellen's mind right now.

"You just want him here so you can torture him for yourself."

"Maybe," he says, laughing. "But we'll do that later. We need to keep him as fresh bait anyway to take him to the boss. He wants him alive. His accomplices though, we can dispose of them like flies. Especially the one he's in love with."

My heart races faster and my tears pool onto the table. Yep. This is it. The last hurrah. I finally felt like I've accomplished so much in my life, and now it's going to be all for nothing, because I'm going to die in the one place I thought I could stay away from. But of course, temptation got the best of me, and this is what I deserve.

I brace myself and I hear the loud sound of stomping into the poker room.

"Freeze!" Someone in a deep voice yells.

Wing gets caught off guard, and drops the gun. Once he does, I try and sit myself up, fast enough so that I head butt him while I make my way up, and he stumbles back a little.

"Ow, fuck!" he yells. He grabs onto his head for a moment, and I try and motion to everyone to get out of that room as quickly as they can. Everyone gets up, screaming in terror as they make their way out of the poker room, and I try and keep his eyes on Wing to see what he's going to do. In the midst of the chaos, security and law enforcement do double duty and file everyone out of the room, while still making sure Wing doesn't move. Once I see everyone's out and safe, I lock eyes with Kellen, who's outside of the room filing people to evacuate the hotel. He's about to run in and grab onto me, but I hear the sound of a gunshot and feel my arm crush like it was hit by a sledgehammer as it enters into it. The last thing I remember is Kellen's face turning to fear as he's screaming for me before I look below and see the blood spewing out from my arm.

Kellen

Hospitals are my least favorite place in the world. The sight of blood and needles scare me, and the ominous vibe hospitals emanate repel me from ever wanting to step into one. But this time, it's the only place I want to be.

I still replay the scene from just moments ago in my head. Marissa reaching out for me to help her, her hand stuck out even though a glass window separates us, but she couldn't have been more happy to see me. And I was immediately ready to be at her rescue, after the pain of watching her be held against her will came up on the screen in front of me.

But I was too late.

She tried to be nice and help everyone else who was held hostage after the poker tournament file out of the room safely, and right before she tried to get out herself, someone working for the Fortune Hunters and the hotel came and pulled the trigger on her. I screamed as she gripped her arm and blood dripped down. The police surged to get a hold of him and I rushed in behind, clutching onto Marissa's limp body as it fell to the floor.

"I'm so sorry," I screamed in between my sobbing as I pulled her limp body close to me. I ripped my shirt off to see if it could act as a stopper for the gunshot wound. "Please hang on."

I pressed her body to my ear. She still had a heartbeat, but it was weak. She had lost too much blood to have any strength in her body to move. Her eyes shut and her face was drained of most of its color.

"Stay with me, please." I whispered, kissing her forehead over and over. "I'm so sorry."

I couldn't stop saying that phrase. I wanted to keep her safe, and I couldn't. By being associated with me, I was giving her nothing but trouble. And now, I'm sitting in a hospital chair while they perform surgery on her in hopes that she'll pull through. And even if she does, I don't even want her to be stepping out of the hotel or leaving my sight.

The police had arrested Wing, the man that shot Marissa, and I hope he rots in a prison cell forever. I wanted to kill him myself after I saw the bullet lodged in her arm. I don't know what I would do if it landed anywhere else and she might not have made it. If she took her last breath in my arms.

The hotel is on lockdown while an investigation happens. I was recommended to stay at the hotel and talk to them, but I adamantly stood my ground. I couldn't leave Marissa, especially since her parents aren't here yet to keep an eye on her recovery. I had to be the person to call them and let them know she had been shot, and they told me very calmly that they were going to be taking the next flight here out of San Francisco to take care of her.

Even my parents told me that they planned to board the jet to come here and assess a game plan moving forward. I wish I was seeing my parents in better circumstances, but them being here will be good for me. Because I have never felt more alone.

"Mr. Zhang?" The doctor comes out and greets me while I sit in the waiting area of the ICU.

"Yes?"

"I just wanted to let you know that Miss Waters' surgery went well and we were able to get the bullet out of her arm and keep it intact. She's recovering in her room right now."

"Can I see her?" I ask eagerly.

"Soon," he reassures me. "We can only let her parents see her at the moment. Do you know when they're due to arrive?"

"Okay," I sulk. "They said their flight out of San Francisco left an hour ago. I expect them to be here fairly soon."

"Great," he nods. "Once they give us the okay, we'll allow you to see her."

"Thank you. Can I ask how she's doing?"

"Good," he smiles. "Very good. She took the blood transfusion very well and we just have her sedated until she can breathe on her own, which we expect to happen rather quickly. She's a tough one."

"Yeah. She is." The toughest person I know.

"Feel free to let us know if you have any questions, but we'll keep you posted." He returns back into the ICU and I lean back in my chair, watching the clock on the wall tick second by second. Time feels like it's moving so slow with all the waiting I have to do. I should have just sent a jet to Marissa's parents so they could get here as soon as they heard the news. But, they insisted on flying commercial. I think it's for my own selfish reasons that I wanted them here faster, so I can get the okay from them to see her.

My phone vibrates in the seat next to me and I pick it up to see who's calling.

"Hey Taylor," I answer.

"Hey, man. How's everything?"

"Not great," I sigh. "I'm at the hospital right now, waiting for Marissa's parents to get here."

"Yeah, shit man. I'm sorry to hear about Marissa. Is she doing okay?"

"Yeah. They just told me they finished surgery not too long ago. Everything went well, apparently. She lost a lot of blood, but they were able to do a transfusion and she took the blood well, apparently. I'm just all sorts of messed up right now, man. The trauma of holding her body as she was losing oxygen. It's the scariest feeling. I tried to use my shirt as a bandage to stop the bleeding."

"Well that sounds like you probably helped save her life."

I don't even want to think what would happen if the blood all fell out in a pool from under her. My shirt wasn't even enough; she still lost a considerable amount. She will likely need a lot of physical therapy in order to get her arm to regain the movement she was once able to do.

"I don't know what I'd do if she died in my arms." Nothing would even feel like it'd be worth fighting for.

"Did you know? About the whole Janessa thing?"

"Yeah. She told me the night before the tournament." While the news of the shooting was all over the news and social media, the news of Marissa's, or Janessa's, true identity blew up around the world. I really did not see this coming. Of course I knew Janessa Frost was a huge name in the poker world, but it was a worldwide name. International poker players knew of her and her skill. And when Wing proclaimed to the rest of the room that he knew exactly who Janessa Frost was, and that she was a fake persona played by a nobody from Las Vegas, someone had their camera ready to record the video of the confession.

I felt for Marissa, who originally had created the persona of Janessa Frost: a confident, well-skilled poker player who flirted with fate and others to become some woman who everyone wanted to be with, but didn't want to be with anyone. Now, she was one and the same, and whether or not she wanted to be a professional poker player anymore, didn't matter because she was exposed by someone who she trusted. Someone that apparently knew her and commended her playing style. Now everyone is commenting on "Who is Marissa Waters?" and if she'd ever make her way back into the poker industry.

"I thought we would use it as a way to get intel on who would be working on the inside and that someone would be naive enough to not know who she was. Turns out she had played with this dealer before and he had remembered who she was when she decided to play a casual game as Marissa. She does some gesture with her hands when she gets a good card, and it was like nothing he had ever seen before." I slump back into the chair and wipe my bloodshot and puffy eyes. "I didn't even think something like this would happen. Just my luck I guess."

"Damn, that's just shit luck," Taylor says. "So, now what? The police arrested him and he's hopefully rotting in jail for...the rest of his life? Have the Fortune Hunters been taken down?"

"I don't know for sure," I tell him. My answer is I can only hope. "The police are supposed to call me once they take him in for questioning and hopefully that will help me get more details about him and Fortune Hunters. But, he talked to Marissa before she was shot, and I can't ask her what happened until she's awake and recovered."

"I have a feeling that he's just another minion. As much as I hate saying that. But whoever is the leader of this whole thing won't just sacrifice himself so easily. I mean, holding a bunch of people hostage in a hotel where there are thousands of people just lurking around every corner? It seems like an amateur move."

"I agree," I sigh. "So, that means that someone else is out there. And they just tried to get rid of Marissa because they knew she was in on the mission. They weren't successful in completely getting rid of her, but she can't be my bodyguard anymore. Not that I don't think she'll do a good job, it's that I will never let her on a mission like this again. It's too much of a risk."

Just as I look back up to the quiet hallway that spans from the elevator to the ICU, I see two adults walking down the hall, hand in hand. One is a tall, lanky white man with parted dark blonde hair and the woman next to him was a short, Chinese woman, whose straight hair is mostly gray now.

"Hey, Tay, I gotta go. I think Marissa's parents just got here."

"Alright man, let me know how the rest of the investigation goes and if there's anything I can do to help."

"Yeah, will do, man. Thanks."

"No prob, man. Hope Marissa has a speedy recovery."

"Thanks. Talk to you later."

I stand up and make eyes with the couple walking closer to me. I get a better look at their faces and see they're both scared and unsure in their lack of facial expression. I also can tell how much of a mixture Marissa is to her parents. She has the same almond-shaped eyes like her mom and full face similar to her dad.

"Hi," I wave. "Mr. and Mrs. Waters?"

"Yes?" Marissa's dad responds.

"I'm Kellen Zhang." I extend my hand out. "I...work closely with your daughter."

"Oh yes, Kellen. You're the one that called us, after Marissa was shot."

I nod. "Yup. That's me."

"Thank you," Marissa's mom whimpers a little, before tears start flowing down her cheek. "Is she okay?"

"Yeah," I reassure her. "She got out of surgery not too long ago. They haven't told me much after that. I think they were waiting until you had gotten here. They've told me only her parents have authority to see her right now."

"Well, we appreciate that."

"Did you know..." I begin. "That she played professional poker?"

"No," Marissa's dad shakes his head. "We never knew that Marissa played poker. She doesn't really talk too much about her hobbies when she comes home. I mean, we know she likes to read books and try new places to eat. But, gambling wasn't anything we were aware of. We're not big on gambling ourselves. Marissa's grandparents gamble, but they kind of just play slots. She never told us about this part of her."

"I see. I had figured as much, but I thought I would ask."

"Is that why?" Marissa's mom pleads. "Why she got shot? Because she's a famous poker player? Was someone out to get her for her wealth?"

"No," I shake my head. "Well, I don't think so. So...this be hard to explain, but I'm gonna try. I am the Director of Operations for the hotel, and my father owns the hotel and runs the management group for it. I found out that there is a group of people that call themselves the 'Fortune Hunters' that have been around for a few years and want to take down my dad, or his company. Why? I have no idea. Maybe because he's a rich and powerful Chinese man and they want to strip him of all the wealth he has. But, Marissa saved me from an attack by a group of these men a few months ago. Like we're talking about some mortal combat self defense and she was able to get me to safety before they kidnapped me. Then I decided that I would enlist her as my right hand person to try and figure out who these people were and take them down before something bad happened to me or the hotel. We thought we had hit the jackpot once Marissa had confessed to me that she was Janessa, that we could use her as bait to draw in a Fortune Hunter who was going to raid the tournament after it was done, since a lot of money was at stake. Turns out, the person we were looking for was someone who worked for my hotel and he picked up on some hand gestures that Marissa does when she plays poker and put two and two together. I had no idea that she had done those things and let's just say, it went a lot worse than I ever could have imagined."

I take a breath before I pass out myself from trying to explain this convoluted situation. "I can't tell you how sorry I am for this happening to your daughter. She means...a lot to me, and I am just feeling so guilty that I had put her in a position that almost killed her."

Marissa's mom rubs her hand along my arm. "Thank you, Kellen. For explaining all this to us. It's scary, yes, but it sounds like you really care about Marissa."

"Yeah," Marissa's dad side eyes me. "Are you two dating?"

"No!" I immediately answer. "Well, not technically. We...oh my gosh, this is so awkward to be talking about with her own parents. We didn't want to date because of work and everything. But, I...really like her. Without being all TMI about it, we've hooked up. If work wasn't an issue, then I would've asked her out a long time ago." I purposefully leave out the word love because I didn't want them to think I was lovesick with someone I couldn't even label as my girlfriend.

"Yeah, I can tell." Her dad laughs and I'm uncertain whether I should feel scared or relieved. This wasn't the ideal way that I wanted to meet her parents for the first time, that so much is certain.

"We like you Kellen, and even though we don't really know you, you seem like a good guy, and someone who is really protective of Marissa. So, you get our stamp of approval, whenever you two do decide to start dating."

"Thanks," I nod. "I don't know how we're going to move on from this though. I feel like I care too much about her for her to be with me. I mean, I don't want her to be with me and have our lives be put on the line again. She almost...she got hurt. And I can't help but think it's my fault."

"Well, you two are smart adults." Her dad pats me on the shoulder. "You'll figure it out. We're going to go and see if we can talk to the doctors about seeing her now, though."

"Oh yes." I motion to the ICU floor. "Please do. And when you're able to, can you let me know when I can see her?"

Her parents nod and make her way toward the hospital rooms. I wipe my eyes and head back down to the seat I've probably made an indent in from sitting for so long. It felt like we had a long road ahead, but I felt better that her parents had seen that I had cared so much about their daughter. Maybe there was something I needed to change about our status after all.

Chapter Twenty-Three
Marissa

I groggily wake up to my eyes being crusted around the edges and dry as a desert.

How long was I out for?

I peer over to my hands. One has an IV poked through it and the other is completely bandaged up from the gunshot wound through my arm.

"Hi sweetcakes," I hear a familiar voice call to me. I turn and look over and see my dad sitting on a chair next to my hospital bed.

"Dad?" I croak out. My throat feels as dry as my eyes do.

"Yes," he nods, rubbing the top of my hand. "We just got into Vegas not too long ago. How are you feeling?"

"Fine," I say, truthfully. I can barely feel any pain. I'm led to believe it's because I'm so drugged up on whatever they gave me after my surgery, that the pain feels practically non-existent. I know that's not going to be the case forever.

"Really?" My mom comes to join me at my other side. "These must be some magical drugs," she laughs.

"How long have I been out for?" I ask. "You two got here so quick."

"Well, luckily for us, there are plenty of flights that come from San Francisco to Vegas. We got here as soon as Kellen called us."

Kellen. The last thing I remember was Kellen holding me, sobbing uncontrollably as blood spewed out of my arms, kissing my forehead as he apologized for all that unfurled. He's not the one at fault, I wanted to reassure him, but as the blood quickly kept gushing out of my arm, I soon lost focus of anything that was happening to me and soon enough, I was too weak to even open up my eyes.

"Where is he?" I ask. Probably back at the hotel, trying to clean up any of the chaos that remained after the shooting. I don't even know how messy the once well-kept poker room was. All the chips that were once stacked on the table, signaling all my winnings are probably strewn all over the floor. Sad to think my winnings will probably all go toward my hospital bills and recovery now.

"He's just outside," my mom says. "Do you want me to go get him?"

Without any hesitation, I nod, being careful of my sore body and aching bones.

"Okay, let me go tell him you're awake."

I turn back over to my dad, who is trying to grin and bear it even though he was obviously pained. Who likes seeing their kid in a hospital bed with needles sticking out of their hands?

"You okay dad?"

"I'll be okay, sweetcakes," he says, using my nickname again. "As long as you're feeling okay."

"I imagine the journey to recovery is going to be a long one, but I think I'm going to be okay. I always tell myself it could be a lot worse."

"Yeah," my dad nods. "A lot worse." The worst case scenario could have been that I could've died, which if the bullet had struck me on my back, or my head, would have happened a lot more easily. I got lucky, even though I still got shot.

My dad looks up near the door and I turn my head. He smiles as he makes eyes with who's standing at the door.

"Hi," Kellen waves as he approaches the other side of my bed.

"Hey," I smile. He looks like he's pulled an all-nighter in the span of a few hours, with his eyes having dark bags under them and drooping down. He's barely cracked a smile when he sees me, but he manages to flash one when he sees me. "How's it going?"

"Better now that you're awake." A tear trickles down his cheek and he quickly wipes it away before anyone notices.

"Crybaby," I say, in a mocking voice. I don't really say it to make fun of him. I know he's probably cried more today than he has in his entire life.

"So?" He laughs. "You make me feel things." Good, I would be kind of sad if his heart was just a big block of stone and that he didn't show any emotion at seeing me awake for the first time post-surgery.

"Speaking of," he begins. "How are you feeling?"

"Fine," I shrug a little. "My arm is pretty numb. But whatever anesthetic or drugs they got me on is making the pain feel almost like it's not there."

"It's the recovery that you'll start to feel more of the pain," my mom chimes in. "We have to make sure your wound heals completely and doesn't get infected."

"How long is that supposed to take?" The worst part about this whole me getting shot thing is that I can't do anything. No work and lots of rest. I can't even cook anything because it'll put too much strain on my arm. But I can't stand doing nothing. Sure, I like watching tv in bed like the next person, but this is such a busy time at work, that whatever time I'm away from it will put me back so far.

"Well, you'll need to do physical therapy on your arm to get it moving back to normal. And your stitches will need to heal from the gunshot wound. The doctor was telling us it can range from two weeks to a month."

"That long?" I whine. "But, there's so much happening at work! The world's biggest Asian pop star since BTS is coming to stay at our hotel in a month!"

"Honey," my dad grips onto my good arm. "You got shot. Don't you think it's good to take it slow for a little bit?"

"There's barely any time to take it slow, Dad! You know how much I can't stand to relax. I don't default to it. Not when I can be spending my time doing something else, like being productive."

"Your dad is right, babe," Kellen says, rubbing my arm. Did he just call me babe? I didn't hate it, I just was kind of shocked by it. In front of my parents too. I wondered what they thought when they met him for the first time. Oh, Mom and Dad, this is my coworker/not work superior but he does have a higher position in the hotel than me that I've fucked multiple times. Oh did I mention that I saved him from a kidnapping from a Chinese mafia group that was founded because they absolutely hate his father and that's kind of the reason why I'm here in this hospital bed right now? Oh, and I'm a secret professional poker player that somehow was ousted by someone I thought wouldn't pick up on my weird hand gestures when I play? This is going to be one interesting visit while I basically regurgitate a memoir to my parents of all the things that have happened to me since I became a poker pro.

"You really need to rest up," he continues. "Don't worry, there are plenty of people that can help with the Andrew Tseng Group while you're out. Everyone understands you need to take this time to recover."

"Okay," I sigh. "So I'm just going to be at home doing nothing while I recover? I guess I can start adding things to my watch list on Netflix."

"Well, we're probably going to be staying here for at least a week to help," my mom chimes in.

"Where are you guys staying?" I would be nice and offer up my apartment, but it is very small and only one bedroom. I don't think my parents would be as happy with sleeping on my couch or an air mattress. Especially if they're planning on staying for a week.

"Well...we haven't thought about that yet," she admits. "But you live in Vegas! There are plenty of places we can stay..."

"At the Blossom!" Kellen interrupts. "You're more than welcome to stay at the Blossom for as long as you need. It's not an issue at all."

My eyes widened at Kellen. Sure, it was possible. We're not at full occupancy, and I think I could extend the friends and family rate to my parents if they wanted to save some extra money on a room. We're not the most expensive hotel on the Strip, but I think our average rate right now is going for at least $200 per night.

"Oh, thank you, Kellen," my mom was beaming at his offer. "Please let us know how much it'll cost and we'll make sure to take care of it with the front desk."

"Oh," he looks at them with a kind of dumbfounded facial expression. "No, you don't have to pay anything. I can talk to my dad, it should be fine. I mean, it's the least I can do on behalf of the hotel, because you're here to help with Marissa's recovery."

"Are you sure?" My dad asks. "We know the hotel needs to make money too. We'd be happy to help pay anything to stay and help Marissa."

"Of course, but really, it's the least I can do. You can stay as long as you need just as long as Marissa's well taken care of. I mean," he turns his head and looks at me. "She can even stay in my spare bedroom. That way your parents don't need to drive back and forth from your parent's."

"Oh," I utter. That would be really nice. I mean, the beds they have at the Blossom are way more comfortable than the bed I have at home. And if I'm staying at Kellen's villa, then he can just ask the restaurant to bring any sort of food I want. It's a lot better than the food I'd try to cook.

"Thank you," I smile at him. I know Kellen would also just drop anything to make sure I'm taken care of. Something as small as my pillows are fluffed.

He nods and continues to rub my arm.

"That's very kind of you, Kellen. We really like this one. You two should really think about dating."

I groan. "I don't know if that's a good idea mom, Mom…"

"Thank you," he butts in. "Sorry, what Marissa meant was, because we're coworkers, we can't be really labeling ourselves as a couple."

"Also because we haven't talked about a relationship at all…"

"Shh." He shoots me an evil glare and I shoot one right back in his direction.

"Ah, that makes sense," she nods. "Well, whatever you two kids have planned, we like him. Anyway..." she motions for my dad to stand up and head towards the door with her. "We're going to go to the cafeteria and get some coffee. That flight really took us out. We'll only be a minute!"

They awkwardly step out of the room and leave me and Kellen in the hospital room while the only thing that can be heard is the steady beeps of my heart rate.

"What the hell?" he says to me. "Can you just go along with what I had planned?"

"Why are you upset with me?" I yell. "I was being honest. To my parents, who are the two people I would want to be honest to the most. We're not a couple yet. And I know we were being exclusive but I don't know, maybe I am starting to think that being in a relationship is a bad idea!"

"But it isn't! I don't think it is. Don't you see, Marissa? You almost died, and forget what anyone tells us. I want to be with you. I'm in love with you!"

My heart skips a beat. That's the first time that Kellen has ever told me that he was in love with me. But the problem now was I didn't know if he meant it, or that he was just saying that because he's in a vulnerable state right now. I'm laying in a hospital bed, with a gunshot wound to my arm bandaged up. And he watched me get shot. Obviously he was going through a lot of trauma right now to be saying anything that made sense.

"But that's the thing!" I started to cry. "Are you really in love with me, or are you just saying that because I'm in a hospital bed right now? I know you're feeling a lot right now Kellen, I fully recognize that. But obviously as you can tell, my life is kind of a shit show right now! I was ousted at a tournament because someone caught onto my weird hand gestures I do when I play poker. And I paid for the consequences. I'm a walking target, Kellen, and there's nothing I love about myself right now."

"Maybe it's the drugs right now," he grits out. "I'm going to give you the benefit of the doubt and say it's the drugs, but you are really saying a lot of stupid shit right now. I should get back to the hotel and make sure everything's...okay." He quickly stands up and begins walking to the door. He turns around and gives me another angry glare, before shaking his head and walking away.

When he disappears out the door, a part of me wants to reach out to him and tell him that I love him back, but my numb arm is preventing me from even making such a move and my coward mind is preventing me from even uttering such things.

Chapter Twenty-Four

Kellen

I promptly storm into my office once security drops me off at the lobby. Everyone had looked up and stared at me walking with such an angry stride that I could see them cowering back to the wall instead of the usual smiles and waves.

I hated how upset Marissa was making me feel right now. She would have to do a lot for me to reach a point where I could genuinely say I hated her, and she's not quite at that point yet, but I am definitely frustrated with her.

It's complicated. Our relationship, the stress of everything going on, and now Marissa's recovery has weighed a lot on our mental well being. I could put a smile on my face and say we're getting through this for the sake of making everyone happy, but all I'm feeling right now is scared for what the future is going to bring.

Maybe Marissa was right in some ways. I am feeling a lot of emotions right now, and my confession came out of left field. But, it was true, whether she wanted to accept it or not. Even though we were never officially a couple and promised ourselves that we wouldn't take it to that point unless we really felt ready for it, I developed strong feelings for Marissa the moment I met her. Her perseverance, the way she makes me laugh, the stubbornness she's feeling because she's stuck in a hospital bed and can't work for at least a month while her arm is recovering... the list feels like it's infinite. But, I rushed to be the person that tried to help as much as I could, and in my feelings, in that hospital room, I was afraid of what the end was going to look like that I rushed to tell her all the feelings that I had stored in my mind without stopping to give it much thought. If I had it all planned out, I would want to tell Marissa that I loved her, that I wanted to pursue a relationship with her somewhere romantic. An intimate dinner, a stroll down the Strip, a moment where we kiss while the booms of the Bellagio fountains sound out behind us. Saying it while she has needles sticking out of her hands is less than ideal for someone who weirdly feels like doing romantic things for the woman who's changed his life for the better.

I don't even get to my office when I hit my back along one of the walls of the back office and I slide down until I'm sitting on the floor. I don't think there are any tears left for me to cry, but I let out a loud sigh at how everything just went south in my life so fast. I don't know why Marissa defaults to feeling incapacitated because of this, I'm ready to ignore all my responsibilities for the foreseeable future and just let fate run its course. Sorry in advance to everyone I've let down because I don't have any motivation to work or fix all what's going on at the Blossom at the moment.

I hear footsteps approach me as my head's between my legs and my arms are wrapped around them. I see a pair of pink and blue Hoka shoes on the floor and peer up to see who's the person behind the feet. When I look up, my eyes are shocked at who's standing next to me.

"Kiera?"

"Yeah, yeah, surprise! Bet you're not that jazzed to see me right now though."

"No," I quickly stand up and rush to give her a tight hug. My sister and I were never much to show affection to one another, I feel like that's because we're so different, both in personality and stages of our life, that we only show affection if we're forced to. But right now, I am genuinely happy that I get to have her in close proximity to me versus if I had to call her on the phone.

"You don't know how happy I am to see you," I murmur into her shoulder. "I've had the worst day of my life today."

"I know," she reaches up and rubs my back while I still keep my arms around her. "I'm so sorry Dai Dai. How's Marissa?"

"Fine. Or probably not right at this moment. We kind of ended things between us. It's probably my fault, if you really think about how it all went down. I told her I loved her and she didn't believe me. She thought I was only saying it because of the circumstances."

"And? Was that the case?"

"No!" I quickly respond. "Maybe. I do care about her. But, love is a strong word, and I haven't said that I'm in love to someone in a long time. I mean, the facts are there: we're not a couple, we've never been a couple, and for the duration that we were hooking up with one another, we needed to keep it a secret, because of my job and hers."

"Well, you don't need to be in a relationship with someone to love them. Making it official kind of ends up being the next step."

I nod. It takes me back to how much everything has evolved between us. That night when we met, I didn't really know who she was or if I'd ever see her again, but she made some kind of imprint on my life just from the first time that we made eye contact with one another.

"You're right. I also don't think I'm very well versed with how to be a good boyfriend anyway. I'd want to do all these things to show her that I really care about her, but she's feeling her own emotions right now that I don't know how to properly tell her that I'm in love with her."

"That too," Kiera nods. "You know, they say that you can't love someone unless you're able to love yourself, and by what you're telling me, it sounds like she's having a hard time doing that right now."

"Yeah." If there was ever a time that Marissa could not hate herself more, it would probably be right now. She's not able to work and utilize the skills that make her good at her job, she was ousted by someone she trusted in her own happy place, and she's being showered with all this affection when she'd rather be alone. Maybe I was the bad guy because I was doing too much for her right now.

"And I think I'm making things worse because I'm trying too hard to make things better, and she just needs to think about her game plan alone."

"Ding ding ding." She taps my forehead to signal some "brain activating" motion. "I think you've figured it out."

"So, what should I do? It's not like I'm enjoying not being the supportive friend that I think she needs right now."

"Just be patient. You can't rush your way into her heart, especially now that she's carrying more trauma and emotions than other women her age. You two will be okay," she reassured me. "Couples fight. Friends fight. Your love for each other, whether she's ready to admit it or not, will get you through this tough spot in your life."

"Thanks," I mutter. "I guess you're not the devil I used to call you when we were teens."

"And I guess you're not the hit and quit guy you used to be in your younger years. Vegas did change you for the better. Landon misses you though."

"I miss him." When he doesn't have snot dripping from his nose and throws garbage trucks my direction. "You didn't want to bring him on your first time to Vegas?"

"It's not my first," she scoff. "I've been here pre-Mom days on countless bachelorette parties. I suppose you could say it is my first work trip though. And he's too young. I don't want to go out to a bar when I have him attached at my hip crying for milk. Mom decided she'll take care of him so I can have some fun when I'm not working my ass off to fix you."

Ah, the puzzle pieces all start clicking in my head. I knew that there was a reason that it was going to be Kiera here instead of my mom. She's the VP of Marketing for Fortune, whose essential duties include cleaning up any possible PR scandal the hotel might be facing, whether fault of its employees or not. Who would have thought she had to work to clean up her own brother's messes?

"I always knew there was a catch anytime I see you now. Alright lay it on me, tell me how much trouble I'm in now that our sibling sappy moment is over."

She sighs and pinches the temple of her nose. "Kellen, don't take this as a way of saying I hate you, but you have made my job ten times more difficult with what's happened. Fortune has never had to deal with something this big since the robbery with Mom at the Grand."

"Wait, you know about that?"

"Ba told me. Probably the same day he told you. He needed to fill me in on what all was going on here, in the case that something bad were to happen. And lo and behold, can't say he didn't warn me."

"It's scary, Kiera. First when you almost get kidnapped somewhere that's supposed to be your home, and then get robbed when you think you're safe enough to explore the Strip, and then your girlfriend, friend with benefits, whatever, tells you she's a world famous poker player and is ousted and shot by an employee of your own hotel. Can't say this is what I signed up for."

"I know," she says, wrapping her arm around my shoulder. We're still sitting on the ground in the hallway of the operations office, and I kind of like it. I don't want to go back to my desk right now for fear that I'm going to have to deal with this PR nightmare Kiera has been hinting at. "But, if it wasn't for all of it, then you wouldn't have gotten to know Marissa as much as you did."

"Touche. So, lay it on me, what's our recovery plan?"

Kiera sighs and pushes herself up from the floor. She extends her hand and I grab onto it to stand up myself. "This is more than just a you and me conversation," she says. "Come on."

To my dismay, we head into my office where a familiar face is sitting cross-armed behind my desk.

"Hello son."

"Hi Ba." My father is wearing a full three-piece gray suit with a maroon tie. Even after he's been on a plane for five hours, he never willingly wears casual clothes when he's on hotel property. Even if he was relaxing behind a slot machine, he would only opt to wear a polo and some khakis, never sweatpants or jeans.

"How are you?"

"Fine." I really need to stop saying I'm fine when I'm not, but it's so easy to default to being fine.

"I don't think you're fine," my father retorts. For a man who's focused on the bad qualities I had to offer during my time on Earth, he was extremely astute.

"Ugh," I huff. "I'm terrible. Thanks for asking."

"Of course. You know better than to lie to me and you know it's okay to not be okay, Kellen."

"I'm just trying to put on a good face for everyone. I know it's a stressful time right now."

My father laughs. "Yep, you are definitely my son. How's Marissa?"

"She's okay," I shrug. I wonder if my dad and I were at a good enough spot for me to disclose my love life further with him. He does know of Marissa, just not the attempted "love" slip or how I want to crawl into bed right here right now and spoon her until all our problems went away.

"They had a fight," Kiera chimes in.

I scowl at her. There's that conniving sister I've grown to love and hate.

"Thanks, Kiera." I murmur.

"Everything okay?" my dad asks. My eyebrows shoot up. I guess he cares more than I give him credit for. We should have more heart to heart conversations more often.

"Not really," I sigh. "I told her I loved her, but she thought I was just saying that because I was vulnerable seeing her in a hospital bed. And now I'm wondering if she was right."

"Well, wouldn't you be the best person to know your own feelings?"

"Yeah," I shrug. "But maybe what I'm feeling isn't always the right thing to feel."

"Kellen's just not used to falling in love," Kiera chimes in. "He never does."

"Not true!" I retort. "I just had other expectations when I moved here."

My dad folds his hands in front of him and looks at us standing across the desk from him. "Well, you'll get through it. Like I told you, falling in love comes with its challenges. It's overcoming them where you see where exactly you need to be."

"Thanks, Ba. Or should I say, Si Fu?"

"Stop," he chuckles. "But thank you. Okay, heart to heart moment over. This is a huge problem, Kellen. For the Blossom and for you. As an employee and as a Zhang."

My heart sinks. I was expecting to feel pain, but I thought I would brace myself enough for it. When my dad finally uttered the words "huge" and "problem" one after another, it still stung.

"I know," I nod.

"When did you find out Marissa's true secret?" he asks me.

"Not long ago. She only told me because she wanted to enter the tournament. She thought she'd be safe here, that I would have no idea who she is. But she had to tell me when I started telling her I was going to use Janessa as bait to lure in the mole from within the poker tournament. She was afraid that she was going to get hurt otherwise. I guess it was my fault that I made her panic when I said she'd get in trouble from who Janessa might attract, but how was I supposed to know she dressed up as the one of the best female poker players in the country in her spare time?"

"I know," my dad says. At least he feels sympathetic about the whole thing. "I shouldn't blame you for finding out who her secret identity was. The poker community is just breathing on our necks now about this. They want answers and in depth interviews from Marissa now on her secret identity. For someone who might not like the world paying attention to her, she kind of has no other choice now."

Yeah, that was what I was afraid of. If we could have masked Marissa's identity and caught the mole, then we would be able to continue our lives as we were. Maybe Marissa would finally retire Janessa, go out with one last bang, and not the literal one that happened.

"I know. If there's a way we can make a statement on her behalf, I think that might be the better option than to have her speak herself." I felt more confident putting together a BS statement than her being forced to talk to people that only want to bombard her with cameras and questions and make her feel more anxious than she already was.

"We don't know yet," Kiera pipes in. "I know that you want to help her wipe away all her problems, but then problem two comes up."

I turn to her. "Which is?"

"Your relationship with Marissa Waters-slash-Janessa Frost."

"What exactly about my relationship?"

"People have put two and two together that you two are romantically involved. Not by anything you did before the incident, but when someone catches you kissing a newly shot Marissa, they assume you're romantically linked rather than you being an overly affectionate guy."

Damn it. Of course I wasn't thinking at that point to hide my affections for her, because my flight or fight response had prompted me to hold her and kiss her frantically. But there were people that had just left that room that would blab about us to the press, especially because I was a prolific person, even if everyone was still coming to terms on who Marissa was.

"I should've known." I slump. "Even when you're trying to comfort someone you really care about while blood is spilling out from their body, people will still shift their focus on the fact that you kissed someone in public.

"Again, it's not something we're blaming you for," Kiera says. "We're just telling you what we're dealing with right now."

"You would be surprised at how many people are on social media right now that are crying over the fact that you are off the market. The Blossom's social media is flooded with comments saying how they're deeply saddened that Kellen Zhang is off the market."

"And how Marissa isn't pretty enough or good looking enough to be with someone like you," Kiera adds. "But we're choosing to ignore those comments."

Yeah, and now I wish I could ignore them too. Now I just wanted to destroy anyone and everyone who even tried to comment something as vain as Marissa's "ugly" appearance.

"Easier said than done," I murmur.

"You know those comments are irrelevant anyway," Kiera rolls her eyes. "You have people talking about you all the time, now it's time to not let these people talking about Marissa affect you."

Just another thing that I wanted to shield Marissa from. First it was anyone that was out for her blood, and now it was also strangers who didn't even know her but wanted to talk like they did.

"So, what kind of game plan have you thought of to help fix all this going on?"

Kiera sighs, and her and my dad made glances at each other before they settled back to looking at me.

"We're sorry Kellen," Kiera begins. "But Marissa can no longer be an employee here, effective immediately. It's the only thing that we can do to protect yourselves and the company."

My heart feels like it shattered into a million pieces.

Let.

Marissa.

Go.

She was terminated. Effective immediately. Which meant we weren't going to be allowed to see each other anymore. I start to panic that now that we're not working with each other, and how big the chasm feels between us, we'll never see each other again.

And here comes the downward spiral again.

Chapter Twenty-Five

Marissa

The time had finally come when I was discharged from the hospital and could do the rest of my recovery in some place more comfortable and less intimidating. It was nice that Kellen had extended an offer for my parents to stay at the hotel to be nearby for my recovery, but I still feared that we were at a bit of a crossroads with our relationship and he didn't even want me staying there with him.

I know that I overreacted when he told me that he was in love with me, and that I could have responded better. I know that a majority of people would be overjoyed when someone tells them they were in love with them; I apparently am not a part of the majority.

I reach over to grab my phone and see if Kellen had texted me any new information. I didn't tell him that I was being discharged today, so he probably won't even know that I'm arriving at the hotel right now. My parents helped me pack up a suitcase full of items from my apartment, and we made our way toward the Blossom's lobby.

When my dad pulled up the car to the valet entrance, I notice a horde of paparazzi standing in the lobby, mingling amongst each other.

Oh shit.

I'm really hoping that these people are here for a celebrity that just so happened to be staying at the hotel right now.

"Mar," my dad says with a worrying glance over to the group standing by the entrance. "How much of a famous poker player did you say you were?"

I don't know if this is the right time to be humble, rather than telling my parents that this might very well be for me whether I want it or not.

"I might be kind of famous." I bite my lip. "Like, on the top ten poker players list?"

"Oh god," he sighs. "Well, we have no other choice. We'll tell the valet who we are, and I'm going to try and shield you as best as I could until we can get into the lobby. Just don't break apart from me. Okay?"

"Okay." I nod.

The valet circles around the driver's side window and smiles as he's greeting us.

"Hello, welcome to the Blossom!"

Before he could say the rest of his spiel, my dad softly grasps onto his arm and pulls him closer to him.

"Hi. My name is Tim Waters and my daughter, Marissa, is in the back. We just got discharged from the hospital and I know you see those paparazzi hovering by the entrance. We need to have you take our bags and we need to blockade her from entering the hotel without them bombarding her with questions. Think you can help us?"

The valet person, while looking shocked after my dad quickly explained the situation to him, nods softly and whispers into our car.

"We'll grab your bags. Drive to the service entrance just around the corner to the lobby, we'll get you covered."

My dad nods and presses the button to pop the trunk open. Quickly, the valet gathers our suitcases and rolls them into the lobby. Once they close the trunk, my dad coasts off out of the lobby's entrance road and to a separate entry way that we'd often use to unload large boxes and deliveries. Huh, I'm surprised I had forgotten this was a thing. Maybe because it'll load us to a long corridor to a storage room whose insides look like a Costco, and it took us way off the beaten path where the lobby was.

My dad put the car's hazards on and steps out to shield me and my mom until someone came to greet us at the service entrance.

"Hi," the man greets us. "I'm Gerry, one of the bellmen. We're gonna escort you to the lobby."

My mom and I nod at him as he leads us back into the hotel. I feel like a celebrity, being escorted in a place that was so familiar to me. I didn't like using the word celebrity to describe myself much. Maybe it was because I thought celebrities were on a completely different level in terms of social status, following, and wealth. They were things that I thought I wasn't ever able to obtain.

We open the door back into the hotel and find out that we are now in the area near the guest room elevators. Some people look at us while they wait for one of the elevators to come, but no one stops me or points at me like they know who I am.

We get to the lobby and I'm delighted to see that there's hardly a line to check in. I rush over to Kayley, who's working the front desk right now. She hasn't seen me post-accident because she hasn't caught much of a break at the front desk, but she's texted me every day to ask how my progress is going.

"Hey stranger," I smile at her as I'm leaning on the desk.

"Oh my gosh! You've been discharged?" She runs from the computer and swoops me up in the biggest hug. It stings a little bit on my wounded arm, but I'm happy to see her that I wince through the pain as much as I can.

"Kay, my arm's a little..."

"Oh god, sorry!" She lets me go and throws her hands up. "My excitement caused you pain. Okay I will remember to be more gentle. Anyway, how are you feeling?"

"Better," I nod. "My stitches are supposed to be healed up in a few weeks and I'm just instructed to rest until they give me the green light to start working again. Not that I'm really in a rush anyway. I can barely lift my arm."

"Yeah, I heard you're staying here? With Kellen? I mean, he only told me the day you were admitted because I'm the closest one to you, but he's kind of been MIA since then. That still happening?"

I shrug. "It's a little up in the air at this point. I haven't spoken to him since that day either. I guess we didn't break up because we were never together, but I don't think we're in a good spot by any means." Or at this point, he even wants to be with someone as complicated as me.

"Well, he's been kind of quiet since you were in the hospital. He doesn't really talk to us anymore. All he does is just wave and then immediately coop up in his office until someone needs him for something."

My shoulders sag a bit. It hurt him a lot more than I thought. Part of it was that I just didn't even really feel ready to hear the words yet. While I can tell myself that I am in love with Kellen, which if my feelings over the past few months have shown me anything, it's that I have felt more for him than any person I've dated or even considered going on a date with, and I don't like that we're in a place now where there feels like a rift between us. It unsettles me that I want us to have a future together, but there are forces that are keeping us apart, forces that I've brought on because of my own fears.

"Maybe I should talk to him," I tell her. "I don't even know if he made any reservations for my parents. Would you mind checking?"

"Sure thing," Kayley says. She types my last name into the system and combs through the reservations for a bit before she points at the screen.

"Yeah, I have a reservation right here. Tim Waters. Check in is currently for a few days from now, but we have availability so I can push it up to today. And there's even a comment here: 'Comp per Kellen for Marissa Waters' parents to stay during recovery.'"

"And when did he make that reservation?"

"Seems like...three days ago."

I'm numb at how he's kept his word. It almost makes me emotional, that I might have been a complete jerk to him, and the last time we talked, I might not have wanted to see him for a while, but he still made sure that my parents were taken care of. Now it was just a matter of where I wanted to be taken care of. I know at first he had offered the spare room in his villa, but would it be too painful for us to see each other every day?

"Oh. Well, uh awesome. Can I get them checked in then?"

"Yeah, totally."

As Kayley is working to get the keys registered for my parent's room, I make eye contact with who is walking out of the operations office. Kellen, and Joelle following behind him. Kellen meets my gaze and halts in his place, causing Joelle to almost bump into him.

"Kellen," she says, startled. "Why'd you stop?"

"Marissa," he eyes me and my body standing straight, but he doesn't sound excited to see me at the front desk. "I didn't know you'd be discharged today."

"Yeah, the doctor said the recovery was going really well so they let me out a few days ahead of schedule."

"Um...that's wonderful. I'm glad to hear you're feeling better."

"Thank you." I try to smile at him, but I hate that I have to force it out of me.

"Oh, Marissa!" Joelle says, standing to the left of Kellen now. "You're back from the hospital! What are you doing here? Shouldn't you be resting at home?"

"Uh, well, Kellen had offered that my parents stay here while I was doing the rest of my recovery." I didn't bring up the spare room offering, because I technically didn't have confirmation if Joelle knew about us, and if she did, then if I was going to hear the consequences of it upon my return to work.

"Well, how nice of him." She shoots a look at Kellen and then back to me. "Actually, Marissa, while we have you here, would you mind stepping into the office for a moment? We just want to talk about some things, you know, with the incident happening and all."

"Joelle," Kellen warns. "Is this a good time?"

"Yes," she stares back at him. "I think it's good timing since Marissa is here at the hotel, don't you?" She grins back at me. "Don't worry, it won't take long."

This takes me by surprise, but I'm sure it's just Joelle asking if I'm okay and what happened. "Sure thing." I beckon my parents over so that they can grab the keys from Kayley and get settled in their rooms while I head back into the back office and revisit the desk I was soon beginning to get familiar with, that now was just an empty desk in Kellen's office.

"Have a seat." Joelle motions to the chair that is next to hers, across from Kellen's desk. He sits down and looks at us with an unreadable expression.

"Um, first of all, how are you, Marissa?" Joelle asks.

"I'm fine," I shrug. "The bullet wound is mostly healed, which is good. They said that I should regain full motion of my arm in a few weeks."

"That's great!" Joelle beams. "I was so scared when I learned you were the one who got shot. You never think it's someone you're close to, so it was really hard on all of us to hear it had happened to you."

"Yeah, I'm sorry. I wasn't thinking it was going to happen to me either, but I guess everyone knows now about...what I've really been working on, right?"

"Yeah, Kellen explained to me pretty much the gist of the situation at hand. About that group of men who were trying to hurt him, his father's company, and they knew you were a famous poker player. It's a large pill to swallow, to say the least."

Throughout this, Kellen remains silent. I quickly catch a glimpse of him, wondering what thoughts are racing through his mind while I've had to tell my boss about the events that have transpired.

"Um," Joelle takes a large gulp in and swallows. "Kellen has also explained to me that you two were romantically involved with each other. Is that true?"

Dammit, I didn't think this was going to be more of a confessional. I wasn't thinking I had to tell Joelle until at least the day I returned to work, and on my own accord as well.

"Yes," I slowly nod. "It's true."

"Okay. I just want you to know that you aren't in trouble. And I'm not doing this as punishment of any kind, or based on my own decisions."

My hands start to feel clammy as I grasp them tighter together, coupled with the increased heart rate and the weird feeling resting at the bottom of my stomach. Is this what I think it is?

"I'm so sorry, Marissa. But your employment with the Blossom Hotel has been terminated."

I'm caught from left field and my only reaction is to start crying. Maybe a little bit from shock, maybe from sadness. Definitely from me thinking that it didn't have to end like this...but here we are. I try and blink quickly to stop any tears that are dropping down my face. Terminated. What an evil sounding word to make this wound hurt just a bit more.

"I've...been fired? But why?"

Like there's anything I can argue to salvage this. Like Joelle said, it's nothing that I've done linked to my relationship with

Kellen, or as punishment for anything. But, it soon sinks in that I don't have a job, and I'm not even able to make money right now, so I'm scrambling to think how I am going to earn a steady flow of income. Especially off a major hospital visit.

"Like I said, it's not anything that's your fault. You are a good sales manager, a very strong worker, and your relationship with Kellen didn't break any employee rules. But, there is a lot of clean up that the hotel needs to do now, including your recent confession that you are renowned poker player Janessa Frost, that parting ways is the best thing to do to protect you as well as the hotel."

I nod. "I understand." Even though I didn't want to. That of all things that were to get me fired, my own alternate persona would be the one to do it. Maybe it was better to let things retire when there wasn't much more at stake.

She takes a stack of papers from Kellen's desk and hands them over to me. "Here's all your exit paperwork with your final paycheck. Tells you about insurance and all that. And you have my cell number, so you call me if you need anything, okay?" She lets out a breathless laugh. "I think you'll be just fine. Wherever you end up."

"Well, we'll see," I try and force out a laugh. "I'll just take it one day at a time, I guess."

"That's the spirit," Joelle says, patting me on the shoulder. "Best of luck out there." She gets up from the chair and heads straight out the door, letting the door slam behind her.

"Mar," Kellen rushes. "Please know, this was completely out of my control. I didn't want any of this to happen. To us, to your job. I can't tell you how much of a wreck I feel about everything."

His face looks like he's barely gotten any sleep over this. His eye bags are starting to get bags under them, and his hair is the least kept I've seen in a long time. I can safely say I'm over the entire thing: getting fired, people knowing my secret, admitting defeat to the Fortune Hunters, that I just sigh and shrug my shoulders.

"It's okay. I know it's out of your control. I just have to accept my fate." I don't even know if that fate is staying in Vegas, but at least my fate with the Blossom, a hotel I can feel accomplished that I've given my life and everything to, has sealed itself up.

"You don't have to be broke," Kellen says. "I have the money. I'll take care of you."

"It's not about the money, Kellen!" I interrupt, angry that he thinks I want to take the way out by relying on him. "I want to be able to be successful from my own merit and hard work. I don't need to be carried through life by my boyfriend or whatever the fuck we are at this point."

"Okay," he sulks. "I'm sorry, I just...I just want to help."

"I know," I hold the bridge of my nose. "But, I think it might just be best if you left me, left this alone. I...I can't see this working out between us."

"How can you say that?" he retaliates. "I told you how I felt about you, Marissa. I love you and I will do anything to make you happy. Look, I know there's a lot of hurdles that have been thrown at us, but..."

"Exactly! What are these hurdles trying to tell us?" I yell, tear-stricken. "That it's not meant to be. I need to get out of here."

"Marissa —"

"Just, leave me alone. Please." I turn my back to him and start pacing away. Why is it that when I try to put myself in control of my life, it all just breaks into a million little pieces?

Chapter Twenty-Six

Kellen

There has yet to be a day since Marissa walked out of this very office, saying "goodbye" to me, to the hotel, and to us, where I've genuinely felt happy. The moment she walked out the door, the joy that I had with her almost every moment we spent together has been sucked out of my body and gone who knows where. Into the oblivion of Las Vegas where it roams around with the fumes of cigarette smoke and seared meats.

I've worked hard to try and ensure that I stay busy enough so I didn't need to stay cooped up in this office with reminders of what once was, so for the past two weeks I've been walking the casino floor, standing behind the front desk, actually offering to help check guests in, and even going so far as to ask the executive housekeeper, Yvette, if I can inspect rooms with her. Something that can be a distraction to take my mind off Marissa, who I've wanted to call for the past two weeks to hear her voice and tell her how much I miss her body next to mine.

As a result of my incessant longing, I've developed a better relationship with Kayley than both of us ever thought possible. Granted, most of it is her feeding me updates on how Marissa has been doing, but she's more accepting of me once she's learned just how much Marissa means to me, and how lost I am without her.

As luck would have it, she's knocking open the office door right now and steps inside.

"Hey boss," she says, soon hovering over my desk. "Almost time for weekly Ops meeting."

"Ugh," I groan and lean back in my plush office chair before realizing I've leaned too far and now feel like I'm going to fall off. I grip the arm rests and slide back up. "Oops."

"Last week wasn't that bad, right?"

"No." The weekly operations meeting is just as its name implies: members from the operations team - like me, Kayley, Yvette, and Micah, the concierge manager, bring our weekly department updates to Erick and he tells us what we should also be improving on based on guest feedback. Since the poker tournament, our TripAdvisor rating has decreased dramatically. We're still in the top ten hotels on the Strip, but we've bumped down three places because people "don't feel comfortable at a hotel that's being targeted by the Chinese mafia." Newsflash, neither does this guy, but that wasn't our choice. Suffice to say, it's really taken a toll on everyone's workplace morale and as director of operations, I should be the one to absorb everyone's sadness and tell them "it's all going to be okay!" but with my own monsters I'm fighting, I've really dropped the ball on that. Another thing I've leaned on Kayley for support about, but I'm sure she's suffering without her best friend/work wife here to keep her spirits up.

"You know how it's been," I sigh. "Same shit, different day." I wipe my face over with my hands. "Any Marissa updates?"

Last Kayley heard, Marissa had let her know that she was just recovering at home and going to physical therapy for her arm twice a week. Her parents had since checked out of the Blossom because any longer would have felt like they were overstaying their welcome, considering they couldn't use the excuse that their child works here anymore, and have since stayed at another hotel. Turns out they had plenty of points with Hilton and opted for Resorts World instead.

"I asked if she was busy on Saturday so I could pop in and say hello, and she said she's free. So this is your warning to not schedule me on Saturday if you don't want Marissa intel."

"Noted." Kayley's been working her ass off anyway because we had a few front desk agents quit. They didn't give any exact reason, but working for a hotel that might be under attack again without any warning probably has something to do with it. It's also partially the reason why I've come out to the desk more and reignited those front office skills, because manning a front desk alone sometimes can be taxing.

"You know she still really cares about you."

"I know." I don't argue with her about that. If Marissa's face lighting up after waking up from her surgery was any indication, there's still a part of her that feels something for me. Which is why I understand that she is going through a lot right now and that she needs time to herself, to recover and think about what her future looks like. As much as I want to poke and pry, I have to be trusting that she'll choose a future with me in it. I'm not going to give up on us so quickly.

"She's just anxious about the future now, being unemployed and everything. Also with someone still being out there, there's a lot that she should focus on, and even though we're allowed to be together, it doesn't necessarily mean it's healthy that we should be together."

"Yeah," Kayley nods. "Exactly." She slumps in the chair in front of her desk and rests her head on the desk.

"I've never seen her like this. Usually she's the one trying to cheer me up, but now I have to put all my woes aside to make sure she's happy."

"Same here. And there's so much that I want to do, like refer jobs for her, keep her company, tell her it's going to be okay, but those aren't even the best ways to make the situation better. I literally have to just wait it out until she's ready to talk to me."

"Well, I'll see if I can get her to reach out soon." Kayley chokes out a laugh. "I can't believe I'm saying that I'm actually rooting for you. What kind of universe do we live in?"

A really fucked up one, honestly. Not because of Kayley being nice to me, but of how topsy turvy everything else feels. Marissa not working here, the low morale we're somehow forced to keep up here, and whoever the fuck thinks it's funny to keep messing with our heads like this. I thought that we'd catch the right person, the man that shot Marissa, and conquered the Fortune Hunters once and for all, but no. It was just a servant for someone we don't even know. And I don't have anyone to help me anymore figure out who's behind all this.

"It's kind of a nightmare if we're being honest. Not because we're getting along, obviously, but with everything else going on."

"Yeah, it's kind of a shit show here," Kayley laughs. "But we're a team." She stands up and holds out a fist that I go to bump. "We'll get through this."

I give her a slow nod and crack a smile. "We'll get through this." She nods back and steps out of my office where I'm left to ponder the rest of the thoughts circling in my head.

Marissa

My mom walks into my room, carrying a bowl of leftover pho that I had for lunch the other day. It's officially been day fifteen of my stay-at-home recovery, although I don't really have any set timeline on when I'm due back, since I am officially unemployed and have nothing lined up.

My parents decided to not stay past two days at the Blossom. Kellen had tried to persuade them saying that even though we were no longer together, or even friends really, that he still wanted to extend any sort of hospitality that he could, because that's the kind of thing that runs through his veins, but they thought that the situation was awkward all around and that it would just be easiest if they stayed somewhere else. I supported it, even if they had to pay some amount of money in room and tax, because I was mad at the Blossom. Not the hotel specifically, but the people that were running the whole show. I don't know who prompted the conversation about my termination. A part of me believes that Kellen wasn't the one who prompted it, and considering he told me this was out of his control, it must have come from someone who's above him. Maybe Erick did. Maybe his father. Whoever it was, I was upset with them that they wanted to fire me even though I was a good employee and the only "wrong" thing I possibly did was fraternize with a director. Either way, I was stuck at home, plowing through the unread books on my shelf and watching the top ten on Netflix while my parents came to check on me and keep me company for a good portion of the day and feed me food they bought at the 99 Ranch Market.

Today is Kayley's first day that she's able to come and visit me. She's been my gossip girl on all things Blossom drama as it's unfurled. She said she felt weird if she gave me Kellen updates though, because they have been working close together since the incident, and also because they are both commiserating about how people are leaving the hotel due to feeling scared behind the front desk. I pretend to be nonchalant on whether she tells me or not, even though I kind of want her to give me Kellen updates, because I'm very much not over him in the slightest. So, I guess silence is bliss. I am happy that they are seeming to get along with one another, though. It's about damn time those two put aside their differences and actually work like the team they're supposed to.

Kayley texts me that she's here and I press the button to unlock the front door to my apartment building so she can come up. I let my parents know that I'm heading down to the lobby to greet her and my mom is already getting a platter of finger food for us to indulge in before the door to my apartment can close.

Kayley waves ferociously at me once I step off the elevator and walk towards her.

"Hi!" She almost wraps me up in a bear hug before she realizes the last time she did that, I winced from her arms brushing against my gunshot wound. "I was about to give you a hug, but realized that you are very fragile still, and I don't want to indulge you in any more pain." Instead, she rubs my lower arm slowly up and down.

"There we go," she laughs. "How's recovery treating you?"

"It has its ups and downs," I shrug. "I shouldn't be complaining though. I'm apparently recovering way faster than what the doctors were projecting for me." I start to lift my arm up almost in one fluid motion. "I'm almost able to lift my arms high enough to where I'm supposed to."

"That's awesome!" Kayley beams. She's quiet for a moment, her face blank before she blinks rapidly to get the tears out from her eye ducts.

"Sorry," she says, wiping them away with her sleeve. "I guess I just couldn't hold that in much longer. Work has been really hard because no one wants to work front desk because they're all scared, and I've had to fill like three shifts for people and it sucks because I don't even get overtime anymore. And I can't commiserate with you about it because they fired you and I wish they didn't because you're like the best thing that's ever come from working at the Blossom and I don't even have that anymore."

I tug onto Kayley's arm and pull her into me so she can let out her sobs on my shoulder.

"I'm sorry," I say as her snot leaves its mark on my shirt. "I've just been a ball of emotions the last few days. It's so hard to force a smile in front of guests when your entire life is crumbling all around you."

"Remind me that when I'm cleared to start going out again that I need to treat us to a spa day. We've wholly deserved it after everything that's happened."

"Spa day and I want a fully paid for dinner at the restaurant of my choosing for all the emotional distress I've gone through because of you."

I gasp. "You forget that I am unemployed and don't really have much money saved up to even get me past this month."

"Oh yeah," she laughs. "Well I'll just ask Kellen then."

My mouth forms a hard line when she says his name so nonchalantly. Keep telling yourself you're happy that they're friends. Just keep telling yourself.

"Shit, Mar," Kayley's face turns guilty when she sees mine. "I am so sorry. I should have known better. It was a huge slip up on my part saying his name. Won't happen again." She makes a "zip!" motion with her mouth.

I don't have a mirror in front of me to see what kind of face I made that got her feeling so guilty, but I feel bad that I may have had some expression that had her worried sick that she might have ruffled something inside of me. Which, even though she did, I need to be the strong person I want to be and not let something as measly as his name affect how I feel.

"It's okay," I reassure her. "Really. What happened happened and I'm not going to spend any more time wallowing in sadness. If these past few weeks have taught me anything, it's that I've still got a lot of life in me to live and dammit, I have to just move on."

"Yeah!" Kayley pumps a fit in the air a la the final scene from The Breakfast Club. "Fuck them. Fuck them all! You're a strong independent woman, and you are going to get anything you set your mind to!"

"Um...but, hypothetically speaking, if we were, hmm, I don't know, still thinking about Kellen every once in a while, would you care to fill me in on how he's doing?"

I decide to be upfront with my feelings. Yes, I miss Kellen tremendously. Yes, we're not technically dating anymore, so he can be free to date who he wants to, and so can I. But I would rather spend my days alone, turning down others in hopes that someday we will be able to reunite. I know that it would be better off though if I didn't make a move until the bad guy is caught and everyone's moved on. I don't know if there are people out there who might not be able to move on from the Janessa reveal, but I can hope that I can get to a point in my life where people will stop talking about it if they want me to be able to live my goddamn life in peace.

Kayley looks at me, eyes wide and slightly terrified. "You're sure?" She grabs onto both my arms, more gently this time, and shakes me a little bit while staring deep into my eye holes. "You're ready to talk to him?"

"I wouldn't say I'm ready to talk to him yet, I just want to know how he's doing, that's all. I still care about him."

She smirks at me. "I knew you still did. If you're worried that he's moved on to someone else, don't. He's very much not over you. You two are soulmates, whether you want to admit it or not. And I'm going to figure out a way to get you two back to that sweet spot."

"Kay, I just asked if you could fill me in on how he's doing." But, there was that little voice in my head that was squealing at the plausibility that we, Kellen and I, had a strong chance of being a possibility again.

She playfully rolls her eyes and swats the air between us. "Yeah, yeah, I know. I just also happen to know that you were curious if he had found someone yet and just letting you know, he hasn't."

"What a relief," I murmur. "I mean, good things come to those who wait."

"Yeah!" Kayley shot her hands up, exasperated. "So hopefully this was enough time for you two. Kellen's been a mess, Mar. Like weirdly this whole thing has been good because he's actually walking around the hotel, making sure everything is in good shape, really hardly ever leaving his desk. But he's not the same chipper person anymore. Even though he was only chipper when he was with you, but now it's just all work no play. It's kind of draining given everything going on."

"Oh," I mutter. I know that this has been a difficult time, but my heart begins to ache knowing that I've virtually destroyed the likable personality that he was working so hard on maintaining. My heart still wants to chase after him, but I can't keep him from living a life drama free, which is why I had broken things off in the first place.

"I mean, he'll be okay...I think. If you're thinking of keeping things distant."

"I just don't want to." I groan and then plop myself on the couch in the lobby of my apartment building. My parents are probably wondering what the fuck we're talking about that's prevented us from moving upstairs. "I still love him." Which if being in solitary confinement in my apartment for two weeks has taught me anything, it's that I wish that I had told him that I did and I wasn't so much of a coward to face the new and scary future that we had ahead of us. Especially now that I've lived my life always certain that my career was going to carry me and not having that backbone anymore.

"I think that we need to do something about that," Kayley tells me.

"What are you thinking?" I ask. Although, knowing Kayley, she has something up her sleeve that I know I won't see coming.

Chapter Twenty-Seven
Marissa

Kayley's plan is arguably, a horrible one. But, it's filled with good intentions, and arguably will be the push I need to not only get Kellen back, but to also help me realize that I needed to make a change inside myself. So, in the long run, it's actually a genius plan and helped me unearth why I was hesitant to make the move to be with Kellen. Anyone could probably understand that I was angry when I was let go from the Blossom. And it took me some time to understand it. It wasn't the decision that they wanted to make, but they needed to. I was withholding secret information that when unearthed, spiraled into a lot of publicity that the hotel needed to cover up. It was a lot to clean up, and I felt bad that I forced my coworkers into doing it. Maybe doing this will give me closure on a part of my life that I never thought I would welcome again.

We had to get the sales team on board with orchestrating an event that is top secret so that when Kellen sees the event plastered across the hotel, he isn't quickly jumping to conclusions. Thankfully, I also was able to block him off of Janessa's

Instagram so that when I made the grand announcement that I was going to be making a statement at the hotel one morning, he wouldn't know, but the rest of the world would.

They graciously allow us to gather in the hotel's open ballroom area, where we've set up a small stage and await the flock of people to gather to hear Janessa Frost speak for the first time since the truth was unearthed that well, she actually wasn't a real person.

"Feeling nervous?" Joelle asks me. We're both standing behind the makeshift elevated stage before my scheduled announcement in a few minutes.

"Yeah," I sigh. "I didn't think I'd ever need to do this."

"Did you really think that you could've gone your whole life without people knowing that you were a famous poker player?" She starts laughing. "Hannah Montana couldn't do it."

I roll my eyes. "One, Hannah Montana is a work of fiction. And two, I thought I did because I didn't think that she would've wiggled her way into my life again. I don't regret it though, it might have helped Kellen get one step closer into finding out who is behind this once and for all."

"Well, even though you're not an employee with us anymore doesn't mean that you can't come by to check on us in the sales world." She puts a hand on my shoulder. "I'm proud of you. For being able to finally live out your dreams."

I reach over and wrap my arms around her shoulders, embracing her in. "Thank you," I whisper over her shoulder. Joelle went through a lot, being forced to let me go. If she had it her way, she would have willed everything in her power to keep me on, even if I carried a lot of baggage. Now that I'm in between jobs, I could tell that she was trying to make sure that I was secure in whatever job I was going to be entering in, and saying every word possible to make that happen. I never expected it from her, but I couldn't be more thankful that she did.

"You know I want the world for you," she says while rubbing my back. "And I hate that I can no longer have you to myself."

"Yeah, it is going to be weird that I'll be coming to the Blossom as a celebrity in some ways," I chuckle.

As we're wrapping up our conversation, the murmurs of the audience become a little louder and my palms begin to feel a little more sweaty.

"Damn. That sounds like a lot more people than what I was thinking."

"You're telling me! Still can't believe you're Janessa Frost. Were Janessa Frost. Do you know how badly I wished that one day you would grace us with your presence at the Blossom? Granted, I thought it'd be like a VIP guest kind of situation, but she was right beside us all along."

And today, it was going to be the time to say goodbye to her once and for all. I walk up to the stage and take a look around. Kayley told me to give her the signal when I was about to begin my speech so she could quickly alert Kellen. I try to initially survey the audience to see if he was watching me yet, but there are so many people that everyone's face seems to blend together.

Kayley rushes up next to me and gives me a thumbs up that I should begin. Also, that Kellen's probably somewhere in the crowd and I'll just need to trust that he's listening to what I'm going to say.

"Hello, everyone," I begin. "If you're here, it's probably because you were expecting to meet the one and only Janessa Frost. And maybe you don't know what's happened in the last few weeks, but if you don't, Janessa Frost entered her first poker tournament after three years of disappearing from the poker scene. To her surprise, she won, but it didn't come without consequence, when a former poker attendant for the hotel revealed that Janessa Frost was not a real person, just a character made up by a former employee of the Blossom Hotel. That former employee is me, Marissa Waters. To everyone who has felt that I betrayed or misled them, I apologize. I wanted to do something I loved while keeping my true identity separate at the same time. This has led to a lot of people, people I love, to not trust me, and me feeling scared that if someone were to be with me that I would be putting their lives in danger, and I thought it would be better if I just let myself be alone for the rest of my life. But, of course, I didn't love the life that I was setting up for myself, and in turn, thought I needed to do something that would change that. So, if you're listening to this, let this be my official statement. Effective today, Janessa Frost is no more. A blip in history. What once was, now gone. And here's to the future. I am excited to announce that I, Melissa Waters, will be making my return to the poker scene stronger than ever. As a full-time poker player. I know, it is a gamble...get it? To be doing this, especially because I don't have much of a track record going, but I love poker, and I want to be able to play wholly myself. And that's what I'm going to do. Thank you."

Everyone starts clapping loudly that I'm jolted in surprise by the loud eruption of support filling the room. People's hands start going up, wanting to ask questions.

"Marissa, what is your next tournament?"

"Marissa, do you know who the heads of the Fortune Hunters are?"

One of the casino's security guards comes up and announces to the room that I will not be taking any questions before ushering me off stage.

"Hey, if you need personal security support, you know where to find us."

I nod, thanking him before going on a search for Kellen. As I'm rounding the corner, I ram into a body, a seemingly familiar one that almost sends me to the ground. I look up and before I can utter my apologies, I see Kellen's face, panting like he had just finished running to meet me in time.

"Kellen, I wanted to talk to you about..." I begin. But before I get the next word out, he grabs onto my arms and slams his mouth onto mine. I go flimsy in my legs and reach my arms around his back, latching onto him as he hoists me higher up to meet his face. It feels so familiar again, even though it had felt like forever since I kissed him.

"Sorry," he laughs once we've broken apart from the kiss. His arms are still cradling me in him and he's bent down to touch my forehead. "Kayley told me to come here, but she didn't say why. But now I understand."

"First of all, I should be the one who's sorry. I'm just worried about taking the next step. I don't like living life without a plan and being in such a state of vulnerability. But, if this time of recovery and reflection has taught me anything, it's that I could figure out a plan all I wanted, but if you were in that plan, it wouldn't feel complete. I should have never tried to shoo you away, even if I was trying to protect you from my fucked up life. I want my fucked up life to have you in it, because I love you, Kellen Zhang."

"I love you too, Marissa Waters. I love you so much. You're the best thing to ever come from this adventure that I've had living in Las Vegas. And I'm so proud of you for deciding to follow your dreams." He kisses my forehead. "You're going to be the best poker player in the world."

"Thank you." I grin. "I'm terrified, but I told myself I needed to take risks every once in a while to get what I want, and hell. I think I just have to go for it." I rest my head on his chest and grip tighter onto him.

"So," he says, pulling me apart so he can look into my eyes. "Are we doing this? For real?"

"Yes," I frantically nod. I had never been more sure I wanted anything more than that ever in my life. "We're doing this, for real. I wanted to show you that I'm not scared anymore. Of hiding any part of my life. And if you want to go on this rollercoaster with me, please, by all means, I want you always by my side. I want to be yours, Kellen. Me and no one else."

"I want it. I want it so badly, baby." He cups my face and we're kissing again. Our tongues are gliding against each other and I let out a soft moan, before gripping onto his neck and pulling him close to me again.

"Ahem," I hear a voice beside us and jolt back to reality. My cheeks flush with embarrassment as I see Kayley awkwardly standing there, trying to get our attention. Do I ask how long she's been watching us? Am I a little peeved that she interrupted the moment I had been dreaming about for weeks now? All of the above.

"Sorry to intrude in on all the fun," she says. "But we have a meeting in five minutes to get ready for the VIP group arrival."

"Dammit," Kellen murmurs. "It's like our last meeting before he arrives, so I can't really make up an excuse to miss it."

"I mean, I don't think you should anyway," I remind him. Even though I wasn't working on it anymore, I'm still wholly aware that this group arrival should be a priority on everyone's list, even if I wanted to do nothing more than crawl into Kellen's bed and rip his clothes off right now. "You need to make this visit count. To save the hotel."

"You're right," he nods. "Can I see you after work?"

"Of course you can," I grin. "Happy Noodle for dinner?"

"And maybe something else too," he whispers into my ear. He reaches into his pocket and hands me a room key. "Go hang out in my room until we're done."

"Okay." I grab the key and give him another kiss. "I love you. Good luck on the meeting."

"Thanks." He grips my hand once more before letting go. "I love you, too."

Everyone waves to me before heading toward the end of the hallway while I latch on to Kellen's key and begin walking over to his room. No matter how much I will the grin on my face to stop, it doesn't. I'm feeling the happiest I've felt in weeks, and I finally took the step I needed in order to reach the end of my character arc like they have in the stories. The flaws finally feel like they're fading away, and I'm skipping with confidence I finally unearthed in myself, and to top it all off, Kellen and I are officially a thing. We're officially in love, and all the dreams are starting to feel like they're coming true.

Chapter Twenty-Eight

Kellen

We step into the conference room and I feel the pressure of all the eyes staring back as Joelle, Kayley, and I step in. The giddy feeling I just had when my lips were on Marissa's soon fades when both Erick and my father look at me with judgmental eyes. My sister already left to go back to New York, but my father decided to stay a few weeks to ensure everything was perfect for Andrew Tseng's visit and performance. While I thought that the relationship between my dad and I was mended after we had that heart to heart, ties started to sever again. While I didn't blow up at him for it, I wasn't particularly happy that he made the executive decision to fire Marissa. He had a hint of remorse sweep across his face when my sister told me their decision, but it still didn't change the fact that he had the idea in the first place. And then I had to be in the room when Joelle had to tell Marissa. I couldn't even think to be in the room when it happened, but I had forgotten that I had opened the invitation for her family to stay here, for her to stay with me, that when she had actually made her entry through the hotel's doors again, I couldn't let that dread stick with me anymore. I had to rip off the Band-Aid when I got the chance.

And even then, when I thought all hope was swept away for me and the one person I called my soulmate, turns out I just needed to be patient and let things marinate, because Marissa surprised me today. She faced that big fear weighing on her body and made this big speech about how she wasn't going to spend her life hiding anymore. She had her dreams, and she was going to chase after them, by being who she was and not the character she made up in her head. And, as I watched her, speaking in her most raw and true voice, emotional and all, I fell in love with her again. The love never really disappeared, but I know that she did this for me to hear it, or else Kayley wouldn't be tugging at me to get out of my seat and go and reconcile things with her. And she told me the words I've been wanting to hear for months now: I love you. And I told her exactly how I felt: that I loved her too, and I was ready to make things official. Sure, she has no job right now, and she probably will never work for the Blossom again, but she was mine, and I was going to do everything to make sure her and my hotel were safe.

But now, life seemed to ram back into me and tell me life wasn't all rainbows and butterflies, because my dad's scowl was all that was on my mind again.

"Good of you all to show up," Erick chides. "Although, you're here late and we have a lot of ground to cover. Where were you all that affected your punctuality for the meeting?"

I will myself to not roll my eyes right at him. Erick is the biggest kiss-up when my father is in the room. Sometimes, I wondered if he just wanted to be adopted into my family because of how much he looks up to my father. But his constant kissing up meant that I always got put down. He had to make himself look good, so he made sure I looked bad. It made me wonder if he did it because he was afraid I was going to take his job, but I currently had no desire to be General Manager, so I wished he could stop worrying.

He knew that we were at Marissa's "big announcement." Even though we disguised it in all our correspondence as a "poker event," he watched as Kayley and I left our post behind the front desk for an extended amount of time to a mob of people standing in the center of the conference floor. He asks the question not only because my dad is here, but because he's done nothing but say how good it was that we got rid of Marissa when we did because she was the one that brought all the bad omens to the hotel. Not the poker attendant that shot her, of course.

"There was an event," I say, my tone as even as I can make it. I was here because it was a part of my job; I wasn't here to talk friendly to someone that clearly has it out for me.

"What kind of event?" my dad asks.

No one wants to speak up, and I guess I don't blame them. My father has "menacing" written all over his face when he's angry, and you need to brace yourself because he rarely says anything that warrants a smile. What could I say that would make him not question my antics? Some high revenue generating event, I guess. Which this event very much wasn't.

"A press conference," I say.

"For what?" He counters.

The air around us grows hotter and I feel everyone's stares beating down on me. Shouldn't we be actually talking about the event at hand instead of wasting everyone's time with all this interrogation?

"It was for Marissa." I sighed. "She asked if we could host her press conference announcing her official entry into the professional poker world, and her officially confessing about being Janessa Frost. And before you say that we had no power to do that, I okayed it because I felt like we owed it to her because she was literally shot on our property. Not that she'd ever sue us, but we brought in over two hundred people to that ten minute announcement alone, and they probably went off to eat in our restaurants and gambled at our machines. And not that it mattered when she did work here, but we're officially dating, so if you have anything bad to say about her, I'd like it if you didn't say it at all, because I love her and I'm just trying to make things right."

My dad is silent while Erick's nose is flaring. I watch him as he angrily opens his mouth and lifts one finger to speak. But, before he can say anything, my dad stops him from doing so by speaking for himself.

"Thank you for letting us know, Kellen. I am happy to hear that you and Marissa are together, and please let me know if there's anything the Blossom can do to help Marissa's poker career. We'd be happy to arrange any meet and greets for her."

I'm stunned by my father's response. I know that it isn't the first time that he's surprised me before, but when I think that everything seems to be going downhill, he's actually brought it back up. I've never wanted to run and wrap my arms around him more than I do right now.

"Thank you," I nod.

"Okay," he claps. "Are we going to start this meeting soon? We are running out of time and I have another meeting after this." He turns to Erick and his face is burning red of embarrassment. I chuckle. Feels good when my father actually feels like he's on my side for once.

"Uh, yes sir," Erick bows his head. He clears his throat while we each take a seat farther down the way from him and my dad.

"So, we are about a week away from our Andrew Tseng group arrival and our Lunar New Year hotel celebration. Engineering will be setting the lobby with our Lunar New Year decorations beginning tomorrow, and we've confirmed our lion and fan dancers."

"What about the food we are featuring?" My dad asks.

"I've talked to Chef Peter about doing an array of small bites that we can hand to guests upon arrival. We will also have a specialty three course menu at Lotus and hand delivered cocktails to our VIPs arriving with the group."

"Okay good," my dad finally says. "I also would like Kellen to work in close proximity with Chef Peter on amenities for these VIPs arriving."

I stifle a groan so my dad doesn't begin wondering what's got me all bunched up. I don't have anything toward Chef Peter now, because I in essence won out with the battle against him for Marissa. I should be happy that Marissa chose me in the end, but that brief period of time where there was even someone else that she considered, rocks me to my core. Thank goodness he's not at this meeting or else I'd be putting on my best resting bitch face while I've thought about all the ways that I want to express how angry I was when he was trying to take Marissa away from me.

"Sound good, Kellen?" My dad asks me. I'm stuck in a gaze before I realize that was a question directed toward me and I quickly nod to acknowledge him.

"Yeah, great. Will do."

The meeting goes on for a bit, Erick moving through each group that's here. I have to give it to him, he's actually on top of his agenda and I'm not feeling like I'm wasting my time. He's obviously come prepared, and my dad seems impressed by how much he's covering. He wraps the meeting once all the departments are covered and no one has any questions and dismisses everyone.

I begin to stand up and walk to the door when he calls after me to stay.

"Can I talk to you for a bit, Kellen?"

My shoulders slump and I bite my lip to stifle the groan I want to let out right now. This guy just knows how to ruin my plans. I want nothing more than to spend time with my girlfriend right now in my room, but I'm stuck having to follow his beck and call.

Once everyone's left, I look Erick straight in his eyes with the most even-toned voice I got. "Yes?"

"I don't care what your dad says. You are to not have any more events with Marissa Waters in this hotel. She might be your girlfriend now, but she's a threat to our hotel and she's not allowed to put it at risk."

My fist coiled back. What the fuck? Does this guy just think he can be making these kinds of decisions? He might be general manager of the hotel, but what is he going to do if I want to have Marissa come over here and play? At the end of the day, my dad owns the hotel. He makes the final call, and he's made his point clear. He wanted to help Marissa, and so I was going to let him. And no one is going to stop me. Especially not big grinch Erick that seemed to hate my guts more and more every day I stood in his way.

I play dumb. "But my dad said we could…"

"Your dad doesn't know the day-to-day schedule of this ho-tel. And obviously I have to work extra hard to make sure that this hotel is in tip top shape any time he's here. You don't know it yet, but something's going to go wrong if we let her come back here. And I can't be letting that happen. I mean, she already got shot once by someone we let work here. Only a matter of time before the real leader of Fortune Hunters strikes."

I sit up a little in my seat. Wait. How does he know we hadn't caught the boss? The only reason I knew was because Marissa told me. And the only reason she knows is because the man she thought she could trust before he shot her told her that the boss likes to keep his bait fresh. But the only thing that's fishy is what Erick just said. But if my suspicions are correct, I think Erick has something he's been hiding. And I don't want to assume that he's working with the enemy yet, but I knew that I'd be a fool to trust anything that's coming out of this guy's mouth. He's had it out for me ever since I got here, and now I'm wondering if he secretly plotted Marissa's leave from the company. He couldn't have known...or could he?

I open my mouth, but I stop myself from uttering any words. I can't just ask him point blank: "Hey, are you working for the enemy?" That's stupid. This needs to be one of those things where if my suspicions are correct, then I need to catch him in the act. And what perfect timing that we're planning this big event that will make or break the hotel? Erick is going to do whatever it takes to send my ass back to New York, but if I already have the sneaking suspicion, then he's about to have a rude awakening when I catch him in his own game.

"Okay," I nod. "You're right. Sorry, I'll tell my dad that any press releases won't be necessary. Want to keep the hotel safe for everyone."

He doesn't raise any eyebrows in suspicion and simply nods to agree with me.

"Thank you," he says. "Glad to see that we're beginning to be respectful to one another. You keep this up and maybe I'll actually tell daddy you're doing a good job and mean it." His laugh is bellowing and it's fake as fuck. I have no desire to be your bro, your work wife, whatever. I cannot get you into any of the clubs or golf courses here in Vegas, and I would never want to. Well, unless my dad forced me. But now, if this man is working for the enemy, then I'm making it my mission to make sure he's out of this hotel, stat.

Chapter Twenty-Nine
Kellen

I race back to my room, occasionally turning my head back to make sure Erick, or anyone else, isn't on my trail. I tried my hardest not to leave the room in a suspicious manner, so that he'd not question anything, but I can't be thinking he's dumber than he actually is.

I fumble for my key and open the door, shutting it quietly behind me. I walk in through the hallway and spot Marissa eating chips and watching some Korean drama on the tv.

"Hey," she smiles, standing up to meet me. Her smile quickly disappears and her face becomes worried. "Why are you panting so much? Were you running?"

I nod, unable to even speak. I don't know what I'm feeling more, the exhaustion from running, or the nerves from my latest discoveries.

"Just wanted to race to get back to your girl, huh?" Marissa jokes. She wraps her arms around my waist and pulls herself into me. I wrap my arms back around her, taking a soft whiff of her sweet scent and give her a kiss on the forehead.

"Sure," I laugh. "No, well, that wasn't actually the reason I was running. Even though I am very happy to see you. I think I might have just gotten some intel on who's the ringleader for the Fortune Hunters."

"What do you mean?" she asks, pulling back.

I explain everything to her while I'm getting a beer from the fridge and opening it on the kitchen island in the room. Marissa sits in one of the barstools while I lean on the counter across from her. How Erick said "head of the Fortune Hunters" when we thought the only people that knew the boss hadn't been caught was us. We didn't even tell the police yet, so how can he know?

"That is pretty sketchy," Marissa agrees. "And his responses definitely insinuate that he might be hiding something. Man, of all people, of course it had to be the HBIC."

The man needed to be in a position of power to execute his master plan, and now I was freaking out about what he had up his sleeve. I already had an instance where I almost lost Marissa, I could not risk something happening to her again.

I walk back over to her and pull her close to me. I kiss the top of her head, and she waits for a beat before returning the hug back around me.

"What's this for?" she asks.

"What? Can I not randomly show affection to my girlfriend without explanation?"

"No," she answers quickly. "I mean, of course you can. I...I think that's the first time that I've heard you refer to me as your girlfriend."

"Yeah?" I smile at her. "How does it sound?"

"I love it," she says as she goes to bury her face in my chest. "And I know I'm going to love it every time you call me yours. And I hope it stays that way as long as we're both standing."

I reach down and give her a quick peck. "You will be." I already knew it. I knew that with everything we've weathered thus far, that I don't want to spend a day without calling Marissa mine. I wasn't in a rush to marry her, ironic given we're in the city of shotgun weddings, but I knew that I wanted to grow old with her and spend the rest of our lives falling deeper in love with one another, getting to know each other, and eventually raising a family together.

"I love you," I whisper to her.

"I love you, too." She tilts up and presses her lips onto mine and I lean in to deepen our kiss, cupping my hand around the back of her head, stroking my hand down to her waist.

"I have to be honest though, I'm terrified of what Erick has planned next, if he's who we think he is."

I sigh. "I am too. Andrew Tseng is coming in a week, and I have no idea what Erick and the rest of the Fortune Hunters have up their sleeves. But, I can't have his or anyone else's life on the line on a day full of celebration."

I rest my head atop Marissa's. I had been thinking so much about how to make this day seamless, with little or no issues at all. I beat myself up in my head with the realization that there's still someone out there who has a plan to hurt innocent people and bring vengeance to this hotel. And the ringleader is none other than the general manager.

"What can we do?" Marissa asks. "How can I help? How can we get the rest of the hotel to help?"

"I don't know," I admit. "To be honest, I don't want anyone to help if they're too worried their life's at risk." It was a lot to ask because we didn't even know if we'd be successfully able to catch Erick. He's dangerous, and I know he's not extending a soft spot for anyone that works for the hotel, even if he might promise someone it.

"What can I do?" Marissa presses. "I know I'm not allowed to be in your office anymore, but..."

"No," I stop her. If I had it my way, I'd keep Marissa away from every possible thing that could harm her. Right now, that felt like it was the entire city of Las Vegas, even though it wasn't, but with the head of an Asian mafia out on the loose, I think keeping Marissa somewhere safe, even if it was in the comfort of my room, was best.

I groan. This is exactly the same thought that my dad had when I was kidnapped for the first time. And when he told me under no circumstances I was to leave the hotel, I wanted to rebel and go against his wishes and leave, and look where that got us. So, me defiantly telling Marissa she can't help worries me. I don't want her to get angry with me for keeping her from doing something. So much for trust in a relationship.

"Sorry," I add, giving her a kiss on the forehead for added affection. "I don't want to force you to stay here and not do anything because I know that you hate not helping. But, ugh, Marissa. If something happens to you again…"

"I know," she nods in agreement. "I'm scared, too. Trust me, you're not the one that had to have a bullet taken out of your body." She strokes both my arms up and down. "But I'm not going to let you take them on alone. I was able to hide an identity from people for more than a year. I'd like to think that I'll be able to do some work taking them done from behind the scenes."

"Okay," I relent. I nod and pull her into me again. It wasn't the ideal outcome I could have wanted, but I did need all the help I could get. "You can help. But, you have to do everything incognito. Erick knows that I'm staying here and he has a master key, so we need to get you somewhere where he won't find you."

"Sure. I mean, Kayley can make a dummy reservation under a fake name and then check me into it. I can hole up in one of the standard rooms and see if we can get access to the cameras to scope things out."

She sounds slightly unsure, but I think this is the best way to go about executing this plan. We can get security to share access to the camera footage, but have to come up with a convincing enough reason to fork it over. I could try to tell them the truth, but would they believe me? And trust me enough to allow me access to look at every nook and cranny of this hotel and what our guests were up to?

"We might have to tell security the truth then," I said. "If they wonder why we're asking for access."

"I think I can convince them." I try to sound confident for the both of us, because I'm holding out for a hero, while still trying to be the hero for the woman I've confessed my love to recently. While I know there are plenty of people out there whose job it is to save everyone from danger, I'm never going to feel like I've done my job or acted on my purpose of moving here and finding a new start if I just sat behind and did nothing.

"Just work with Kayley to get you set up somewhere in the hotel, and I'll make sure to text you what the next step in the plan is." I give Marissa a quick peck. "Whatever you do, stay safe."

"I will." Her voice starts to break a little at the end. She wraps her arms around my waist, giving my shirt a little tug. "You too. Please."

"I'll be okay," I promise her. I couldn't let her down. "I love you."

"I love you, too." I lost track of how many times we said those three words in the past day, but I will keep saying it and never get sick of it. Eventually, I'll show those three words in another way, but now, I was on a mission.

I speed through the casino floor to the security offices, trying not to draw attention to myself to the unassuming casino guests. The hotel has been booming with business post-poker tournament, which surprises me because I thought we would need to conduct more of a recovery plan after some insider sting that involved a shootout with one of the hotel's employees. Who'd want to go to a hotel that has to clean up dried blood off its carpets? Definitely not me. The chaos feels like it's acting like a magnet, though, as people have been flocking our restaurants, shops, and guest rooms in preparation for Andrew Tseng, as well as people who probably are coming to snag a peek at Marissa. Love that my girlfriend is famous in a way, but I can do without the occasional flirtatious message in her DMs. Only I get to send those now.

I knock on the door to the security offices and Desmond opens it, towering over me. Less so in height, but as an ex-defensive tackle in college football, Desmond can run into anyone and decimate them just like that. I can't wait for him to just break Erick like he's a twig.

"Hey, boss," he greets me, beckoning me to walk into the windowless control room. "How's it going?"

"Eh, it's been okay. A bit stressful. I'm sure you're feeling the same."

"Yeah." He leans back in his office chair and looks up at the screen, which has sixteen camera angles of various parts of the hotel. "We just hired another guard to post up by the eating area. I'm glad Erick is letting us hire more staff to keep the hotel safe ahead of the Lunar New Year celebration coming up."

"Um, yeah, about that..." I gulp. Is Desmond going to believe what I'm going to tell him? Hell, all I can do is hope he will. He's going to be an important part of this mission to take Erick down.

"I think Erick works for the Fortune Hunters."

Desmond looks at me stone-faced, and I patiently wait for him to show any sort of reaction. Seconds feel like hours though as my palms begin to sweat waiting for him to respond.

"You think Erick, the hotel's general manager, works for the Fortune Hunters, the organization that wants to take down your father's company? Not to mention they shot your girl-friend and kidnapped you?"

"Well, when you put it that way, yes." I nod. "I think he might be heading up the operation."

"That...shit." Desmond leans forward in his chair and rubs his face. "No. Really?"

I nod once. "I don't have anything confirmed except his social cues. He basically confirmed the existence of an Asian mafia boss. And maybe he just has been keeping up with the news, but there's something that I don't trust about him. He's had it out for me since the beginning, and I'd be a fool to let myself fall prey to anything he tells me to do."

"Well, we really can't be acting on anything unless we have evidence," Desmond notes. I pout, knowing he's right. We can't technically make calls based on personal vendettas, especially while working on the company's dime. "But, between you and me, I think you're onto something."

I lift my brows. "You do?"

"Hell yeah. Erick is shady as shit. I didn't tell you yet, but the day of the shooting, I was wondering why we didn't have more guards posted around the poker room. Even if we couldn't anticipate what had happened, we know to stage double the amount of guards for a poker tournament of that caliber. But we had the same amount of guards working as any other day. And right before the shooting happened, Victor had to be called to an altercation at the Sportsbook, by Erick himself. He just said he was walking by and heard something. But Victor got there, and nothing happened. There was no altercation. There wasn't even a big game going on to spur one at all. I asked Erick afterward and he just shrugged and reasoned that people had calmed down. So, we think it might have been a diversion to what was about to unfurl."

"Holy shit," I whisper.

"At the time, I went along with it. Believed him because he's the boss, right? But, it didn't sit right with me. He seemed too calm and collected after everything transpired. You'd think after a shooting happens at your hotel, you would be freaking out a bit, right?"

"Yeah. I mean, I did. Not just because of what happened to Marissa, but one of the biggest pop stars of our time is going to be here and I'm terrified."

Desmond grabs a hold of my leg. "Hey, we're gonna get through it. Our team knows how important this event is, and if Erick or whoever is working for him is going to try something, then we're going to shut it down before he can. I might not be able to convey to anyone what we're looking out for, but I will keep an extra set of eyes out for anything he's doing specifically. I have your back."

"Thank you, that means a lot." I'm glad that I was able to get our head of security to keep an extra pair of eyes out. "Marissa and Kayley are trying to set up a stakeout point somewhere in the hotel. Erick's going to be on my ass about everything Marissa does because he wants me to believe the shooting is all her fault, but I know the truth. That just means he's going to watch me too because I've publicly made my relationship status known. So, there's no lying about that. I'm hoping that we can get other employees to band against him so he doesn't have anyone on his side in the end. We team up, and take him down just in time before Andrew Tseng suspects anything."

"Sounds like a plan," Desmond says. "Let's take down the man in charge."

Chapter Thirty

Marissa

This week I've been walking on eggshells, and I feel like I'm about to burst.

I've been hiding out in a standard room, perched on the fifty-fourth floor, trying to gather any information I can to finally take Erick down. That crook. I'm so relieved that I don't have to work under him anymore, because I'd punch him in the face the next time I'd see him again, and I would definitely lose my job at the Blossom. And probably get arrested.

But he arranged one of his minions to shoot me. I wish I could scream. But as the saying goes, "Innocent until proven guilty." And to be honest, I have no idea how I will be able to prove Erick is behind the Fortune Hunters, unless I had him say in verbatim, "I am the head of the Fortune Hunters." Or something loosely along those lines. But Erick's smart. I can say all I want about how I wish he could disappear and rot in a jail cell for as long as he lives, but he's plotting his next move to be one step ahead of us. So he can somehow figure out what we're up to and nip it in the bud so he's off the hook. That's how I got ratted out, and being alone in this hotel room is not helping me feel much better about how careless I was. In the end, I'm thankful that Kellen forgave me. Hell, he more than just forgave me, he confessed his love for me. And now, even though everyone's on high alert, at least I can say I'm happily in love and I don't have to hide it anymore.

As I'm scrolling through our master-plan timeline, a knock comes from the door. It takes me by surprise, but the only people that know I'm here are Kayley and Kellen. Everyone else that has access to the hotel's reservation system just sees an alias name and hopefully thinks of it as just a stayover guest. I leave the DND indicator lit anyway, only requesting towels every once in a while when I need a new one.

I slowly creep toward the door and take a look through the peephole, sighing in relief when it is just Kayley standing outside.

"Hey," I say, opening the door just a crack. Kayley quickly steps in and quietly shuts the door behind her. "You know you can just use your key to get in, right? Seems unnecessary to knock. Especially because I get all scared that it could be someone I don't know and have to figure out a master plan in deflecting."

"Yeah, but you have a DND on. If someone walked by me and saw me do that, I could get written up. Remember, it's all about being inconspicuous."

"Yeah, yeah, I know." I fall back down onto the bed. I miss Kellen's bed. Not just because it's a more plush mattress with higher thread count sheets, but I miss his body flush against mine, the way he'd wrap his arm around my body. How his sheets held his scent so well. All I have now is a less plush, still very comfortable bed and no Kellen scent to help me fall asleep. "I'm starting to lose it ever so slightly, if you couldn't tell."

"Eh, I would too if I had to camp out in a standard king." Kayley sticks her tongue out to mimic her disgust. "Sorry we couldn't splurge at least a junior suite for you."

"Really, Kay," I laugh. "I don't mind. Too much. I can't have staff side eyeing a comp suite reservation. And, while Kellen did politely ask if there was any way that I could stay in his villa to do so, that will definitely be the first place Erick looks when he's on the hunt. And post poker escapade, Erick wants absolutely nothing to do with me. Not that he probably wanted anything to do with me in the first place, but now he's shutting down any appearances, tournaments, anything associated with me to ensure the hotel is in 'tip-top shape.' I wish I could beat his tip top into smithereens."

"Oh god, same here. Kellen and I have been at our wit's end after these meetings." She takes a seat on the office chair and turns to the large window overlooking the Strip. If there's one thing I could keep about this room, it would definitely be the view.

"I bet. Got any intel to spill on Erick from the meetings?"

"Oh for sure. I wish I can record these meetings so you can see how absolutely bonkers he is acting. I get it, Andrew Tseng is a big deal and I want to make sure everything goes as well as the next person that works for this hotel, but the requests he is making to Kellen are so outrageous. It's 'Kellen, check to make sure the carpet is spotless.' Or 'Kellen, make sure each amenity is arranged like this. He is definitely trying to deflect Kellen with tasks that aren't his responsibility and Kellen's dad doesn't sit in on these meetings so he's not acting like that neutral-ish third party that can kind of suss out when something's up. The rest of us know, but we can't say anything or else we'd lose our jobs too. And, I think I'd rather try to get Erick out of his job than just walk off mine."

"Yeah, that makes sense." I wish that I can do more help than what I'm able to offer. It sounds like everyone's quest to try and keep quiet to take Erick down means that they need to be on an extra tip top behavior as to not ruffle any feathers.

Kayley's phone rings and she reaches into her pocket to check who it is. She grins at me once she glances at the caller ID. Once she turns the phone, I can see why.

"Kellen Zhang" her phone screen reads.

"Well look who it is," she tells me. "I wonder if this means he's successfully escorted Andrew to his room." She swipes her phone left and presses the speaker button.

"Hello?"

"Hey," Kellen responds. "The bird is in the nest. Or, whatever incognito way you want to say escort complete."

"Nice. How is he? Is he nice? I always assume celebrities are entitled from the get go."

"Yeah, I know." I smile to myself, happy that my two best friends have reached a point where they're each other's best friends. "No, he's pretty chill. Didn't talk too much. Just asked him how his flight was and if he's ever been to Vegas. Not that I can really recommend anything to him besides what restaurants we have here. I told him if he needs anything, to call me or have security escort him. We have one of our guys stationed at the villa entrance all hours, and have to check ID so that the name of the room matches their list. And all of Andrew's visits are by appointment only, so Erick can't use his general manager card to spur on a visit. Because he would just drop in, and we can't allow him to do that."

"Has he bugged you yet about Andrew's escort or anything?" I asked. I realized that Kayley hadn't told him that she was in the room with me, so once I asked, I realized I might have taken him by surprise. "Oh, sorry. Hi babe. Kayley's in the room with me."

Kellen stutters for a bit before awkwardly laughing into the phone and saying, "Oh, hi babe. I was just about to call you after this too. Are you okay? Everything in the room good? Again, I wished you could just stay in my room, but with the security and Erick..."

"Alright we get it," Kayley interjects. "You two fuck." I shoot her a dirty look, even though she's not lying. It really makes things weird when your best friend knows your boyfriend because she reports to him. While I can be happy they get along, I have a feeling she will get a little too comfortable and say shit that hopefully doesn't get anyone in trouble with HR.

"Kayley," I sneer. "We don't need to be talking about that right now."

"You're right, I'm actually starting to feel traumatized by just the thought of you two...ugh. Anyway Kellen, what were you saying..."

"Shit," he whispers suddenly. We lean in closer to the phone, and I'm blinking nervously at what he might be saying that to.

"Kellen, what's wrong?" I ask.

"Erick's coming this way. Fuck, what could he want? I have to go. I have to confront him and make sure he's not going to do anything. He knows about it too, but he thought he could be sneaky. Not this time, motherfucker."

"Please be careful," I warn him. "Call for help if you're in trouble."

"I will," he promises us. "I'll call you back when I'm done talking to him. I love you. Uh...that was for Marissa. Obviously. I mean, Kayley, keep up the good work. I'm going to talk to you guys later."

"Okay, I love you too," I tell him. "Bye."

Kayley shakes her head when I give the phone back to her. "I don't have a good feeling about this."

"Me neither. What should we do?" I feel the restraint of the room making me claustrophobic. I can't sit idly by and wonder all the what ifs when it came to what was going to happen with Kellen and Erick. "I'm scared Kellen's getting himself into danger." My eyes start watering and I bend down to bury my face in my hands.

I hear Kayley walk over and feel her arms pull me closer to her. She rubs her hand up and down my arm and rests her head on my shoulder. "He'll be okay, Mar. Don't worry."

"I know, I just...there's so much I'm not sure about. Like what is Erick capable of? If he had no remorse for having one of his minions hurt me, what's going to happen when he's got Kellen alone right where he wants him?"

"Kellen's smart," she reassures me. "He wouldn't have made the decision to confront Erick if he didn't know the risk. He'll be okay. Especially because he's already almost lost you once, he's not going to let you feel the same way about him."

"True." I still feel the remnants of remorse as I recall that fateful day. Kayley's right. I have to trust that Kellen knows what he's doing. And if he's in trouble, he'll tell us. I just need to be on high alert in case my senses tell me otherwise.

"If it makes you feel better, we can head down to the security offices to be closer in case of an emergency."

"It does," I nod. "We need to make sure that we've got them surrounded."

Chapter Thirty-One

Kellen

I stare Erick down as he strides toward me and the entrance to the villas. My blood boils seeing his smug face stare back at me.

He passes me and heads straight for security, and I stop walking when he tells the guard to let him through.

"I'm sorry boss, I don't see your appointment until tomorrow."

He grows frustrated and raises his voice a bit at the guard. "I'm the general manager, I don't think that I need to be making appointments every time I need to talk to Mr. Tseng. Can you just ask him and say 'It's important?'"

"No, sir. Unfortunately I cannot."

"This is nonsense!" His voice raises, and the guard is holding his hands out to calm him down.

"Sir,"

"No." Erick points a finger at him. "This protocol is idiotic. I should not have to comply with Mr. Tseng's wishes when he's a guest in my hotel."

"Just because you've been put in charge doesn't mean it's yours," I interject. He's fuming when he looks back at me and the audacity I had to put him in his place.

"And you think it's yours?" he asks. He takes a few steps closer to me and narrows his eyes at me. "News flash, Kellen. Your father requested you work under my management. You report to me and that means I have the power to terminate you at any point."

I roll my eyes. I had absolutely no respect for his man anymore, and if he wanted to fire me, which I know was just him bullshitting to feel like he can have the upper hand, then so be it. But I needed to figure out if my instincts were correct if worse comes to worse and he tried to fire me.

"You can't terminate me. Not only because my family owns this hotel, but because I know who you really are."

He smiles coyly and just starts to laugh, sort of maniacally at my discovery.

"Well well well, you think you know everything don't you, Mr. Zhang."

"Tell me I'm lying." I seethe. "I dare you. Tell me you're not the leader of the Fortune Hunters. Either way, I tell my dad the truth, or I tell him a lie but convince him to believe me because I'm his son. And tell him you told me an Asian mafia boss was the one who was behind my girlfriend almost dying."

Erick doesn't say a word, and it's a tell for me that he's freaking out that I've been able to see through his secret.

"Let me say this." He steps closer to me so I can feel his hot breath on my face. I want to recoil at the evil stench he radiates. "I will never confirm nor deny your rather...baseless accusations, but even if you were to try and get me off these hotel premises, I'm always going to be one step ahead of you. And I will find a way to bring you down. You and your crooked family. Mark my fucking words." He turns around and walks away and I feel my heartbeat quicken.

"Holy fuck," I whisper. I do nothing else but run. I take an alternate route around the pool area to avoid bumping into Erick again. I try to call Marissa while avoiding running children in their sopping wet bathing suits. They're not supposed to be running anyway, but I don't have a beat to tell the lifeguards to keep their eyes peeled.

The phone rings once before Marissa answers.

"Hey babe. How'd it go with Erick? Oh, and you're on speaker phone with Kayley and Desmond so don't say anything...provocative."

"Noted," I pant. "Y'all in the casino security office?"

"Yeah. Do you want to wait to tell us when you get here?"

"Yes, I can do that. I'll be there soon. Just trying to avoid Erick as much as I can."

"Okay, we'll see you in a bit. Love you."

"Love you too." I hang up the phone and speedwalk through the casino, amidst the sounds of coins clashing and whooping sounds. The people that get excited over big wins hollering that they've made it big, but having no idea what's going on behind closed doors.

I knock on the door leading into the casino office and see Marissa, Kayley, and Desmond huddled around a computer screen.

"Hey guys, what are you..."

"This son of a bitch!" Kayley shouts.

"Oh my god," Marissa whispers.

"Wow, you know I never thought I would see something like this on a work computer, of all places. Also, what an idiot. Both him and me I guess. I knew I should've just asked IT to tap into his computer when he wasn't at his desk."

"Doing?" I finished. I walk up closer and stand behind Marissa. I lean forward and rest my chin atop her head and she tilts her head up slightly to catch a glimpse of me.

"Hey babe," I smile at her.

"Hi. Desmond found a way to remote into Erick's computer. We've been able to find a bunch of his files and there's tea." I chuckle at the way she emphasizes tea. I look closer at the screen, where Desmond has pulled up a zip folder simply titled "FH."

"What were you able to find?" I ask.

"Pretty much everything that solidified what you had suspected about Erick being the ringleader. I know we both had a hunch, but once I realized IT could just remote into any device that's registered on the hotel's server, then it was easy to see if he was keeping anything on his computer. I was worried he might have kept it somewhere else, but it looks like he was too cocky to believe that no one would think of what we did."

"He's not at his desk when you're doing this, right?" I start to feel worried that maybe we're the idiots if he was. Desmond would know better than to have an autonomous looking computer going with Erick in the office, wouldn't he?

"No, of course he isn't." What a relief. "Made sure he would be away from his desk long enough for us to do some investigating. A few days ago I caught a glimpse of his schedule when he was on a lunch break. He's over at Caesar's for a general manager round table. And then they have a happy hour following that I know he's going to take full advantage of. So he's probably not going to return to his desk for another...two hours? At least? But if he does, we have eyes on the lobby and employee entrance. And all I need to do to get out of the computer is just press a button."

"So, what's the dirt you found on Erick so far?"

For a blip I forget to tell everyone about what happened in front of the villa entrance. In a way, I didn't need to try to make everyone believe me anymore, I guess Erick had his true colors shine through from the things that he left saved on his computer.

"Well for starters, he's totally plotting to kidnap Andrew Tseng during his performance and hope he can get rid of you beforehand to make that happen. There's just an entire folder dedicated to Andrew Tseng's stay. All of his press meetings, rehearsals, where he's going to be at what time. And then I found his run of show and next to it, Erick put names of people who we believe are Fortune Hunters stationed to keep an eye out during rehearsals, meet and greets, and what song we believe will be the moment the Fortune Hunters will essentially snatch him from the stage."

"Hold up." The memories of my kidnapping flood my brain again. Does Erick have some weird obsession with just kidnapping everyone that he wants gone? And does he think he's going to be successful kidnapping a celebrity who has an arsenal of security around him? "What does this master plan look like?"

"You know, I have to hand it to him, it's quite complex and damn near foolproof. If we had no idea what he was doing, then maybe we wouldn't have been able to catch it." Desmond goes on to explain what he thinks Erick might have up his sleeve, while we intently listen and I plot how I'm going to best him at his own game.

Andrew's Lunar New Year spectacular is going to be an experience that's almost out of this world. There's going to be a point in the show where Andrew will be on a platform, singing and playing his guitar. As he's performing his song, the platform will slowly rise, and he'll be suspended in the air and everyone will be in awe as indoor pyrotechnics go off and the lights go dark.

What's planned to happen next is that the lights will come back on and everyone will cheer at his epic performance. But, he won't be on the platform anymore. It'll be like a magic trick, except none of it will truly be magical; it'll be the work of a kidnapper gleefully hoping he's bested me by taking a worldwide pop superstar from my grasp. But, with this information, I'm going to try and be one step ahead. Be there when Erick strikes, and kidnap Andrew before he can and get him somewhere safe. Whereas for Erick, I'm having him cornered and hopefully arrested.

"It can work," Desmond reassures me, when I tell the group my initial thoughts. "We'll make sure to get you somewhere safe once you're off the stage. Talk to Taylor and get a spot at Cyberscape that we can hide in once we can get Erick somewhere where he can't escape."

"Ten-four. I'll talk to Taylor, and figure out how to convince Andrew to let me kidnap him before he gets kidnapped. And then convince him to still play a residency here. I mean, if my entire goal is to get the ones in charge out, maybe he'll be convinced."

"I think we'll be fine," Kayley chimes in. "He seems like he's not one of those people who are super uppity about everything. Surprisingly."

"Yeah, he's cool." In many ways, he's like the people I let into my social circles: cool, charismatic people that flaunted their money around like confetti. But in a few ways, he's like who I'd hang out with now: the down to Earth, let's play some games and chill kind of people. If I wasn't trying to protect him, I'd actually try and get him to move here just so I can have another friend.

We exit the security office once we wrap up talking strategy, and I plead with Marissa to come back to my room with me instead of holing up in the room upstairs.

"Come on," I beg. "Just for tonight?"

"Kellen," she sighs. "It's not safe and you know it. Especially now that Erick literally disclosed his identity to you."

"Erick's not on premises right now. And won't be for a few hours at least. All I need is to get you in my room, and keep you there for the night. We'll order room service, take a dip in the pool for once, and snuggle in bed until we fall asleep. Or until you fall asleep and then I'll go play games with Taylor because I'm too nervous to even think about sleeping now."

I'm trying to not push Marissa because she's right, it's not safe. But this entire hotel is not safe. Marissa would still need to go up to her room perched up on whatever floor it's on and sit alone until the sun rises. I know this time I can keep her safe and sound. I'd rather have her wrapped around me, to give me a little more security at night, instead of asking to watch her with some baby monitor mechanism that lets me see her room from a screen.

"Please," I ask her with begging eyes. "Just for tonight. Because we don't really have much time left."

She sighs and reaches to wrap her arms around my waist. The gesture surprises me, but I quickly return it by wrapping my arms around her and squeezing her so tight, almost to the point of cracking her back.

"Kellen," she giggles. "You're squishing me!"

"Good," I whisper in her hair. "I never want to let you go."

We make the trek back through the villas and to my room. I flash my key to the guard, so he can let us through. He questions for a moment why Marissa's accompanying me, but I tell them it's only for one night. Plus, with the guard posted at Andrew's door at all times, it's not like we'll see him anyway.

Once we get into the room, I order room service for us from Lotus. I think it's been enough time for Chef Peter to stop having a vendetta against me because I'm dating someone he fell at first sight for, if he ever had one. I order a spread of food: beef chow fun, salt and pepper pork, honey walnut shrimp, and some hot and sour soup. Once it gets here, I fix Marissa a plate and bring it to her on the couch, where we've set up a comfort movie we both enjoy: Rush Hour 2.

"Thanks," she murmurs, taking the plate from my hands. She's been quiet since we got into the room, and I sense she's not feeling her usual giddy self.

"What's wrong?" I ask.

She tries to deny she's feeling upset. "Nothing. Why?"

"You've been quiet since we got to the room. I'm just making sure you're okay."

"I'm fine," she tells me, but her monotone voice tells me otherwise. "I don't think you should be worrying about me."

"Mar, I'm your boyfriend. I think worrying about you is outlined as one of the duties of being your boyfriend. And you know you can and should tell me whenever you're worried about something." I put my hand on her thigh. "I just want to make sure you're okay."

"I know. I just find it a lot easier to keep my feelings bubbled up so I don't need to have you worried about me and everything that's going on. Even if it makes me feel like I'm not always present or happy all the time."

"But I don't want you to do that. What's making you worried?"

"You of course!" She shouts back. Her face softens and she turns back and looks down at her plate. "Sorry, I don't mean to shout." She places the plate on the coffee table in front of us and scoots closer to me, going to rest her head on my shoulder.

"I'm nervous. I'm nervous out of my goddamn mind about what's going to happen with this concert. Erick's dangerous, and...if he's set out to kidnap Andrew and sees you're in his way, he'll kill you. There is absolutely no doubt in my mind he has an idea planned on how to do that. I just don't want to lose you the way you could have lost me. And I know I was extremely lucky to have survived almost scot-free, but you're going to be elevated thirty feet in the air when you do this. If you fall..."

"I won't," I stop her. "Or, I'm going to do everything to not fall. Or let Erick try and kill me. I'm racking my brain around all the possible scenarios, and I just have to trust my gut everything's going to be okay. And I want you to also."

She reaches over and presses her hand to my cheek. I lean into her touch and feel her warmth spread into the rest of my body. She chuckles. "We really just have to go through all these obstacles just to be in love, huh?"

"Seems like it," I reply. "But I'll do anything if that means I get to be in love with you. Forever."

I lean over to her and kiss her, holding her face in both my hands. I feel her eyes stream down tears, and I use my fingers to wipe them away. She wraps her arm around my neck and pulls me closer to her and I obey. I put my hands down to circle her waist and guide her to lean down on the couch.

She laughs as soon as she realizes that I'm hard and she can feel it, through my jeans and onto her.

"What?" I ask, momentarily breaking our kiss.

"Nothing," she says, her voice a lot lighter this time than the first time she told me nothing was wrong. Instead, she reaches and strokes where my hardness is over my pants.

"Should we do something about this?" She asks.

"Oh, we absolutely should."

In no time at all, we're undressing and I go back on top of her, planting kisses down her face and neck, until my mouth begins sucking on her breast. She lets out a gasp and I laugh, giving her a little bite.

"I love when your nipples are pointed for me," I tell her. I start to stick my fingers inside her. Starting with one and then another, before I start feeling around inside her. "When you're wet for me. When you groan for me."

"Kellen," she cries.

"Just. Like. That." I lean down and begin using my tongue to explore. Holding her thighs apart, I lick her folds and smile when she moans.

"Oh god," she says. She gives my hair a little tug and I grunt a bit.

"Sorry, did I pull too hard?"

"Abso-fucking-lutely not," I tell her when I come up for air. "I just love it when you pull my hair."

"Good," she wraps her hand around my dick and starts pumping. "Here," she whispers. "Let me do a few more things that you love."

"Marissa." I close my eyes and my heart rate quickens. I'm trying not to burst before I can inside her. "Can I come inside you?"

"Yes," she nods. "Should we...finish this in your bed?"

"Let me just grab a condom from the room, but I want to finish you right here."

I shuffle to the bedroom to pull out a condom from my nightstand, quickly putting it on myself so when I return, I'm ready. I see her naked body kneeling on the couch and I lead her to lie down.

"Wait," she stops me. "I want to try something different."

My eyebrows perk up. "What are you thinking?"

She turns around and rests her palms on the cushion and right in front of me, is her ass in full view.

"You want me to take you from behind?"

"Yeah," she nods. "I, uh, I kind of like doggy."

This girl. I'm definitely not complaining. I scoot closer and stick myself into her from behind, placing my hands on her hips. It only takes one thrust and my body to make contact with her ass and I already know I'm not going to last long.

"Ugh, Marissa. This might be quick."

"That's okay," she reassures me. "Keep it going."

I pick up the pace a little bit, and give her ass a light slap. I lose myself in the sight of its vibrations and after a few rhythmic thrusts, we're both shouting in unison when we finish.

She turns around to face me, panting. "Good job."

"Thanks, back at you." I give her a kiss to show my appreciation.

"Eh, you did most of the work."

"But you have the nice butt."

She blushes. "I do, don't I?"

We head to the bathroom to clean up and rinse ourselves off before going back to eating dinner and watching the movie, before Marissa falls asleep just as the movie pans to the fictitious "Red Dragon" hotel in Las Vegas, an inspiration of my father's for a lot of Blossom architecture. It's weird how everything going on feels like it's straight out of a movie. I go up and turn off the lights, returning to kiss a sleeping Marissa on the forehead.

"We're going to get through this, babe. I'm going to always protect you, even if it means I get hurt. I promise." I drape a blanket over her and walk over to the kitchen to call Taylor.

He picks up on the second ring. "Hey man, what's up?"

"Hey, I need your help. How confident are you in holding an international pop star hostage?"

Chapter Thirty-Two

Kellen

"Man, I don't know," Taylor says after I've repeated my plan to him for what feels like the fifth time. "Are you certain that this is going to work?"

"It has to. Otherwise there is going to be no other way that I will be able to get Andrew Tseng to a place that's safe and secure. Unless you know someone who works for Area 51, then you're my next best hope."

We're in one of the suites of the Cyberscape, officially owned by the Cutler Group and managed by Taylor, which makes me happy because these past few months, Taylor and I have become close. We were always considered "acquaintances because our dads worked in the same circles," but in our late night adventures turned to random video game nights, I now consider Taylor a friend. And now, a partner in crime. He could have chosen to ignore me, or tell me that I needed to go about this alone, but he didn't. I'm just hoping that because I've chosen his place to hide out, that he or his hotel staff aren't put at too big of a risk. The entire point of my plan is to be somewhere

Erick least expects, and I don't think he knows Taylor and I are friends. Once he sees we're out of the hotel, then we can escape in just enough time for him to guess which hotel we've turned to. And given that the Strip has over thirty hotels, it's safe to say our odds are pretty good.

This was my first time actually standing in a room at the Cyberscape. The rooms are extremely well themed: LED light strips circle the ceiling that can change color, or do a rainbow effect all around the room. There's neon light signs in the room, and art that screams "Cyberpunk." Just need to throw in a computer with a colorful desktop case, and it'd be the room of my dreams.

I'm glad Marissa's going to be working here - Taylor's also the MVP for telling her about the job opening and basically Marissa's new boss that she's the best fit after she couldn't work at the Blossom anymore. She'll have no trouble selling this hotel. This decor sells itself, dare I say better than the Blossom's decor.

"I mean, I'm happy to help however I can, you know that. Just as long as you don't think Erick is going to suspect any-thing."

"Erick doesn't know anything about me other than who my father is and who I've chosen to date, sans her secret identity. And I don't want him to know anything else."

"Yeah good thing." Taylor straightens out some of the signage on the desk, displaying QR codes for restaurants and events happening at the hotel. "I'm excited to be working with Marissa," he adds. "She's cool."

"She is." I raised an eyebrow. Taylor wouldn't be that person to steal her away from me, right? "And she's mine. In case you forgot."

"I didn't," he lightly shoves his side against mine. "And I'm not going to. I'm not a homewrecker, dude. Some may say I'm actually very happy for you."

"And I will be for you," I remind him. "Whenever you decide you want to settle down."

"That might be a while, man. I've got a lot of baggage, I don't think I want to subject anyone to that. Or you know, get my heart broken all over again."

I raise a brow at him, but I don't ask any follow up questions. Secretly I hope that Taylor will settle down and find someone he'd be happy to spend the rest of his life with. In a city where people make spur of the moment decisions when it comes to love, I'm somehow proud of myself I found someone that makes me wish time stopped, so I can savor every moment of us together.

"Well, sans the mafia that's out to get me, I think that we've made it quite well for us here in Vegas. Who would've thought?"

"Not me," Taylor laughs. "My dad sent me here to 'make me do something productive with my life.' He had to have some confidence in me to basically manage a newly acquired hotel, which I never thought he had any faith in me to begin with."

"Hey, my dad too," I laugh. "All it took was a near-death robbery to have him open up to me about why he parents me the way he does. Apparently, these Fortune Hunters have had it out for my family for a while."

Taylor goes and touches me on the shoulder. "Well, we're going to make sure they aren't going to hurt anyone anymore."

I'm waiting in the wings of the Blossom Theatre as guests begin to arrive for the show. The last twenty four hours have been a rush, and not just because Marissa and I shared a passionate make-out session in my room before I needed to show up for Andrew's rehearsal.

The hotel is completely covered floor to ceiling in Lunar New Year decorations. Red lanterns hang from the top, and fabric gold dragons zig zag from wall to wall. It's a major dent in our budget, canvassing the hotel in all these decorations, but it makes me happy that we're going all out for the Lunar New Year. When I was in high school, as I started to get accepted into different colleges, I wanted to feel happy for even having a place to study. But, my dad had a more critical response. Why did I get rejected from Harvard, then Yale? I was happy with being accepted into NYU and fell in love with the campus, but once I was accepted into Columbia, my dad basically forced me to go there because it was an Ivy League. Sure, I had a good college experience, but I wondered, if I didn't have an immigrant father, would I have had more of a say on where I was going and what I was doing. The answer, unfortunately, is probably. But, as I look up at the hotel that my dad and family helped build and imprint some aspect of our family's culture in, I tell myself that everything happens for a reason, and I'm proud to be where I am, and where I come from. And after all this, that I'll be able to celebrate that with the person I love.

"Kellen," a familiar voice cries out for me, and I turn and almost start to cry.

A short, red-haired woman smiles. She has more wrinkles now than she did when I was born almost thirty years ago, but she still makes sure to dress to the nines, even if she's going to get coffee. It's not like I've seen her in years, but I hadn't realized until now that I would miss her so much.

"Mom," I smile and walk up to her, embracing her tightly. I sniffle, and she pulls back to help me wipe the tears off my eyes.

"Oh sweetie, what's wrong?"

"It's nothing bad. I'm just happy to see you."

"I'm happy to see you too, Kellen." She pinches my cheeks and in my older age, I'd tell her not to, but I've missed her enough that I think she's allowed to pinch her own son's cheeks. "I cannot wait to meet this new lady of yours. Is she coming to the concert?"

I haven't kept my mom in the loop regarding The Plan, because she would uncontrollably freak out, so I try and conjure up a response that's both convincing and somewhat factual.

"No," I tell her honestly. "She doesn't work here anymore, so it wasn't really easy to get her a ticket. But, you'll get to meet her before you fly back, don't worry."

"I better. It's the least you can do after almost giving me a heart attack when I learned you are going to try and escape from a thirty-foot hang during this concert with Andrew Tseng?"

"Mom," I gripped her shoulder and pulled her close to me. Erick can't hear what we say in the mix of other guests, right? Or other guests passing us didn't hear what she just said, hopefully. "Shush. I don't want to scare the guests. Who told you about the plan? I told Ba not to tell you. You know, because...I didn't want to give you a heart attack."

"Your father cannot hide anything from me," she counters. "He tried. You can give him credit for trying. But, I asked him if he knew how Andrew's concert planning was going and he couldn't help but get flustered. And then he told me everything."

"Ah, great. Well, I don't want you to be worried, Mom. I know what I'm doing."

"You say that, Kellen, but these people are scary. They will stop at nothing to make sure our family suffers. And now that he thinks he has you right where he wants you, he's not going to make it easy for you to escape."

"I know." I don't; I wish I did, but I don't like that I've also worried my mom about my plan. Sooner or later she was going to find out, and maybe it's better she found out now instead of wondering why Andrew Tseng wasn't coming back down with the platform and hearing the screams of Erick and his team as I whisk Andrew away.

"Trust me, Marissa's told me how she's felt about it, too. And I don't want to let her down."

"You really love this girl, don't you?"

I nod, my face somber as I think about all the what ifs again. But, the warmth floods in again, and I nod confidently. "Yeah, I do. I want to protect her, even if it means I'm risking my life in the process."

"You've turned into a really good man, you know that?" She grips onto my arms. "Your dad and I are so proud of you. And when you take down this man, and become GM, I know you're going to make this hotel succeed. And make us proud, even if you already do."

"Wait," I shake my head. "Become GM?"

"Yeah," she says. "When Erick gets arrested, which he will, there's going to be someone that needs to run the hotel. I don't think anyone is better suited for the job than you, honey."

"Yeah but isn't it up to Ba?"

"Well, of course. But your father would want no one else to run this hotel more than his own son. I think that was kind of his plan all along. Why, do you not want to?"

"I..." I think about it. Me, General Manager. I'd be in charge of every single department in this hotel. Every decision gets run by me. Did I truly have the experience and leadership capability to run a hotel all on my own? Taylor seems to think he does, but why did I feel so unsure?

"I do," I conclude. "But what if I don't do a good job?"

"Then we're a phone call away if you have any questions. Look at this hotel, Kellen. These decorations, the crowds of people smiling and having a good time. You're a part of making this happen. I think there's no one else who will dedicate themselves to making this hotel succeed more than you will."

"Thanks, Mom." I give her another quick squeeze, and start walking to the theatre. "I'll see you after the show?"

"Yes you will, honey. I love you."

I smile. "I love you, too."

I watch my mom disappear down the hall and suck in a breath. Now's as good a time as ever to make my way to the theater. I walk past the line that's almost to the lobby of people waiting to be let in. This theater isn't small either. It holds almost five-thousand seats, and every single one has been bought for this concert. Five-thousand eager fans that are about to have their minds blown...and hopefully no panic attacks.

I sneak through the back door entrance and walk through the corridor that puts me behind the stage. I peer over, eying the set stage. There's a few props that assist the show in becoming a cinematic masterpiece. A smaller LED sphere to mimic that new venue that's drawing eyes all to Vegas that's going to show different things throughout the concert: blossoms falling, fire burning, the Earth rotating. There's also those pyrotechnics that will shoot up fireworks around the stage, and the stage. The iconic stage that will be pulled up in the air. The audience can't see the suspension bridge that hangs above the stage, where I will wait to pull Andrew aside. I turn around and look over at the spiral staircase that is supposed to act as an emergency exit, but is going to be our escape route. It's going to be tough to run down and not trip and fall, but maybe the adrenaline will make me not be a total klutz this time.

"Shit," I look up and realize just how high the bridge is. It is so easy to take one misstep and fall. I'm not afraid of heights, but I also don't know if I'll be able to look down and not want to hurl.

"Hey Kellen, are you okay?"

I jump and sharply turn to see who's talking to me. "Oh, Andrew. Yeah, I'm fine."

"Are you sure? Your face looks really pale."

Is it right to throw the "I'm half white" joke as a response? To mask that I might be feeling this way because I just realized that the ground below me in my great escape will be wobbling under my feet and I could fall and potentially badly injure myself? Probably not.

"Yeah, I'm fine. I just..." Exhale. "I just want to make sure the show goes well, you know? Stage fright? Even though I won't be on stage?"

He tries to laugh to make it seem like I don't sound like I'm spewing nonsense from my mouth. "Yeah man, off-stage fright. I get it. It'll be okay though. There are a ton of people out there that are excited for a good show. And I'm excited to give it to them."

"Yeah," I nod. "I am too."

"Hey, and I know we haven't really talked much with how busy we've both been, but I've really enjoyed my stay here. You've been super nice and hospitable, and seem like a really cool guy to hang out with. I'm excited to do a residency here."

I freeze up for a moment. Verbal confirmations don't equate to anything official, not unless it was documented and signed, but he told me what he's excited for and that was to have his residency here. I can't tell him what's about to happen, because once I do, that verbal confirmation will just become my word against his. And he'll go back on his word.

"Yeah man," I smile and nod. "I'm excited for you to perform here too. It's gonna be great."

"Well, I'm going to just spend some time in my dressing room before it's my cue to go on stage. We should hang out after the show. Come to my villa, I'll order drinks for us. We'll celebrate all your hard work paying off."

I gulp. That's if I can even make it to then. Don't think about that, Kellen. Just smile and promise that everything's going to work out. You've had to tell all your loved ones the same damn thing. You can tell a complete stranger with a net worth that's double yours that too.

"Yeah, we'll talk after the show?"

"Sounds good. See you then."

"Okay," I whimper, exhaling a long slow breath. Show time.

I quietly make my way up the spiral staircase as Andrew begins his ascent above ground. I'm dressed head to toe in black: black beanie, turtleneck, and face mask to blend in with backstage so no one can see me trying to take Andrew when they'd be trying.

He finishes his solo, with a bit of riff on the guitar, and soon the fireworks go off. It brightens backstage ever so slightly, and across the bridge, my eyes widen as I see Erick, and some of his men ready to pounce. The bridge is not the sturdiest thing in the world and I gasp when I step down on it and it wobbles.

"Fuck." I whisper as the crowd finishes cheering and the stage goes black.

I have no other thoughts in my mind right now than to just grab Andrew and run. I take his arm as Erick runs across to try and grab his other one and pull him closer to me.

"Ow!" he whisper-yells. "What the fuck is going on?"

"Run!" I yell back and guide him down the spiral staircase back down to the floor.

"Get them!" Erick yells at us and I hear a gunshot go off.

"Was that a gunshot?" Andrew shouts.

I groan. I should have known he had some sort of weapon on him.

"Just keep running," I reassure him. "I have an idea to get you to safety."

"Wait, who are you?" he asks me. I realize that I'm pretty good at disguising myself then. I guess Erick probably knows who I am at this point. I rip off the face mask and toss it aside and turn around to face Andrew.

"It's me, Andrew."

"Kellen? What-what are you going to do with me?"

"Making sure you don't die, for starters." I tell him. I radio Desmond from the walkie in my pocket. "Kellen to Desmond, are you there?"

"Copy that," a muffled response comes in. "What do you need?"

"I have Andrew," I tell him. "But Erick is armed. Tell Taylor to drive up to the villas entrance and take Andrew to Cyber-scape."

"Wait, but what about you, sir?"

"I need to hold Erick down. This isn't just about getting Andrew to somewhere safe. It's making sure no one else gets hurt."

"Where are you?" Desmond asks me.

Another shot goes out and we reroute to behind a wall of one of the bars. "We're exiting the theater. Desmond, evacuate the hotel now."

An alarm blares, with an automated voice telling everyone to evacuate the hotel immediately. I open the door to the hotel and hold myself against it to barricade it from Erick coming through.

"Andrew," I talk to him straight to his face. "You need to go to the villa entrance and get into a black Mercedes. That's my friend Taylor; he's going to take you somewhere safe. I would go with you but I have...other things that I need to deal with. I'll explain everything when I get there."

"Kellen, but..."

"No," I warn him. "Just run to the villas entrance right now. Time's running out."

"Okay," he relents. "Stay safe."

He runs, and even though people try to stop him to get a photo with him, which is an absurd thing to ask given the circumstances, he tells people they need to evacuate the hotel with him. I try to barricade the door shut with my body weight, but with three men on the other side of it, my knees start to buckle.

I try to run a game plan in my head. What I need to do is to ensure that they get caught. I lean forward to peer down the hallway to see if anyone's coming — probably too busy making sure everyone is out of the hotel safely.

If they hear me make a call to Desmond about calling for reinforcement, I fear they might run to escape through a different way. I need to bite the bullet. In as close to a literal sense as possible.

I open the door and hide behind it, watching them lose their balance and stumble out of the doorway. They look confused, turning their heads in all directions wondering where I am. I tackle Erick from behind and thankfully, startle him enough that he drops the gun. He mutters a "fuck" but doesn't think quick enough to dive for the gun. But I do.

I push him aside and get in front of everyone to get the gun. I grab it before anyone else can and point it to Erick.

"Freeze!" I yell.

"Or what?" he jeers. "You expect me to think that you'd actually shoot me?"

I'm not going to. I would rather have him rot in confinement than be dead. I tease by putting my hand on the trigger. Desmond, a little reinforcement would be great right now.

"I will." I try to make myself sound convincing. "So I never have to deal with you putting my loved ones in danger ever again."

"And risk ever seeing them again? Yeah, right. I know you Kellen Zhang. You're just like your father. A coward. Your father could have avoided this entire mess if he never fired my uncle. For what? Because my uncle wanted to actually make some change to the Grand Fortune and your father refused to hear any of it. My uncle was a damn good general manager and his reputation was ruined in the hotel industry because of your father for being disrespectful. For going against the authority. He never financially recovered. Thank god he didn't do a background check about who my family is when he hired me. Poor guy didn't see it coming. And now what is he going to do when his precious son, heir to the Fortune Hotel Group empire, is locked behind bars forever?"

"Maybe he'll be thankful that I finally bested the group of people that have haunted him for so long."

"Or maybe he'll be crying when he discovers his son no longer has a pulse."

Erick takes me by surprise, tackling me to the ground and wrapping his arm around my neck, pulling tighter so I have trouble breathing. I try to raise the gun to shoot his leg so he lets go, but he chokes me tighter causing my breaths to shorten. I want to gasp for air but I can't. Just as I'm about to pull the trigger when I hear a hoard of voices yell, "Freeze!" and I slump to the ground as Erick lets me go. Everyone's voice around me sounds muffled and I struggle to keep my eyes open, suddenly feeling fatigued and trying to keep my breaths regular.

"Kellen. Kellen." Someone shakes me and I try to talk but my voice is so raspy that it's hard to decipher what I'm saying.

"Hey!" It sounds like Desmond's voice. "We need help here now!"

"What's happening?" I try to use my raspy voice to ask him.

"We're going to get you somewhere safe, okay Kellen? Just hang on."

I try to control my breaths but soon, my eyes become more and more heavy and I shut them. All I'm hoping is that Erick's being taken into custody and maybe I was able to make sure everyone was safe after all.

Chapter Thirty-Three

Marissa

"Thanks," I nod to Taylor and Desmond after exiting the room. I brace for the worst, knowing that Kellen may not make it back in one piece after word from Taylor and a panicked Andrew got to me that Erick was armed and dangerous and Kellen was trying to take him down all by himself, but it still pained me to see Desmond carrying a limp Kellen in his arms.

"He's not dead," Desmond makes sure to lead with. But I look closer to a sleeping Kellen to find dark bruise marks around his neck.

"Thankfully," I add. I'm too exhausted to be hysterical. I'm just glad he's breathing and safe. And that Erick would soon be behind bars and away from us, probably forever.

"We're going to let him rest. We checked in with paramedics already. Just get some ice on the bruising and check in on him when he wakes up. He'll be okay otherwise." Taylor was generous enough to give us a double queen to sleep in for the night, so I didn't have to disturb Kellen if he was still sleeping into the night. I don't know if I could sleep though, if by some chance he'd wake up and I wouldn't be awake to see it.

"Any news on Erick?" I ask.

"He's in custody," Desmond says. "That's all I know. Obviously later down the line we'll have to go to court for when he's sentenced, and Kellen will have to testify while running a hotel in Vegas at the same time, but we'll get through it. Together."

I smile at his reassuring tone, that he's grown to have some fondness for the man that he had little faith in to get the job done. It wasn't too long ago that Kellen stepped in front of an entire hotel's operations team and introduced himself as the new director. And when all I could feel toward him was animosity for being so careless and so full of himself. How could you see the rich hotel owner's son and not think that he's incapable of operating a hotel and caring about anyone but himself? But, he proved all of us wrong, and now he's done more than just the bare minimum; more than just executing a grandiose Chinese New Year event in the hotel. He saved a huge pop star's life, and got thousands of guests out of danger. Even though I fell in love with him a while ago, I couldn't be more proud of how much he's matured over these past few months, and how supportive everyone is in ensuring that he's taken care of. I don't know who's going to fill the role of general manager yet, and it's a much larger responsibility than just handling operations. I feel confident that Kellen will be a good GM, if his father decides he wants to hire from within, but it'll be a lot on his plate. Slightly more than trying to capture a mafia boss from executing turmoil on the hotel and anyone who walks in it.

"I know." I don't work at the Blossom anymore, but all the people I met and befriended still have a place in my life, and I want them to succeed. Not a lot of big scandals happen to Vegas hotels. Sure, there was that cyber attack that happened a while back that compromised thousands of hotel reservations, but an inside sting that could have resulted in near death? I'm surprised that people still flocked to the hotel after what happened to me.

"And we're here to help too," Taylor chimes in. "We might be competitors, but Kellen's my friend. And helped me out when I didn't feel like I could run a hotel myself. I want to have his back in the same way. Besides, it looks like I might be working with his girlfriend on some future poker tournaments."

As we continue milling about, a door opens and I jump thinking that it was Kellen. When I look up and see that the room to Kellen's door was still shut, and the person walking out of the room next door was none other than Andrew Tseng, I still feel surprised, just not wanting to run up and wrap my arms around him.

Andrew looks...rough. Despite his hair losing its structure and looking like he was a mad scientist, he is still beautiful, but don't let Kellen hear that. He also looks like he couldn't fixate on anything except ending his show prematurely and having to escape from Erick. I can't even imagine what his social media looks like right now, with everyone blowing up his phone wondering if this concert was a good idea and him having to explain himself, when he doesn't even know what went on.

"Mr. Tseng," Desmond turns to him frantically. "Are you okay, what do you need?"

He holds up one hand, and doesn't say anything for a beat. "I'm fine. Can I talk to you?"

He was looking at me when I asked that question, and it caught me off guard. "Me?" I pointed to myself.

"Yeah," he nods. "Marissa Waters, right? You're Kellen's girlfriend?"

"Yes. Um, yeah. We can talk. Wanna head down to the lobby? Wait, you're like a superstar celebrity, all of the above. You probably want to go somewhere private."

He shrugs. "No, I don't really care actually. Are you hungry? I could eat something right now."

I'm in the weird place of "yes I am starving" and also "my anxiety has taken me on a journey and eating is the last thing I want to think about." But, I put a hand to my empty stomach. Eating is probably a good idea.

"Yeah, I should probably eat."

"Got any recommendations for food places here? I know you guys work here. I mean, this guy's family owns the place. Just uh, as long as there's no like...astronaut ice cream or whatever."

"You like sushi?" Taylor chimes in.

"Love it," Andrew says.

"We have a good Japanese restaurant. It's managed by the guy with that popular hand roll spot."

"Oh yeah," I nod. "I like it there."

"Let's do it then."

We begin down the hallway and down the elevator that quickly takes us down the fifty and some change floors to the ground. I keep a distance between Andrew and I, for fear that people will recognize him. I'm surprised he didn't want to wear some disguise or something to shield him from people that will come up and ask for a photo, autograph, hopefully not to touch him and cause a stampede.

"Are you sure you're not afraid of people coming up to you?" I ask once we've exited the elevator.

He shakes his head. "Not really. I'm not really in the mood to talk to fans right now, so if anyone comes up to me asking for something, I'm just going to say maybe some other time. You know, when I'm not trying to think about this group of people that ruined my show and almost kidnapped me."

"Valid."

"You felt that way too, right? After people found out you're Janessa Frost?"

My eyes widen. "You know about that?"

"I, uh, followed you when you were active in the community. Might've...fantasized about you a little bit. But, to be fair, I didn't know that Janessa was an identity you made up."

"Wow," I ruffle my hair back a little bit. "Well, I kind of did the same, when I was younger and you released your first album. My favorite of yours to this day is still 'midnight escape.' And then ten years later, I'm living proof of the girl you sang about in that song. 'I'll sneak out of my window at midnight, just to tell you how I feel. Your father said you couldn't see me, but I wish I could tell him I don't care.' Forbidden love is so...weirdly swoony."

"Thanks," he chuckles. "It was all the rage with teens."

We ask for a table in the restaurant, and then Elli, the hostess, goes speechless when she sees who's next to me. We try to tell her to calm down before she screams in excitement, but she catches herself and takes a deep inhale, probably realizing she's still on the clock.

"I'll put you both somewhere near the back of the restaurant. It's right before the dinner rush, but we'll seat people closer to the entrance."

"Thanks," Andrew says. "I appreciate it."

We look at the menu and decide we both wanted a hand roll sampler. I check my phone every few minutes to see if there's been any updates about Kellen.

"Seeing if Kellen's awake?"

I jump a bit in my seat and quickly put my phone face down on the table. I'm with a celebrity and it looks like I could give two shits.

"Sorry. Yes. It's rude of me though, to be looking at my phone when you want to talk to me."

"It's okay," he reassures. "It is your boyfriend who you're checking on. I think that's valid for ignoring someone who's invited you for a meal."

"Sure. But also, you wanted to talk to me about something? What was it?"

"I wanted to just check in and see if you were okay. And also tell you, before I talk to Kellen about this because I know that he's going to advise against it, but after I get home and talk to my manager, I'm going to proceed with the residency at the Blossom."

"Wow. That's awesome. I know Kellen will be happy to hear that. Were you thinking that he'd tell you not to because he feels so bad with what happened?"

"That's exactly what I think. I mean, it was a lot of emotions going through my head when Kellen pulled me out of the theatre and...hearing those gunshots. I just wanted to make sure that everyone in the hotel would be safe. Because it's my show, and they paid a lot to attend. But, I want to just perform and settle down a little bit. And I think this is the perfect place to do it. And Kellen is a great guy. He's someone that I definitely could see getting along with. Spending the night playing video games with him and Taylor. I want to try this out, for real, and see where it takes me. And if people are skeptical about coming for the first few shows, then we'll just try and work at making them excited to come. But, I like it here. I like the hotel and the workers. Plus, the bad guys are captured, so we don't have to worry about anything anymore. That's kind of what Kellen wanted all along, right?"

"Yeah. We kind of started working together because I helped rescue him from one of the Fortune Hunters that tried to kidnap him at the hotel. Then when his father said that he wanted to try and get you signed on as a resident, then Kellen started feeling like he needed to get this whole thing figured out because he didn't want to disappoint his dad, make you feel worried, or let everyone down. At the time, I had this animosity against him, because we'd actually met before working together at this nightclub, and kissed. But, turns out I wasn't the only one locking lips with him that night and I kind of just thought he was a playboy. But, he proved me wrong. And...one thing leads to another and we kind of just started liking each other. I was kind of worried because I hadn't told him about Janessa, and I wasn't even thinking I'd play much again, but I thought I could use my persona to lead people into my trap. Which in hindsight, worked, just...I had to get shot because of it. But, I realized that I didn't need to hide behind a persona anymore, and I hoped that I could reach a point where I could love Kellen and not feel guilty about it, and it turns out I can. And...yeah. I know he's a good guy, and I'm happy that others are seeing it, too."

I take a deep breath. I feel like I just dumped a novel on this guy, and he just wanted to tell me that he's doing his residency here. I'm happy to hear that he's thankful for Kellen, after hearing Kellen worry about how he'd react when he whisked Andrew away from danger.

"Sorry. Didn't mean to dump our life's story on you. Do you uh, have anyone you're seeing?"

"Me?" He points to himself. "No. Not dating at the moment. I, um, have a son though."

I almost spit out my tea at this tea I just learned. Not that I read Andrew Tseng's wiki, but I definitely learned just now that he has a son.

"You have a son? How old is he?"

"He's ten. Brayden. I love the kid, but I had him when I was twenty-one, at like the height of my career, and I was more focused on pursuing music than having a family, so I kind of tried to work something out with his mom. I send child support, she takes care of him."

"Does he know you're planning on moving to Vegas?"

He shakes his head. "I will tell him. He might not be very happy with me, but I'll fly him out here every month to visit. I know that I'm not a good dad, but I still want to be there for him. Especially since it feels like he acts a lot older than his age. Figuring out he has a broken family and all that."

"Good luck," I tell him. "I hope everything goes well when you do."

"Thanks." He smiles. "Yeah, I just wanted to thank you. For working with Kellen on making all this possible. And if there's anything either of you need, please let me know. I owe him everything for saving my life."

"I will, thank you."

We finish up dinner and my phone buzzes. I look at the caller ID and almost drop my phone seeing Kellen's smiling selfie and his name in big letters on top. What is he doing calling me right now, when he should be resting? Although I'm excited, I'm also worried that he's trying to do more than he should right now.

"Sorry," I tell Andrew. "I'm just going to go take this."

"You're fine."

"Hello?"

"Hey, babe." Kellen greets me with a slightly raspy voice. "I wanted to see where you were."

"Sorry." I feel like I'm just apologetic Marissa today, saying sorry about every freaking move I make. "Andrew wanted to talk to me, and he was hungry so we got something to eat. We're walking back now."

"Andrew?" Kellen sounds a little panicked. "Is he okay?"

"Yeah, yeah babe, he's fine. He's good actually. But I'll let him tell you that himself."

"Well, um. I wanted to see if you wanted to come back and see me? I'm not cleared to really do any strenuous activities, but I miss you."

I laugh. Even in his weakened state, he still has a big heart. "I'm coming soon, okay? Just hold your horses for like five more minutes. Probably less than that."

"Okay. I love you."

"I love you, too." I hang up the phone and Andrew turns to me, grinning.

"You two are so cute," he says. "How's Kellen doing?"

"His voice sounded raspy, but he didn't sound exhausted, so that's progress."

"Good."

The elevator takes us back up to our floor and I knock on the door leading to Kellen's room. Andrew walks up to his door and presses the key to the lock, waiting for it to click open.

"Well, this might be the last time I see y'all for a bit. But, when I'm back, we'll properly celebrate, okay? Thanks for everything, Marissa. Best of luck with y'all."

"Thank you Andrew, looking forward to seeing you again too."

He enters his room and I lightly knock on the door to Kellen's. He opens the door, looking tired but dawning a light smile on his face when he sees me. I leap into his arms, being gentle with his still fragile state, and he gently wraps his arms back around my waist.

"You don't know how happy I am to see you," I tell him. "I tried to keep it together when Desmond brought you over, but I almost thought I'd lost you. I guess now I can say I know what you've been through."

"Yeah," he says gently. "At least there was no blood this time."

"Thank god," I murmur, cheek pressed against his chest.

"So, you and Andrew got something to eat together? How is he?"

"Nice. Despite the rollercoaster of a journey he went on during the concert, he actually is really thankful for you. But I told him to tell you that himself. And he has some other news to tell you."

"What's that?"

"He wants to do the residency. Yes, even after everything that happened, he still feels like he wants to give it a shot. And he wants to genuinely be your friend. You know, the whole saving his life thing made him realize that."

"Wow." Kellen's surprised, and starts fumbling over his words. "I can't— wow. That's awesome. Well, I'd love to have him and give him another shot at performing. Or multiple shots. I was kind of worried after what happened and Andrew being nervous being whisked out of the hotel for his own safety that he'd never want to go to this hotel again."

"Funny enough, that's why he wants to come back. Well I don't think it's because he wants to get kidnapped again per se, but he's really thankful for you practically saving his life and if anyone would offer him a residency, he thinks he wouldn't get along or feel a connection to them like he did with you. He wants to set up a video game night with you and Taylor soon."

"Well then. Looks like I'm playing video games with a pop star. When Andrew was just about to go on stage, he actually did tell me that he was excited to do his residency here. And looks like he's staying true to that. Maybe it won't be so hard to recover from this after all."

"Come on," Kellen takes my hand and leads me to the room's balcony with a gorgeous view of the Strip. We see the other hotels across the street, and a few spaces down, The Blossom. Only a select few rooms, notably all of the suites, at the Blossom have balconies, but a nice touch to the Cyberscape is that quite a few of their rooms have balconies.

"Wow," I beam. As the sun has now set, the lights are on, and we're even out at the right time for Bellagio's fountains to be dancing. "Vegas is so beautiful," I sigh to myself.

"I think the view I'm seeing is more beautiful," Kellen says, looking at me.

I roll my eyes. "You are so corny. But I love it."

"I love you." He reaches down and lightly kisses me. He sighs. "We did it."

"We did it." We bested the beast and survived to tell the tale. I couldn't believe that my life in Vegas would include such a Vegas-esque plot line. "Together."

"I never thought when I'd move to Vegas, I'd fall in love with someone I goofed up with when I met her at the nightclub, but I did. And we had quite an adventure along the way, didn't we?"

"Yes." I don't know if almost dying was something I wanted to have on my adventure, but it truly goes to show that love conquers all. "Yes we did."

I lean to give Kellen another kiss, as the fountain spurts up again to Today's Hits. As we parted and held each other, looking over the Vegas skyline, I couldn't wait to see what sort of adventures await us next.

Chapter Thirty-Four
Marissa

A few months later

A "Ha!" I grin. "Looks like my hand comes out on top again!"

"Not fair," Rory grumbles. "I've been dealt shit hands. Not my fault that you can see through my bluff."

"Just have to rework your tactic, Ror."

Rory Vinland, one of the highest-ranked poker players, side eyes me and my grinning face. Rory and Janessa were close acquaintances, frenemies to be precise, but now that I've buried who I once was, Rory and I have been rekindling our friendship and constantly practicing with one another. Rory still hopes he can beat me in the next upcoming tournament, but I'm not going to make it easy for him.

"Lucky for me my next tournament is at the Blossom so I don't need to worry about competing against you. Although, I do understand why you're taking a back seat."

"Yeah." I'm not participating in the next poker tournament at the Blossom because it's still fresh in my mind what happened six months ago. Instead, I promised I'd meet up with some play-ers after and dish on how everyone performed. Everyone's say-ing they're happy I'm not participating anyway because they're worried I'll sweep the tournament. Happy to know that I can be a successful full time poker player, which I never thought imaginable. I miss working in hotels, but thankfully Taylor and Kellen have used their respective authorities to get me on as a tournament consultant at each of their hotels.

Speaking of my handsome and amazing boyfriend, Kellen has been doing great as the new general manager. When he first arrived at the Blossom, the staff was uneasy about him and didn't make any effort to get to know him, or believe that he could run a successful staff. I guess all you needed to do was stop a hoard of people trying to kidnap an international pop star and film it for the world to see for people to trust you again. And lucky for me, he and his new Director of Operations, Kayley, are still getting along swimmingly. They even are making plans for a poker night with Taylor. They said I had to be the dealer, of course. Someone else should be given the chance to win, right?

They have a busy few months ahead of them, as business is booking up with the news of Andrew Tseng arriving for his Las Vegas residency in a matter of weeks. That, coupled with the huge poker tournament coming to the Blossom in a year that I've started coordinating, the hotel is set up well for its success going into the new year.

Kellen <3: Swing by Blossom when you're done playing with Ror, need to run some errands before dinner.

Me: sure, just swept him anyway no surprise there. I'll be over soon.

Kellen <3: that's my girl!!

Between Kellen in meetings and me practicing with other pros for WSOP, we've hardly been able to enjoy some quality time for ourselves. It also doesn't help that we don't live together yet. I do spend the night over at his villa when I can, but I forget that I have an apartment with food that needs to be eaten and clothes that need to be washed. Kellen said once everything settles, he wants to find a place to live, but he doesn't say for us. I don't force him to anyway. We're a few months into our relationship, and while I'm two months from my lease being up, I don't want the "living together" next step in our relationship to be a burden for him to think about.

I bid Rory adieu and start making my way to the Blossom. The Strip is full of pedestrians milling about on a Friday night. Their bodies occasionally look up at the marquee of each hotel and what their offerings are this month, and when I make it to the Blossom, I smile when the sign with LED blossom leaves shines with Andrew Tseng's body signing into a microphone announcing his upcoming residency. I always had faith we'd be able to get him, but I'm so proud of Kellen for overcoming all the odds and making it happen. I know he'll say he just had to do it or else his dad would be upset at him, but he really does love this hotel, and me a few months ago doubted that when I watched him introduce himself in front of us. Because then, he was just a player who seemed like he was forced to work to make his family proud. Now, he's a general manager of a hotel on the Vegas Strip. And throughout the stressful times, he grins at how much he's accomplished so far.

I meet him near the food court, and smile when I see him standing in the walkway, hands in his pockets, smiling back at me. I pick up my pace a little bit and skip into his arms, like it's been an eternity since we've last seen one another.

"Hi," he says, squeezing me tight across my waist and reaching to give me a quick peck. "So your game with Rory went well?"

"Yeah, I mean, I think I just got lucky. But he put up a good game. He told me he's using the next Blossom tournament as practice so he'll beat me at the next one. Which just means I have to keep practicing to stay good. You don't mind if we'd just do some practice games after dinner right? You know, so you can get good too."

"Well, I'd be happy to, but you know there are other things I'd much rather be doing." He grips my ass and gives it a little squeeze and I can't stop laughing at the tickling sensation it sends down there.

"Kellen," I try to grit out without laughing every other word. "Enough with the PDA!"

"Absolutely not. I've had to keep us a secret for long enough, I'm publicly showing my affection for you and I don't give a fuck who sees."

He whispers that last part with such a fierceness, it causes my insides to get hot and bothered. Maybe we should detour to his room to take care of business before we head to dinner...

"Kellen," I whimper. "We can also partake in more...secret activities too, if you know what I mean."

"Oh." He says, pulling back. "We can, definitely. Actually, that's what I wanted to talk to you about."

"Sex?" I ask. That's a weird thing to bring up. "Wait, am I pregnant? Wait, no I'm not. I would know that before you. I'm not pregnant. Yet. You'd be the first to know, of course. Okay, I'm going to stop rambling. What did you want to talk about?"

He takes my hand and leads me to start walking to the front of the hotel. "Come on, I have to take you there to show you."

We head to the parking garage, and get into Kellen's new car. It's a beautiful, and rather speedy sports car that he's taken out on the desert and led me to feel like my organs were about to pop out.

"Where are we going?" I ask once he's started the engine. I'm listing out ideas to match my secret activities comment. Sex shop? Place to get desserts to play with? A movie theater where we can make out in private to whatever movie's out right now?

I'm partial to animated movies, but I'd also like to focus on the movie in that case.

"You'll see," he says. I eye him suspiciously. We're going kind of far from the Strip, into the more residential parts of Vegas and once we start passing large mansions one after the other, I think I know where we're headed.

He pulls into the driveway of a one story modern farmhouse home that looks like it's been built not long ago. The white exterior has no signs of chipping, the walkway is pristine, with stones on each side and small porch lights illuminating the walkway.

"This is nice," I say. I kind of wish he asked me if I was up for seeing friends, but then I think to myself, who lives here that might be throwing a party? Taylor lives in an apartment near the Strip because he, and I quote, still wants to keep some semblance of bachelorhood, and truthfully I don't know who else Kellen hangs out with that might live in such a big, lavish house as this. Oh god, he's not coming here to introduce me to his richer, prettier girlfriend he found that understands his wealth and lifestyle, right? No, Marissa, he said he loved you and was just about to damn near rip off your clothes in public because he was that excited to see you.

"Thanks," he says, taking out a set of keys to unlock it. "I bought it."

"Wait." I stand in the doorway as he opens the door to an empty, echoey home. "You bought a house?"

"Yeah," he says, taking my hand to lead me inside. "Just got the keys today. I know I've been keeping a big secret from you, but I wanted to surprise you with the news when it became official."

"Oh," I nod. "Makes sense."

The house, while very unfurnished, is still beautiful. It has an open floor plan, with a large marbled kitchen island in a very spacious kitchen and dining room area. The ceilings are high, and small light fixtures dangle from the top. Hell, it even has a wine fridge built into it.

"Here," he leads me toward a large folding door that leads out in the backyard. "Let me show you the yard."

I gasp once we walk through the sliding doors. The yard is another story. Large grass field next to a lap pool that I can lay in all day. I imagine myself with a pool floatie and a margarita and sigh.

"Kellen, this is beautiful," I tell him. I don't say that I wish I could live here, because I don't want to overstep. If he wants to still take it slow, and have me sleep over a few days of the week, I'm not going to be mad. Sure, I'll be a little bummed I can't wake up and shout, "I'm going for a swim!" but, I'll get over it. At least I can indulge in it one day of the week.

"Good," he smiles. "Because it's ours."

"Wait," I look up at him. "What do you mean?"

He chuckles. "I mean, it's ours. I'm not going to live in this house alone with you living in the same city. And, I'm definitely not letting you go home to your apartment when you can come here whenever you want."

"Kellen," I almost feel myself begin to cry. "Are you saying…"

"Marissa Waters," he grabs both of my hands and looks me in the eyes. "Will you move in with me?"

"Yes," I nod. "Of course I will."

I leap into his arms and he carries me over to the pool, teasing me by dipping me so close so that I'm barely touching the pool's surface.

"Kellen, wait!"

"Don't worry," he tilts me back up. "I'm not going to do that to you. I'm going to let you take off your clothes first."

"Wait, now?"

"Yes now! You said you wanted to partake in secret activities. I wanted to take you home first before I decide to do anything."

"Oh my god, Kellen," I roll my eyes. "Okay, well I guess that makes sense then."

We shimmy out of our work clothes and he spares no expense jumping into the pool. I follow soon after him and once I'm done shivering from the temperature of the pool, I swim over to him and wrap my arms around his neck.

"Welcome home, my love," he says, pressing his lips onto mine. I wrap my legs around his waist and he hooks his arms below my ass, hoisting me up to him. Our bodies feel perfect as they touch one another. And as I reach up to tug a bit of the hair at the back of his head, I smile, with his kisses trailing down from my mouth to my chest. Who would have thought that the stranger I kissed at a nightclub ended up being the man I wake up next to every morning, the person I'll cuddle up next to on the couch for the rest of my life.

"There's no place I'd rather be," I tell him, once his gaze meets mine. And we continue to hold onto each other as the sun sets and the stars illuminate the Las Vegas sky.

Acknowledgements

Whew, y'all we did it.

The journey to write this book was an adventure, and truthfully, not an easy one. This is the second time I am writing these acknowledgements, because this is the second time I'm submitting this book. I recognized I needed to fix some things after the initial release of WUIV, and I'm happy to be re-releasing another version of WUIV after working with a wonderful proofreader (thank you, Sarah Ward!)

To everyone who shouts out my work and supports every endeavor I decide to embark on, thank you. I had this wild idea to write a romance set in Vegas (but without the shotgun wedding and a lot of the Ocean's Eleven adventure) in 2022 after taking my first trip back to Sin City after I could do all the things: drink, gamble, spend money how I want to, which included a lot of eating.

To my family: Mom and Dad, thank you for your constant support growing up, now, and forever. Dad, I know you may never read this, and Mom, you might, and I hope that this is just as good as the books you read or the K-dramas you love to watch. Por Por and Gung Gung, I dedicated this book to you, but thank you for taking me to Vegas when I was a child. I don't remember much, beyond the Bellagio lobby and the now-defunct Monte Carlo, but I still love the memories we made going on road trips as a child. My (slight) gambling love is all thanks to you.

To Mario: You're my everything and I love you so much. Thank you for being the "yes" husband, being my favorite person to vacation with, and telling people I wrote a book when I'm too embarrassed to champion it myself. You're my favorite and I love you.

To Sam: thank you for bringing my vision of Kellen and Marissa to life. You are beyond talented and I love admiring my cover every single day. I can't wait for more covers to fawn over as I continue to make more books in the Vegas series.

To Jordyn: my Big/BFF/MOH/Book Lover, thank you for getting excited about books with me. I love that we can chat about books when I can't with Mario. Can't wait to ring in your special day in Vegas soon.

To my bookish friends: Bad Bitch Book Club & Steamy Lit & all the authors I've met from going on this indie author journey together. Seeing my book in your feeds, on your stories warms my heart. I am so blessed to know all of you and your love for romance makes me get warm fuzzies. Can't wait to meet you all in person again at Steamy Lit Con or any other bookish meetups we may have in the near future.

& Finally: to my Multi-Racial baddies, especially Lauren Kung Jessen, thank you for inspiring me to write a book about our experiences. Different, but special. We're a blend and I'm so excited to be giving you more books in the future that will help you if you ever felt like you were not enough. Because to me, you're everything.

Thank you to everyone who has read, shouted out, and reviewed WUIV. Thank you for giving me a chance, and I hope to bring more amazing work your way very soon.

Match Game – A Fake Dating Hockey Romance (June 18, 2024)

About the author

Brittany Arreguin is a mixed-Chinese American romance author based in the San Francisco Bay Area. She is a full time Events Coordinator & loves to write romances she conjures up in her dreams. She lives with her husband and cats, Princess Peach & Boo, and loves to frequent breweries and play video games when she's not reading or writing.

amazon.com/author/brittanyarreguin

instagram.com/brittanyarreguinwrites

www.ingramcontent.com/pod-product-compliance
Lightning Source LLC
Chambersburg PA
CBHW031203010826
48971CB00013B/1274